$$\frac{J\bar{F}}{7}$$

—

—

—

—

—

-

ta

,

Peter Lovesey was born in Middlesex and studied at Hampton Grammar School and Reading University, where he met his wife Jax. He won a competition with his first crime fiction novel, *Wobble to Death*, and has never looked back, with his numerous books winning and being shortlisted for nearly all the prizes in the international crime writing world.

He was Chairman of the Crime Writers' Association and has been presented with Lifetime Achievement awards both in the UK and the US.

Also by Peter Lovesey

Sergeant Cribb series
Wobble to Death
The Detective Wore Silk Drawers
Abracadaver
Mad Hatter's Holiday
Invitation to a Dynamite Party
A Case of Spirits
Swing, Swing Together
Waxwork

Albert Edward, Prince of Wales series
Bertie and the Tinman
Bertie and the Seven Bodies
Bertie and the Crime of Passion

Peter Diamond series
The Last Detective
Diamond Solitaire
The Summons
Bloodhounds
Upon a Dark Night
The Vault
Diamond Dust
The House Sitter
The Secret Hangman
Skeleton Hill
Stagestruck
Cop to Corpse
The Tooth Tattoo
The Stone Wife
Down Among the Dead Men
Beau Death

Hen Mallin series
The Circle
The Headhunters

Other fiction
Goldengirl (as Peter Lear)
Spider Girl (as Peter Lear)
The False Inspector Dew
Keystone
Rough Cider
On the Edge
The Secret of Spandau (as Peter Lear)
The Reaper

Short stories
Butchers and other stories of crime
The Crime of Miss Oyster Brown and other stories
Do Not Exceed the Stated Dose
The Sedgemoor Strangler and other stories of crime
Murder on the Short List

Peter
LOVESEY

KILLING WITH CONFETTI

sphere

SPHERE

First published in Great Britain in 2019 by Sphere

1 3 5 7 9 10 8 6 4 2

Copyright © Peter Lovesey 2019

The moral right of the author has been asserted.

A CIP catalogue record for this book is available from the British Library.

ISBN 978-0-7515-7749-5

Typeset in ITC New Baskerville by Palimpsest Book Production Ltd,
Falkirk, Stirlingshire
Printed and bound in Great Britain by Clays Ltd, Elcograf S.p.A.

Papers used by Sphere are from well-managed forests
and other responsible sources.

MIX
Paper from
responsible sources
FSC
www.fsc.org   FSC® C104740

With affection for my friends and fellow-writers Liza Cody and Michael Z. Lewin, who continue to keep me updated on the Bath scene.

1

The two short words Warren doesn't wish to hear: 'It's on.'

'When?'

'Tomorrow – at unlock.'

'Soon as that?'

'Catch the white-shirts off guard.'

'Right.'

But it isn't right, not for Warren. It's wrong, disastrously wrong. He is playing the good-behaviour card this time round in his prison career, working with the system for early release. He's been one of HMP Bream's model cons for two long years. Two years, three months and twenty-seven days.

A riot has been talked about for weeks on C Wing. Talk is easy. For a time it was no more than that, wishful thinking, like sex with the gorgeous Miss Martindale who teaches black history. But by degrees the chat has got serious. The gorillas on the top landing mean business. 'Together we can do this. We outnumber them. They won't know what's hit them.'

A plan has been hatched. Nothing brilliant. Grab the screws the moment they unlock, disable their radios and body cameras, drag them into the cells, tie them up and take their passes, keys and pepper spray. Then hold them hostage. At the same time, someone else will be disabling the CCTV. Coordinated action, see?

How stupid was that, saying 'Right'?

In this place you get in the habit of agreeing with other people. It's not clever to challenge anyone. Even so, there are times when you should say, 'Count me out.'

No one is under any illusion that possessing the keys will mean instant freedom. The people who designed this coop weren't amateurs. You can only get so far and then you need different sets of keys and different passes. There is a better way to beat the system and the wise guys upstairs have sussed it. Instead of breaking out, you break in.

First, uncage your brother inmates and you'll have reinforcements. Strength in numbers. The screws' master keys will give access to the beating heart of the prison: the association area, servery, workshops, gym and chapel. And improvised weapons. Arm yourselves with whatever comes to hand, like fire extinguishers, socks weighted with pool balls, bits of broken furniture such as iron bedposts and steel rails from bookshelves. There's talk that one of the gorillas has taken delivery of a gun, carried over the wall by drone. Whether that's true only he and his inner circle know.

The prison authorities still have the heavy weapons – hoses, tasers, tear gas, stun grenades, sidearms, batons, armed police and the army if required – but they're supposed to act responsibly. The inmates aren't under any such compulsion. They can create mayhem. The obvious way to make it happen is with fire. Set the place alight and see how that goes down with the governor when some of his team are held hostage.

Warren has no desire to be part of the violence. With good behaviour he is planning to reduce a six stretch to three. Getting caught up in a riot will wreck that. He's forty-three now. More than half his life has been spent inside, if you count the years in the secure children's home. His last probation officer – all of twenty-one and straight out of college – said he was institutionalised, unlikely to survive outside some strict regime like prison or the army.

Bullshit.

What did the little prick think? That Warren wouldn't know how to use a knife and fork? Couldn't walk up a crowded street without panicking? Would get tongue-tied talking to a woman?

People like that know shit-all.

He has managed his anger up to now, hasn't he? He can survive outside. He can thrive. But not the law-abiding way society expects, with the pathetic discharge grant of £46 and a one-way train ticket to London – to exist on charity and roughing it on the streets. And not on Jobseeker's Allowance and filling in forms at the Jobcentre. With Warren's special skills there are jobs to be had that no careers advisor knows about.

His problem is that he just said 'Right' and the mob on the top landing now believe they can count on his support. One short word has fouled up everything. He'll be lumped in with the rioters, liable to be charged with whatever these madmen get up to. No lawyer, however smart, will get him off after that. Another long stretch looms.

I can't be alone in wanting no part of this, Warren tells himself. But who else has the balls to take on the gorillas?

And now there is worse.

'How you doing, Warren?'

'So, so.'

'Feeling strong?'

'Dunno.'

'Because tomorrow, when it happens, you're the star turn, you and Muscles.'

His insides clench. 'Why is that?'

'Obvious, innit? Yours is the last door they unlock, being at the end of the landing. We'll all be waiting for you to

3

clobber the screw, you and Muscles, catch him off guard just when he thinks his job is done. That's lift-off. Then we're on our way, mate. There's no holding us.'

He understands the logic. This isn't personal. He and Muscles are unlucky enough to be banged up in the end pad.

Some rapid thinking is necessary.

'He won't be the only screw unlocking.'

'Don't you worry about that, mate. It's taken care of. Soon as you make the first move, the rest of us swing into action. We'll be taking our cue from you.'

'Who decided this?'

'Who do you think? The lads upstairs. Make sure you get Muscles on board. We all know he's not the full quid, but he's going to be needed.'

Warren's cellmate is six-six and eighteen stone and can't hold a thought in his head for more than two seconds. In a fight he's liable to get confused who the enemy is. But he's strong. There are plenty in prison who pump iron every day and get a body. You aren't called Muscles unless you really stand out.

'I don't like this,' Warren says. 'Nobody told me we were first on.'

'I'm telling you now, aren't I?'

No sense in protesting. This guy is merely the mouthpiece for the high command. With twenty minutes of association time left in the day Warren needs to visit the top landing and speak to the head honcho.

And say what?

Think of something fast.

While climbing the metal stairs he is reminded of something everyone learns to live with on a prison wing – the sheer volume of noise hitting you from the brick and metal surfaces. The clang of barred metal gates. Voices raised in argument, excitement, laughter, threat and desperation,

4

shouting across the landings, vying to be heard in a babel of accents and languages. A modern English prison is more inclusive than the United Nations.

An idea comes to Warren.

The top gorilla, Uncle Joe – nobody calls him anything else – is leaning on the railing gazing through the anti-suicide netting at the atrium below, getting the scenic view of his kingdom. Broad, muscled and shaven-headed, he is dressed in designer sportswear, a black basketball shirt to exhibit the heavily tattooed arms. Silver shorts. Expensive trainers.

'Yeah?' Uncle Joe doesn't turn his head to see who has approached.

'You may have seen me around. Warren, from the middle landing. The end pad.'

'So?'

'So I was told to make the first move tomorrow, me and my cellmate Muscles.'

'Got a problem with that, Warren?'

'I wouldn't call it a problem, more a question.'

'Let's hear it.'

'What's happening about the foreigners?'

The connection isn't obvious to Uncle Joe. 'Come again.'

'The cons who don't speak English.'

'They'll catch on when they see what's going on.'

'But can we count on them?'

'Why wouldn't we?'

'We don't know what they're saying. What they're thinking.'

'You're losing me, pal,' Uncle Joe says.

'They're a sizeable section of the wing. And some of them are hard men with their own agenda and it's not just praying and fasting. They could turn your brilliant plan into a bloodbath.'

'Keep your voice down.'

'Sorry.' Warren sidles closer and mutters, 'What I'm saying

is we're aiming to do this clean, am I right? These ay-rabs need telling in words they understand.'

'You speak their language?'

'I know someone who does.'

'Who's that?'

'A geezer called Haseem.'

'Tell him, then. Sorted.'

'Not quite,' Warren says. 'There's an even bigger risk.'

'What's that?'

'My cellmate, Muscles. He's a slightly different problem, but it comes to the same thing. He's unstable.'

'What?'

'Brain damaged. You can't reason with him. He's got the attention span of a two-year-old on speed. And a history of violence.'

'Who hasn't?'

'With him, it's something else. Let me tell you what will happen. Muscles will see me grab the screw and he'll join in and snap the guy's neck like a biscuit. That's what he does. It's why he's in this place. Instead of a hostage we'll have a corpse.'

'We don't want killing,' Uncle Joe says.

'Too right we don't. It gives the riot squad a reason to open fire on us.'

'So tell Muscles.'

'No use. It won't sink in. His memory's gone. He can't even tell you what his name is.'

'He could foul up the plan.'

Warren is starting to think Uncle Joe is not much brighter than Muscles. 'He will, for sure.'

'Why are you telling me this now? I could have got him ghosted.' Ghosting is when a difficult offender is moved to another part of the prison or another jail altogether.

Suddenly the heat is back on Warren for the delay in

6

mentioning the problem of Muscles. 'I only just heard what you want us to do. I came as soon as I could. Too late, isn't it?'

Uncle Joe says, 'Put something in his drink.'

'Dope, you mean?'

'What do you think I mean, dumbo – a lump of sugar?'

'No, I understand.'

'Enough so he sleeps through.'

'But that means I'll have to clobber the screw myself, without any help. They're well protected, those fuckers.'

'So?'

'There may be a better way,' Warren says as if the idea just dawned. 'I don't like it – I really wanted a piece of the action – but it will work.'

'I'm listening.'

'Instead of me and Muscles making the first move, you fix it for the lads in the next cell to deal with the screw.'

2

Warren is up as usual at 5.30 to boil water for coffee and his shave. Then he tries working for an hour on his Open University assignment. Hard going with his mind on what will happen next. He returns his books to the shelf and settles to watching the door. Roll check has to be completed first. He's long ago learned that the screws are as enslaved to routine as the inmates and some of them are more scared than any inmate of making a mistake.

The eye appears at the Judas hole. So far, so normal.

From the landing comes the familiar rasp and creak of cell doors being unlocked, followed by sleepy voices. Warren steps across to Muscles, still out to the world, feet the size of French loaves hanging over the end of the ludicrously small bunk.

'Better move, mate.'

The cell feels colder than usual, and Warren's head is aching. Stress, he supposes. He can't be certain if last night's suggestion to Uncle Joe has been acted on. No one is likely to tell him. He can only be sure of one thing: he won't himself be attacking any screw this morning.

He grasps some of Muscles' bedding and pulls it back from the tattooed shoulder. 'Time to get up, mate.'

A large fist grabs the sheet and pulls it close again.

Warren gives up trying. It isn't clever to upset Muscles. He really did snap the neck of a man who bugged him.

Leave the beached whale to wait for the next tide. Won't hurt him to miss breakfast.

There is a thump from next door that could be the lad from the top bunk getting out – or the heart-warming sound of the screw being smacked against the wall. Either way, something is up because the unlocking hasn't reached their cell yet.

Encouraging.

More noise than usual starts coming from the landing outside. You get to know the level of sound to expect, the tones of voice. These aren't the mutterings of people starting another boring day of bird. A definite air of urgency is coming through.

And this door hasn't been opened.

Good sign. The lads next door must have got the message from Uncle Joe and duffed up the screw.

Five minutes go by.

Quite a bedlam of noise now. The excited voices of a mob that realises this is a day like no other.

Warren moves closer and puts his ear to the sheet metal to try to hear better. Someone out there must have keys by now and ought to be unlocking the bloody thing. He yells, 'Oy!'

No response.

Muscles sits up in his bunk and yawns.

'What's up?'

'They're not letting us out,' Warren says.

'Prison, innit?' Muscles says.

Can't argue with that.

'They were planning to clobber the screws and grab the keys.'

Muscles isn't impressed. His face has gone blank again, his standard expression.

'It was a plan, all set for now.'

'No one told me.'

'They could let us out any moment.'

'I need a crap.'

'Be my guest. Then you'd better get dressed. I don't think we'll be going home today, but if the plan works, we'll get to negotiate.' Warren is talking to himself more than Muscles. A hostage negotiation is a concept too far for the big man.

Still no sound of the door being unlocked. The ugly possibility is forming that their fellow cons have decided to keep them banged up. There is no knowing what version of last night's conversation filtered down from the top landing.

Muscles says from the toilet seat, 'Where's breakfast?'

Breakfast, so-called, consists of teabags, cereal, bread and jam with sachets of whitener and sugar, all in a clear plastic bag shoved through the hatch. 'I wouldn't worry about that if I were you.'

'I'm hungry.'

'They've got other stuff to think about.'

'Like what?'

'Like taking out the CCTV.'

'Whassat?'

'The cameras that spy on us all day long.'

Thinking it over, there is something to be said for being shut up in the cell. The cons might think of it as punishment for opting out, but when the riot comes to a bad end, as it surely will, he and Muscles can't be blamed for the violence and damage.

'Banged up all day?' the big man asks.

'Could be.'

'And nothing to eat?'

'They won't forget us,' Warren says without the certainty he would have liked.

The level of noise on the other side of the door is increasing. No question: something unusual is going on. A bad-tempered

10

debate, probably, about the next step. Trash the place or prepare for a long siege by pooling resources? Prison inmates aren't the best at evolving strategies. Surely the gorillas upstairs must have formed a plan. They ought to exert their authority over the hotheads.

'All we can do is sit it out, however long it takes,' Warren says.

Muscles is sitting it out on the toilet.

The rigid prison routine is on hold for sure. Being banged up is harder to endure than usual, not knowing what to expect. If you know you're there for hours because of staff shortages you can pass time reading a book or watching telly.

Muscles eventually works the flush and gets dressed.

The commotion on the landing subsides in the next hour. Just the occasional shout, impossible to interpret as speech.

'Do you have to do that?'

Muscles looks up. 'What?'

'Grind your teeth. It's getting to me.'

There's a sound at the door and the hatch below the Judas hole opens. Muscles, eager for food, gets to it before Warren.

Something is pushed through and the hatch slams shut before words can be exchanged.

'What's this?' Muscles asks, holding it up for Warren to see.

A sheet of soiled toilet paper has been pushed through. The word SCABS is scrawled across it.

'Dickheads.'

Muscles is frowning. 'What does this writing say?'

'Scabs.'

'What do they mean by that?'

Warren doesn't try to explain. 'Flush it away and wash your hands.' He puts the telly on.

11

Two or three hours pass and no one unlocks the door.

Something is on TV about doing up houses and selling them for a profit. Top viewing for a prison inmate. Warren watches it blankly, his thoughts still on the significance of the insult from their fellow cons. Uncle Joe has obviously dished the dirt and put them in trouble with everyone. The toilet paper could be a sign of worse to come.

'I should be lifting weights now,' Muscles says.

'It's not going to happen today,' Warren says.

'Smoke.'

'No thanks.' He gives Muscles a second look. Weird thing to say considering both are non-smokers – the main reason why they are sharing a cell. Then he sniffs the air they are breathing and understands what the big man is on about. 'They've started a fire.'

'What for?'

'A quick result. The screws aren't interested in a bunch of cons rampaging on the landing, but a fire can't be ignored.'

'Where is it?'

'Your guess is as good as mine. Somewhere upstairs if they've got any sense. Keep it from spreading down here. We don't want the whole sodding wing alight.'

'Why not?'

'Give me strength. Because we're in it, for Christ's sake.'

'I don't want to get burnt.'

'You won't know much about the burning part. The fumes kill you first.' Warren runs at the door and kicks it repeatedly.

No one comes.

3

Magda Lyle's day has started no differently from any other. Up at six, shower, quick decision what to wear, strong, bracing coffee followed by a short, brisk walk along one of the local woodland trails with her boisterous West Highland terrier, Blanche. They always make for the same open area where the dog can come off the leash and fetch the ball and challenge Magda to get it back, with the result that both have a joyful, energising start to the day.

This will be the only exercise she gets today because there is no chance at HMP Bream, where she is a governor. Long hours, mostly behind a desk, with few days off, will undermine anyone's fitness. True, there is a gym in the basement supposedly for the use of staff as well as offenders. Some of the prison officers work out there, but Magda is sure anyone of her level shouldn't use it.

She's young for the job, at thirty-six, having earned a reputation for managing prison staff and offenders with firmness tempered with fairness. With a good degree in law from Edinburgh, she signed up for the National Offender Management Service graduate course and sailed through. Successful spells of three to five years at various Category C prisons were rewarded by an assistant governor post at the women's closed prison at Eastwood Park, Gloucestershire. From there after four years she became the only woman governor at the privately run Category B men's prison at

Bream, and now she's into her third year. The move to an all-male institution was a daunting step-change, but a necessary one to make to progress in this career. So far so good.

Now she lives alone in a two-hundred-year-old iron-worker's cottage on the edge of the Wye Valley with a magnificent view over Tintern, a fine compensation for the confines of the job. Boyfriends? A few, over the years. Relationships? Only one that she'd call serious and that ended when she'd moved south. There's a lot to be said for the single life spiced with dates with male friends she has got to know since moving to this part of the country – two farmers, a sculptor, a taxi driver, and a church organist who turned out to be the hottest of the lot.

This morning she and Blanche have met no one. Occasionally on their walks they wish the time of day to backpackers making an early start, burdened with so much that it's hard to see how they can stay on their feet for an hour. Often they are foreign tourists wanting to know if they are on the right route to the Devil's Pulpit, the local viewpoint. By the time you get there, sunshine, you'll be in need of a chair, Magda thinks. You won't find one.

Blanche can go off the leash now.

Scampering ahead in the morning sunlight, familiar with the route, she regularly goes out of sight on the winding path, but it's never a worry. For one thing, the little dog's white coat will soon be visible again, and for another, she is so responsive that she'll always come when called. Today she is waiting with ears pricked and tail going like a windscreen wiper on high when Magda rounds the next bend.

She seems to have found an item of interest and wants congratulating.

When Magda steps closer and sees what is lying across the path, her blood runs cold.

'Blanche, no!'

A snake, with the unmistakable marking of an adder, head propped against its coiled body, poised to strike.

Westies are doughty fighters. They will take on anything. Adders aren't usually aggressive, but they'll bite the face or foreleg of a dog that comes too close.

Magda swoops, grabs Blanche under the chest and scoops her up in one movement. The serpent slithers away into the bracken.

You never know what lies in wait for you.

Blanche wriggles in Magda's arms, wanting to give chase. Being snatched up and squeezed is no reward for a fine discovery.

As for Magda, she is shaking. She isn't sure how she would have coped out here on the hillside with her dog bitten by a snake. In other stressful situations – say with a troublesome offender inside prison – she has no trouble controlling her emotions, but this has come as a shock. None of the locals have ever mentioned adders. Here on familiar terrain in the sunshine she'd never dreamed of danger along the way. Somewhere in her memory is a line from Shakespeare about the bright day bringing forth the adder – 'and that craves wary walking'.

Ultra-wary. She won't let Blanche run free for the rest of the walk.

Fully five minutes pass before it crosses Magda's mind that clutching the dog to her chest like Dorothy with Toto in *The Wizard of Oz* is an overreaction. After a careful check of the path ahead she clips on the lead and lowers Blanche to the ground.

She allows Blanche, straining for more freedom, to tug her as far as the open stretch where they usually play fetch. No chance of going off the lead today. A few pathetic trots across the glade have to suffice for entertainment. Quite soon Magda decides they've done more than enough for this blighted morning. With time in hand, they start up another trail that will lead them to the cottage.

She is still going over the incident in her mind, wondering if the hillside is infested with adders and thinking there is no certainty that a different route will be any safer, when the cottage chimney comes in sight. At this point, Blanche likes to race ahead and be waiting by the front door. Poor little pup, she hasn't had much fun.

Magda takes pity, stoops and unclips the lead.

Blanche hesitates and looks up for a clue as to what to do next. People can be unpredictable.

'Go on, then. Race me home.'

The terrier doesn't need a second bidding. She's off like a greyhound, or as like a greyhound as a Westie with six-inch legs can be.

Magda pockets the lead, takes out her key and follows. There's time for more coffee and a bite of toast before she drives to work.

Unusually, she hears barking from Blanche. In the garden two pigeons take flight with a clatter of wings and she guesses the reason. Pigeons were put into the world to be bullied by small dogs.

She lets herself in, drops two slices into the toaster, goes to the bathroom, puts on some face, returns to the kitchen, microwaves a mugful of coffee from the pot she made earlier, and switches on the TV. Not much is happening in the world. Yet another survey about chronic problems in the health service is being debated. Some time they'll get around to the overcrowded, underfunded prisons. It will take a mass breakout to achieve that.

Time to leave.

She empties the dregs of the coffee, fills the dog bowl with dry feed and mixes in a tablespoonful of wet food from the tin and then looks down.

16

Where *is* the dog?

Still in the garden no doubt, distracted by those pigeons.

Magda goes to the door and opens it.

Blanche should have charged straight past her and into the cottage, huffy at being forgotten, but she hasn't.

A missing dog is the last thing Magda needs when she's about to leave for work.

'Blanche, where are you? Come on, sweetheart.'

No response.

'Blanche.'

She steps out and looks right and left. The pigeons have returned and brought reinforcements. Six or seven are strutting all over the front lawn as if they own it.

She calls out again and moves around the side of the cottage towards her vegetable patch and the woodshed. This is so unlike Blanche, who will know breakfast is ready and adores her food.

Still there is no sight of her. No sound except the territorial cooing of the pigeons.

A horrid possibility lodges in Magda's brain. Has Blanche gone back to search for the adder? If she has, and she finds one, the outcome doesn't bear thinking about.

One last place remains to be checked. Behind the cottage is a stone wall with ivy growing up it. Magda rarely ever looks along the narrow space between the building and the wall.

She turns the corner and gasps.

A hooded man grabs her by the arms and forces her face against the wall.

4

Magda sees enough of her attacker to register that he is male, taller than the six-foot wall, broad-shouldered and wearing a dark tracksuit and a balaclava with slits for eyes and mouth. The weight of his body presses her hard against the rough stone. Her arms are grasped behind her back and pinioned with what feels like a strap being fastened a short way below her elbows. A hood is dragged over her head, execution-style. Unlike the man's balaclava, this has no openings. When she tries to cry out, the fleece-like material muffles the sound.

In this captive state she is hauled away from the wall and forced to stumble blindly back in the direction she has come. He prods her with the flat of his hand. An extra hard shove forces her to the left, off the gravel path and across the turf. Then her heels start sinking into the soft soil she recognises as her vegetable patch. One shoe sticks in the mud and she loses it. Off balance, she almost drops to her knees, but her forearm is grabbed from behind, steadying her. She kicks off the second shoe to keep her balance. A couple of steps further on, she feels his hand on her shoulder.

He stops her.

What now? She half expects some sort of coup de grâce, a crack on the head or a gunshot that will put an end to this nightmare, but it doesn't come. Instead she hears the creak of rusty hinges as a door is opened.

The woodshed.

He has decided to bring her here rather than out in the open. She hasn't used firewood for months, but she remembers the shed is half full of cobweb-covered logs stacked along the two sides. Somewhere inside is an axe, but there is no chance she can use it to defend herself while trussed like this.

A sudden stronger push in her back pitches her forward. Felled like dead wood, she hits the floor of the shed. The main impact is to her left shoulder and hip. Sharp pain, but nothing broken, she hopes. She'll be left with heavy bruising. Instinctively she lies on her side and draws her knees to her belly, expecting him to fling himself on her. If he's a rapist he'll have no difficulty with her clothes. She's in the loose tartan skirt she wears for work and it has rucked up, showing most of her thighs and probably more. Nothing she can do about that.

She can hear his breathing as he stands over her.

Enjoying her helplessness?

She moans, partly from tension, but also to make it sound as if the fall has injured her. Unless he's a total sadist he might think a victim with a cracked hip is a turn-off.

That small hope is snuffed out.

He takes hold of her shin.

She moans again and tries to draw her knees right up to her chest but he doesn't let go. He tightens his grip.

More angry than scared, she straightens suddenly, kicks with her free leg and feels her foot make sharp contact with his arm. If she were still wearing shoes she might have hurt him. As it is, he grunts, loses his grip briefly and immediately grabs her again. This time she feels more than just his hand. A cord is passed around her ankle and tightened. She guesses what it is – blue nylon braided rope she threw into the shed one winter morning after she found some pieces in the garden.

He's binding her legs together, winding the rope several times around her shins, pressing painfully into her flesh. Kicking him wasn't such a good idea. Before he has finished knotting the rope her toes are turning numb from lack of circulation.

But why is he doing it? Is it a bondage thing?

Roped and strapped, hot and blind under the hood, she can only lie there and wait to discover what he will do next. She holds her breath.

When the move comes, it is wholly unexpected. First she feels the back of his hand against her thigh and then the soft fabric of her skirt. He has straightened it and restored decency.

Hardly the action of a rapist.

Her heart is thumping, even so.

But she can tell he isn't looming over her any more. He's backed off. He's finished tying her up and has moved away. Job done, apparently.

Better still, she hears him turn the handle of the shed door. Is he about to leave? He still hasn't spoken a word and it seems he has dealt with the problem she represents.

Her sensation of relief is overwhelming.

The shed door slams shut and she hears him lock it. How annoying that she keeps the key permanently in the lock.

What was he, then – a thief? Did he want her powerless and out of his way while he ransacked the cottage? He must have been lurking in the garden waiting for her to go to the car and drive off. Instead, she'd come looking for Blanche and found him instead.

He won't need to break in now. She's left the cottage door open.

Her bag is in the kitchen and contains her phone, all her credit cards and about £200 in cash. Also her car key. Her Skoda is parked in the road, a good car, less than a year old, the most valuable item she owns, but will he risk driving a stolen car? He'll find a few antiques in the living room and some jewellery upstairs that she inherited from her mother. Not a lot, but most theft is random and they don't know what they'll discover.

Alone now, thank God. No one wants their house burgled and no one chooses to be locked in a shed indefinitely, but either option is preferable to a sex attack.

Wanting to be sure he's gone, she squirms closer to the door and listens.

Steps on the gravel. He has crossed the lawn and reached the cottage for sure. He's going to be busy there for some time. Then will he steal the car and drive off?

To her surprise, she hears voices.

He's talking to someone in front of the cottage. She can't think who. Nobody ever comes calling at this hour. Too early for the postman.

Impossible to tell what is being said. Male voices for sure, and the tone is business-like rather than hostile.

The longer they talk, the more likely that this isn't some local person who happened to be passing by. So he has an accomplice.

Magda's theory of a random burglary is unravelling.

Even as she strains to hear what might be happening outside, a sound much closer hits her with the force of an electric shock: the whimper of an animal in distress.

Blanche.

Somewhere here in the shed.

She catches her breath with such force that she sucks in the fabric of the hood.

She cries out, 'Blanche, darling?' and has an instant response, the same unhappy sound, but louder. Is her small dog cowering in a corner? Why doesn't she come over? Has she been kicked?

This is easily the worst moment of her ordeal, being unable to see what is troubling her beloved pet.

There is a phenomenon known as hysterical strength that in extreme situations allows people to perform astonishing feats like lifting one end of a car from a trapped accident victim. Scientists suggest everyone has some extra energy they can tap into. Magda's heightened emotional state triggers an exceptional reaction. She bucks and bumps across the floor until her head comes in contact with the stack of logs. By rubbing the back of her skull against the hard edges, she starts trying to remove the horrible hood, damp with spittle and sweat, ignoring the pain in the hope that the fabric will gather and slide over her hair.

Moving her head a short way left, she feels a stab of pain above her ear. Something is projecting from the bark and it seems to be a spike of wood, the base of a broken twig. Ignoring the discomfort, she works the hood against the angle until it hooks on.

One more big effort from her entire body and she squirms out of the vile thing.

Her first need is to breathe some air. She takes several huge gulps. Dazed by her efforts, she blinks, raises her head and looks round. There isn't much light in the wood-shed, but she can see movements from a hessian sack by the wall just inside the door. The top of it has been gathered and tied into a large knot.

'Blanche!'

The brute has captured the little dog and thrust her into the sack. Blanche must have been an easy catch, she is so trusting. Right now, she'll be terrified and in danger of suffocation.

Another heart-rending wail.

With her limbs still pinioned, Magda wriggles, maggot-style, towards Blanche, repeatedly calling her name to try and comfort her. She'll need to untie the large knot without using her hands. Without thought whether such a feat is possible, she props herself against the door, leans over and gets a grip on the coarse sacking with her teeth. Inside, Blanche is in a frenzy, hitting the sides, desperate to escape.

The simple overhand knot is effective enough at keeping Blanche imprisoned and eventually suffocating her, but not impossible to untie if Magda can find a way to loosen it. She bites hard and tugs at the cross-over, rasping her face as she works. The whimpering and struggling inside reach such a pitch that she has to pause and speak some words of comfort. But she can't stop for long. Head down, she tries again. If this doesn't work, she tells herself, I'll bite through the bloody sack.

Finally the knot gives a little. Encouraged, she puts even more into pulling the bunched material. It definitely gets looser.

One last effort.

Arching her back, clenching her teeth, she tugs the thing free and creates an opening.

Blanche emerges, panting and bewildered. After some hesitation, the little Westie looks around, takes in her owner lying beside her, props her front paws on Magda's shoulder and licks her face. Her tongue feels like a hot flannel.

'Poor little soul – what did he do to you?'

All of Magda's distress has transferred to her dog. She is hugely relieved to see that Blanche shows no obvious injuries. Some stiffness in the legs, understandably, and hyper-quick breathing.

The small tail wags furiously and the face-licking seems as if it will never stop.

'That's enough, sweetheart, really,' Magda says, wishing her hands were free to stroke and pet the brave little creature. She can offer no more than sympathetic words. No way can she free herself from the straps and rope. She and Blanche are locked in and stuck here until someone registers that she is missing and comes looking for her. And then she can only hope they have the sense to unlock the woodshed and look inside. The alternative doesn't bear thinking about.

After Blanche has calmed enough to sit a short distance from her, Magda turns her mind to what was going on before she heard those dreadful distressed cries from her dog. Two voices in earnest conversation. Quite probably this wasn't a random break-in but a planned operation that she'd interrupted by going to look for Blanche. If they knew her timing, they'd be able to break in after she'd left for work confident that she wouldn't return until late in the evening.

What do they think she owned that was worth stealing?

Or is all this for another reason?

She fears so.

5

The first indication of trouble is picked up in the control room at 8.10. The day shift has just taken over and a supervising officer and two operational-support-grade officers are seated with their first coffees in front of a wall of split-screen surveillance monitors. Just about every part of this Category B prison is covered by CCTV cameras, the inner walls, the front gate, every landing of each wing and all the association areas. In theory the staff are supposed to be checking the images constantly, but limited human resources can't cope with technology on such a scale. Besides, at the start of the day there are vital things to be talked about like the weather and the journey in and last night's TV. It is ten minutes into the shift before Wendy Hunt looks up and notices an irregularity.

'Something's wrong with the second screen, third row. The top two sectors have gone out of focus.'

'Switch the bugger off and restart,' prison officer Crawley says without even a look. 'It's like most of the women I've met, temperamental.' Inside the prison, where almost everyone is given a nickname, Crawley is known as Creepy, but the people who work closely with him call him Creep.

With a shrug, Wendy cuts the power and then restores it. Same result.

'Makes no difference.'

Gordon Crawley doesn't need this. The damned shift has

only just started. With his two silver stripes he feels entitled to better back-up than two wet-behind-the-ears female OSGs. He hasn't much time for gender equality. Privately he is thinking they shouldn't be doing security work. 'We're getting a signal.'

Privately Wendy is thinking Creepy Crawley needs stamping on. 'That's what I said, but half of it is blurred.'

'Everything else is normal. Switch the channel.' Clear views of four landings in another wing appear on the screen that was giving trouble. 'There you go. Now back again.'

The blurred view returns.

A tad more concerned, Crawley steps around the console, reaches up and taps the monitor. 'Funny. Looks like a focusing issue. Fault with the lens. This is C Wing second floor, right?'

'When it's working.'

'Okay, call up the officers on that landing and ask them to check the CCTV.'

Wendy switches on the two-way radio, tunes in and speaks into the mic. A short time later she says, 'I'm getting nothing back.'

'Oh, come on. They've got to be there. They're on unlock. Move aside.' Seated at the console he jams on the headset and speaks loudly into the mic. 'Control room. Let's hear from you. Over.'

All he gets back is an earful of static.

The second support assistant, Bryony Hall, has offered no opinion up to now, but she speaks up. 'Take a look at the screen at the end. Something's bugging that one as well.'

'What did you say?'

'Another camera malfunctioning, and – Oh my God, that's so weird.'

Crawley tugs off the headset, flings it down and stares at the bank of monitors. 'What is?'

'Third row at the far end. C Wing, top landing.'

Now he can see the strange effect Bryony is talking about, several round or oval shadowy shapes moving about on the screen not unlike beachballs bobbing on a choppy sea. Presently the images are gone, leaving the section of screen as blurred as the one Wendy noticed.

'What the fuck . . .?' Crawley says.

'If you're asking me,' Wendy says, 'it was somebody's fingers smearing grease over the camera lens.'

'Jesus, yes. They're disabling the CCTV. We've got an incident in C Wing.' He reaches across and slams his hand on the general security alarm. 'What are the bloody officers doing? Why haven't they reported this?' His way of coping with the crisis is to shout a series of questions that are barely audible above the piercing beep-beep. 'What time is it? Have we made a note? Where is everyone? When does the duty governor get here?'

Bryony decides an answer is wanted to the last. 'Same time as us usually. She'll be on the road.'

'She?'

'Miss Lyle.'

He rolls his eyes. Having a female on the team of governors of an all-male prison is the ultimate imposition for Creepy Crawley.

'Who's in charge when she's not here, then?' he shouts.

'You are, aren't you? Senior person in the control room.'

'Me?' It takes half a lifetime to sink in. He turns pale and tugs at his hair. 'Correct. That's the protocol. What do I do now? Assess the level of disorder, but I can't if the officers on the spot aren't calling in.' His thoughts are bumping together like the buffers of a shunting train. 'Oh my God, I was getting static when I tried. Do you think they're in trouble?'

'We'd better assume the worst, hadn't we?' Wendy shrills, trying to be heard above the alarm.

'Speak up. I can't hear you.'

She leans closer and repeats the suggestion.

'The worst?'

'If their personal radios are down they could have been taken hostage.'

'Makes sense,' Bryony chimes in.

Crawley clutches at his throat. 'What can I do about that?'

Wendy speaks up again. 'If it were down to me I'd check with the other wings, see if the trouble is spreading.'

Bryony adds, 'Especially the segregation wing.'

'Christ Almighty,' Crawley yells, imagining the psychos and sex maniacs running free. 'Do it now.'

But already calls are coming in responding to the alarm, mostly from sections of the prison unaffected by any disturbance. It doesn't take long to verify that the breakdown in communication is confined to C Wing.

So far.

Upwards of two hundred prisoners are housed in that part of the prison.

'Shall I order a lockdown of the wing?' Crawley asks. He's been found out. He is incapable of making decisions.

Wendy has to raise her voice still more. 'Bit late for that if they're on the landings disabling the cameras and our guys aren't answering calls. You may want to lock down the rest of the prison.'

'Should I?'

'Definitely,' Bryony calls out, and adds, 'Isolate and contain.'

'Isolate and contain.' The mantra seems to make an impression on Crawley, but he is terrified of committing himself. 'On second thoughts the governor may want to decide on that. I'll hold fire on that one. She should be here soon.'

'Your choice,' Wendy tells him, conveying a whole lot more than those two words.

'Maybe you're right after all.' He slaps a hand against his forehead. 'Yes, do it. Order a full lockdown.'

'Might be an idea to cut the alarm first,' Bryony shouts.

Wendy waits for Crawley to act and then announces the lockdown.

The silencing of the electronic beeps comes as a relief. Without that assault on the ears it's easier to think.

'I've done the right thing there,' Crawley says, nodding and trying to sound cool. 'Nothing more I can do until the governor gets here.'

'Is she definitely due in this morning?' Bryony asks, more from devilment than uncertainty. 'She goes to meetings some days. We could be in for the long haul if this is one of her mornings off.'

Crawley looks stricken.

More tense minutes pass.

'Hold on,' Wendy says suddenly. 'I'm getting something from C Wing.'

'Shut down everyone else,' Crawley says. 'Let's hear it.'

The voice coming through on the speakers is saying, 'Hello, anyone there?'

'Give me the headset.' Crawley uses his wheeled chair to shove Wendy's aside and take over. 'You're through to the control room. What the fuck is going on there?'

'Who's this?' the voice enquires.

'I was about to ask the same thing.'

'We're in control here and we want to speak to the governor.'

It is already obvious that the inmates have taken possession of the radio and at least a section of C Wing, but Crawley is unable to believe this nightmare. 'Am I speaking to a prison officer?'

'Are you deaf, or what? It's a takeover. Get off the line, jerk, and put the governor on.'

Crawley turns as pale as the whitewashed brick walls. 'The governor isn't here. You can say what you want to me.'

The voice from C Wing says in what is clearly an aside, 'It sounds like Creepy Crawley.'

A second, just audible voice says, 'Tell him to piss off and fetch the governor.'

All this is overheard by Wendy and Bryony, wearing their earphones. They pass no comment and avoid eye contact.

Gordon Crawley tells the offender that he is in charge and anything they want to say should be addressed to him.

'Creepy's no use to us,' the voice in the background says. 'He's only a screw. He can't fix shit.'

The spokesman says, 'Put the governor on or one of your screws gets it.'

Crawley isn't amused by what he is hearing. 'Are you listening? You can speak to me or not at all.'

A scream of pain is heard and it isn't faked.

'Bop him another one,' the second voice says. 'They didn't hear.'

'Cut that out,' Crawley says. 'No violence. Say what you want and I'll see what can be done.'

There is a consultation among the inmates, too indistinct to be overheard.

Their spokesman comes on again. 'We have certain demands you'd better obey if you want your screws to walk out of here alive. First, no dogs, no snatch squads, tasers, tear gas. In other words, you lot had better stay calm. You have a situation and if you want it to end peacefully you lay off, okay?'

'I heard you,' Crawley says. 'What else?'

'We'll speak to the governor when you can put her on, tell her what she needs to come up with. Miss Lyle and no one else. We're not dealing with pesky screws, got that?'

'I told you—'

'And I'm telling you, mate. If you don't produce her in the next hour one of these screws will be over and out. Over and out, right?'

30

After the sudden end of radio contact, Crawley, still deathly pale, turns to the others. 'They're bluffing, of course. They'd be idiots to kill a prison officer, and they know it.'

'This place is full of idiots,' Wendy says.

'Who have they got?' Bryony asks. 'Who was doing unlock?'

Wendy checks the list. 'Bob Vint and Charlie Rowell, two of the nicest guys you'll ever meet.'

'Two stupid pricks, to let themselves get collared by cons,' Crawley says. Any sympathy he might have felt for brother officers has been snuffed out by this emergency. 'The governor will blow her top.'

'How are you going to handle this if she doesn't show up in the next hour?'

'She will.'

'Let's hope you're right. She's running late already. Can we phone her?'

'She won't answer,' Bryony says. 'She wouldn't use the mobile while she's driving.'

Wendy tells Crawley, 'I think you'd better prepare for a no-show.'

'Fine fucking support you are.'

'Do it your way, then.'

After a short silence, Crawley tries to justify his management of the emergency. 'If the governor was here, there's nothing she could do that I haven't done already.'

'I don't know about that,' Wendy says. 'She'd alert the Tornado team, wouldn't she?'

Tornado is a squad of trained prison officers prepared and equipped to deal with riots. Rather than bringing in the police or the army, each prison has its own specialists capable of defusing violent protests, including hostage-taking. At any point in the day or night some of them would be on site on other duties and some at home.

'I don't think it's come to that,' Crawley says.

31

'Alert them, I said. Tip them off so they're on standby.'

'They're supposed to be on standby twenty-four seven.'

'They'll want to be informed of a serious incident as soon as possible.'

He chews the end of his thumb. 'You could be right about that.'

'Want me to do it?'

'All right. Do it.'

She calls George Pitman, the Tornado team leader, a prison officer who has served with the army in Iraq. Pitman goes through the disturbance procedure with her, making sure the essentials have been acted on. When she tells him the governor hasn't yet arrived he asks who is in charge of the control room. She tells him and after an eloquent silence he says he'll get on the road right away.

'Will George take over when he gets here?' Crawley asks.

'He's not supposed to,' Wendy says. 'He's got his work cut out leading the Tornado team.'

'Where's the governor, then? She's bloody late.'

Bryony has been watching the monitors. 'All the cameras in C Wing are kaput now.'

'How did they do that?' Wendy asks. 'They're supposed to be out of reach.'

'One guy on another's shoulders, I expect. The grease will be butter or peanut butter.'

'What do they really hope to get out of this?'

'Relief from the boredom, for one thing. A sense of empowerment. And publicity. It's a way of getting back at the system.'

Crawley twitches at the mention of publicity. 'Who's going to find out what goes on inside these walls? They can't possibly escape.'

'Get real. They've got smartphones. They're smuggled into

every prison in the land. They can call the media any time. Prison riot – it's a juicy story.'

'I hadn't thought of that.'

'They'll get people on the roof,' Bryony says as if it is a done deal. 'That's the way it goes. Hang out some sheets with slogans on them. They're guaranteed to make the front page that way. The tabloids really go for roof protests. They're probably removing tiles as we speak.'

'We don't want that.'

'We can't do anything to stop it until the Tornados go in and restore order.'

6

Magda is hurting. Whichever way she turns, joint and muscle pain drills in after a short time. Her feet have lost all feeling and her trapped arms have gone beyond numb to a strange sensation of the flesh being worn away and the bones fused together, turning her into a stick creature. Her throat is parched. She can't see the sun but it is obviously high, turning the shed into an oven. Her watch is trapped behind her back, so she can only guess at the time. Late morning, she supposes, or into the afternoon. Hours more are sure to go by before she is found.

Or days.

Her best hope is that her absence from work will be noticed and someone from the prison will try phoning and get the voicemail message a few times and eventually have the gumption to come out here and check. But who? As a governor, she isn't under orders to tell anyone about her movements. She hates admitting this to herself, but there is a strong possibility nobody will do anything.

Dehydration is a killer.

For no obvious reason Blanche looks up and barks twice. The exhausted dog has been curled up sleeping all this time.

A bad dream, most likely.

'It's okay, sweetie. You're safe now.'

But the pricked ears have heard sounds that reach Magda herself a few seconds after.

A tense moment.

Two male voices again. The same, presumably. It seems they didn't drive off with her possessions. They must have been inside the cottage all this time and now they are approaching the shed and Blanche is acting as a guard dog, making it all too obvious she has escaped from the sack.

'No, Blanche!'

The barking gets louder.

'Stop it!'

But you can't make a dog ignore an unseen caller. The little Westie dashes to the door and stands squarely on guard behind it, barking fit to burst.

Magda is petrified. There is nothing she can do.

The men aren't put off. The key turns in the lock and the door opens.

The first foot to enter the shed gets Blanche's full attention. She clamps her jaws over the toe end of the training shoe.

'Bloody hell! Get off!'

The man shakes his leg. Blanche hangs on, snarling.

He has to be the tall guy who tied Magda up. Just behind is a shorter, wiry companion who is rocking with amusement. They are both in balaclavas.

The second man says, 'Didn't you tie a knot in the sack?'

The other is too busy with Blanche to answer. He didn't speak a single word when he took them prisoner, but now he is yelling a stream of obscenities. He aims swipes at the small dog's head with the back of his hand and doesn't land many. She snarls even more and refuses to let go. In the end he swings his leg at the log-pile with Blanche attached and when her small body thumps hard against the wood, her jaws open and she falls. He takes a kick at her and misses. She has already backed off to carry on barking at him from a safer distance.

'By Christ, I'm going to slit its throat.' He has taken out a knife with a vicious curved end.

Magda cries, 'Don't you dare.'

The second man is still laughing. 'It's only a wee pooch, for fuck's sake. Here.' He reaches down and grabs Blanche by the scruff and swings her one-handed on to the log-pile. She was caught off guard and this man seems to know how a dog behaves. 'Put the blade away and hand me some of that rope.'

The tall man picks up a length of the blue nylon braided rope. 'You going to strangle it?'

'For the love of God.' His companion loops the rope under Blanche's collar, knots it, tethers the end to a hook on the wall and returns her to the floor. She seems to understand she is no longer a threat, shakes her coat, goes silent and sniffs at the floorboards as if they are far more interesting than the two intruders.

Thinking the second man may not be totally cruel, Magda says, 'She's seriously dehydrated and so am I.'

'You want water?' the short man says. He turns to the other. 'They need water. It's bloody hot in here. Get some.' He is clearly the boss out of these two and he's shown some compassion. Already she is thinking of him as Good Crook.

Left alone with him, she tries to reason. She is experienced in dealing with violent men, if usually from a position of strength. 'You could untie me. You can see I'm in no state to take you on.'

He eyes her without a word. He doesn't seem amused by the remark. She can only hope he is weighing the truth of what she said.

His hand moves to his right thigh.

From the zip pocket of his tracksuit he produces a knife every bit as vicious-looking as the first man's and unsheathes it.

Good crook or bad? Magda sends up a silent prayer.

He leans over her and cuts the rope binding her legs. She gasps and sighs as the pent-up tension is released. Then she cries out with pain. The rush of blood to her feet is like needles forced through her veins.

'Turn your back.'

He unfastens the straps round her arms. Huge relief is followed by huge discomfort as the blood flow is restored. She would certainly have fainted if she wasn't lying on the floor. She tries taking deep breaths.

In a moment she has recovered enough to sit up.

Bad Crook returns with a large bottle of Evian from the fridge. He's also brought the dog bowl for Blanche to drink from. Not all bad then, or is he trying to redeem himself with Good Crook?

Held in thrall by the spectacle of two litres of water disappearing so quickly, the men look as if they might applaud at the end.

Whilst swallowing, Magda is making a rapid reassessment. They've untied her and revived her, yet she isn't dumb enough to believe they are acting out of kindness. They have something planned and she was wrong about the burglary. She's had time while lying helpless on the floor to go over every scenario. It is now screamingly obvious that their actions have a link to her job as governor.

She comes straight to the point. 'What do you hope to get out of this?'

Bad Crook says, 'Shut it.'

His companion takes out a mobile, glances at the display, and steps outside the hut to take the call.

'Is he trying to do a deal?' Magda asks. 'It won't work, you know. It's been tried before. They have a game plan for every situation.'

'I told you. No lip.'

She addresses her remarks to her dog. 'You and I are being excluded from the debate. Pity. Knowing how things work, I could have offered some help.'

Bad Crook raises two fingers.

She says to Blanche, 'Must be hot under those balaclavas. I can understand our visitors being secretive, but a plastic Mickey Mouse mask would have been more practical.'

She's chancing her arm here. Bad Crook's hand goes to the pocket where his knife is.

'You won't use that on me,' Magda says. 'I'm the bargaining chip, aren't I?' Even as she is speaking, she recalls accounts of severed ears and fingers being sent by kidnappers as proof of identity.

Good Crook returns and says to his accomplice, 'It's on.' To Magda, he says, 'On your feet. We're going over to the cottage.'

'Not without Blanche, we're not.'

'Who the fuck is Blanche?' He looks alarmed and she realises she hasn't mentioned the name in his presence.

'My dog.'

'Get you.' He nods, looking relieved that there isn't some extra woman to deal with. 'Okay, but if she gets in the way . . .' He draws his forefinger across his throat.

They allow Magda to hold the rope that is doing service as a lead. Blanche trots confidently ahead of her.

And stops halfway across the vegetable patch.

Good Crook says, 'Move.'

'It's my shoe. She's found my shoe. Good dog. And look, there's the other one.' Without asking, Magda stoops and puts them on again.

She hears Bad Crook ask, 'How long to lift-off?'

'Dunno. Could be soon.'

Lift-off? What does that mean? A major action under way? Normally in a hostage situation you sit tight and discuss terms. Maybe they plan to move her to another location. Makes sense. Once the prison authorities are told she's been snatched, they'll send police to the cottage. Obvious.

She wonders how far this has gone already. She's been locked in the woodshed at least five hours. Her kidnappers have pointedly avoided showing their hand. The terse phrase 'It's on' suggests some high-up has just authorised the operation.

Magda's duty is to stop it – or at least cause some delay.

As soon as they enter the cottage, she says, 'Thank goodness. I need the bathroom – badly.'

Plausible enough, and true.

'He's going in with you,' Good Crook says, tilting his head at Bad Crook.

'He's not.'

'Don't fuck us about. No way are we letting you shut the door. If you really need to go, you put up with him. There may not be another chance.'

'What does that mean?'

'What I said, lady.'

'Where's my handbag?'

'Kitchen table, where you left it.'

'You've been going through it, I suppose?'

'Only to make sure who you are. Your cards and cash are safe. We're not here to steal.'

She crosses the living room to the kitchen and checks her bag. Everything seems to be in there, including her phone and keys. She picks it up.

'Leave it on the table,' Good Crook says.

'I need a comb.'

'You're not going visiting. Leave it, I said.'

She obeys and endures the humiliation of using the bathroom under the scrutiny of Bad Crook. As for Blanche, she sensibly made a comfort stop while they were walking across the garden. She is now curled up in her basket under the kitchen table making snuffling sounds.

'Okay, governor,' Good Crook says after Magda has washed her hands and face, 'time to go.'

Proof positive that they know who she is. This whole episode is definitely linked to the prison. 'Go where?'

'For a ride in your car. You'll be driving me. My mate will be in the van behind and make sure nothing goes wrong.'

'What's the object of this?'

'You'll find out. Play along, and no harm will come to you.'

'You ought to know by now that I won't be "playing along", as you put it, with anything criminal.'

'You will, lady.' He's taken a gun from inside his tracksuit, a black automatic. 'Let's go.'

'I need my bag.'

'Why?'

'Car key.'

'Empty the bag on the table.'

She does so. Her hand goes to her phone.

'Only the key. What do you take me for?'

'What about Blanche? I'm not leaving her here after what she's been through.'

'Listen, governor. I've had it up to here with this pooch of yours. She's got food and water. She stays.' He motions to the door with the gun.

In her Skoda, with Good Crook beside her, gun in hand, Magda waits.

'Start her up, for fuck's sake.'

'Where to?'

'Where do you think? The prison.'

Of all places.

Get with it, woman, she chides herself. Of course he

wants the prison. His plan is bolder and more ambitious than you imagined and he can't do it without you. She presses the ignition.

HMP Bream, her place of work, is outside a one-time coal-mining village on the southern fringe of the Forest of Dean, only five miles off, along a shaded, leafy route through one of the quietest parts of Gloucestershire. They will be there in ten to fifteen minutes.

Not long to decide what she can do.

She says, 'I would have thought the prison was the last place you'd want to visit. Anywhere but.'

'You thought wrong,' he answers, and adds no more.

She steers on to the winding lane that passes the cottage. In the rear window she can see the small white van driven by Bad Crook. He's dangerously close. 'Does he know we're driving through a deer park?' she says. 'I may have to slam my brakes on any time.'

'He's okay.'

'Yes, but I don't want him shunting me from behind. I'm fond of this car.'

He makes no comment.

'Boar, too,' she says. 'I've had to stop for wild boar before now.'

He says as if she hasn't spoken at all, 'When we get to the jail and the guards recognise your car and open up, tell them the van behind is coming in with you.'

'I don't think that will work. They'll be suspicious.'

'You're the fucking governor. Tell them.'

'Me, with a stranger sitting beside me and a white van following? It's abnormal.'

He ignores her.

'What's this about, anyway?' she says. 'Are you hoping to spring somebody?'

'Hoping, no,' he says.

41

His phone sounds. In the car, she is going to hear every word he says. He operates the tab with his left hand, keeping the gun in his right.

Magda checks in the mirror to see if the caller is Bad Crook. Evidently not.

Her passenger turns towards the window and shields the phone. She strains to hear the muttered words. There aren't many of them.

'Ten minutes, no more than that.' He ends the call. Not much learned from that – except he probably has a contact inside the prison.

She is under no illusion. Phones are smuggled into every prison in the land. The latest miniatures are the size of matchboxes and weigh only thirteen grams. They are blatantly advertised as BOSS-approved, meaning they won't activate the body orifice security scanners installed in the visiting areas.

She glances at the gun, now held loosely and resting on his thigh. He will make sure it isn't visible to a prison officer on gate duty looking in. They will be admitted and so will the van if she doesn't find some way of alerting the guard.

'Who are you hoping to spring?'

'I wasn't born yesterday, lady.'

'It's a Category B prison. All the offenders are behind several sets of security doors. If you think I can spirit him out in some way because you're holding a gun to my back, you're mistaken.'

He doesn't seem troubled.

They pass through St Briavels, the last place of any significance before the prison will come into view. The village is dominated by the castle that once served as King John's hunting lodge and in later years was put to use as the local prison until the Victorians built the ugly replacement three miles up the road.

Plans of action are whirling around Magda's brain. All have their element of danger. With her enemy beside her with an automatic in his hand, the best she can do right now is make the effort to get him talking and learn what might be ahead.

'Whatever you do will be on CCTV.'

'So?'

'They'll have the van's number.'

'We're not amateurs.'

She takes that to mean they are using fake plates.

'They'll want to look inside the van.'

'Empty, isn't it?'

She tries another tack. 'Are you going to take off the masks?'

He doesn't answer.

'No prison guard is going to let two masked men through the gate.'

'Leave me to do my job,' he says. 'Make sure you do yours right or the pooch won't get another meal.'

The chink in her armour. He's struck home.

She fights the upsurge of panic. Whatever happens, someone will think of Blanche, won't they? Prison colleagues have seen her. People in the village know her.

They have almost reached the end of the lane that links with Lydney Road where the prison is. She needs to be ice cool. She has a massive responsibility and she can't be fretting over Blanche.

He has put the phone to his ear again.

'Me.' Giving nothing away. 'Are you there? . . . Okay . . . Straight in, straight out and no messing.'

She looks in the mirror again at the tailgating van. Bad Crook isn't holding his phone. The call was to someone inside Bream.

She makes the right turn on to the main road and the van stays so close that she could be towing it.

Up ahead is the prison. One more curve in the road and it will be in view three hundred yards away. Even before the road straightens, she catches her breath in horror.

Black smoke is billowing above the trees.

'God in heaven.'

Good Crook is unmoved. He must have known.

'Don't they realise what a death trap it is?'

She has the full view of the old Victorian building now, the grim castellated gatehouse flanked by twin towers. Behind the razor-wired walls, C Wing is enveloped in smoke, with flames at two of the windows. There are inmates running about on the roof.

'Crazy.'

But she knows it isn't crazy at all. There's a cynical logic behind this. When there's danger of a riot inside a prison, your first duty as governor is to enforce a lockdown. But if the place is burning you are likely to kill some of the inmates, so you are compelled to allow them to roam the landings and the association areas to escape the worst of the flames and fumes. They know this, of course, and they get on the roof to protest and be seen from outside.

Into this mayhem Magda is about to make her entrance, already hours late. She will be recognised by the guards and the gates will be opened. She'll drive in, followed closely by the van. The escapees will have used the confusion to force their way through the system of security gates to the gatehouse yard. They'll get in the van and so will Good Crook and they will drive off.

'Give my mate a signal,' he tells her out of the blue. 'We're stopping.'

'What?' Has he changed his mind?

She does as ordered.

'On the verge. Here. Leave the engine running.'

She watches the van pull in behind.

No other traffic is in sight. No pedestrians either.

He lowers the window. Surely he isn't about to light a cigarette. Maybe he wants a word with his sidekick.

Neither man moves.

Rigid with tension, Magda stares at the smoke engulfing the prison only a short way off. She should be in there, taking charge. She has a duty to act, to prevent loss of life.

Flames appear at a third barred window on the second floor. This is what rioters do to create a distraction, typical of major prison disturbances. And it sometimes ends in tragedy.

She says, 'People are going to die.'

'Shut up, will you? Turn the engine off.'

'You told me to keep it running.'

'Shhhh.'

He seems to be straining to listen for some sound. All Magda can hear is the rustle and swish of the trees.

Then she rejoices. Carried faintly above the sound of the foliage comes the two-tone note of a siren. Fire, police or ambulance, it doesn't matter as long as the emergency services are coming. Someone has acted responsibly.

Her passenger has heard it, too.

'When they come past, pull in behind and follow them through the gates.'

Now she understands. The siren is his cue.

She waits, looks in the mirror, possibilities churning inside her head.

The siren's wail increases and she spots the flashing light. It's a red vehicle. A fire engine.

'Start up,' he says.

The fire engine is fully in view now, coming at speed.

She touches the ignition and watches in her wing mirror.

He smacks his palm on the dashboard. 'Now! Go, go, go.'

The siren is his cue for action and she has to think why he

45

has delayed so long. It was all in the timing. The men inside need the prison gate opened to make their escape.

She starts up and eases the car back on the road.

'Faster.'

You want faster, she thinks. I'll give you faster.

She glances in the mirror to make sure the van is in close attendance. Then she jams her foot hard on the accelerator. The Skoda responds and so does the van behind.

Fifty.

Sixty.

But she doesn't follow the fire engine when it swings left and through the prison gate. She drives straight past.

'What the fuck . . .?' Good Crook yells.

Seventy.

Eighty.

A clear road ahead.

She grips the wheel hard, shifts her foot to the brake, crushes it down and squeezes her eyes shut.

A screech of tyres, a bellow from the seat beside her and then the impact as the van concertinas into the rear of the braking Skoda.

Metal on metal. Shattered glass.

Oblivion.

7

31 July 2015

ONE DEAD, SEVERAL INJURED
IN PRISON ESCAPE BID
KIDNAPPED GOVERNOR'S BRAVE ACT
By J. Ballard Peck

A riot and escape attempt yesterday in the Category B prison in Bream, Gloucestershire, resulted in at least one death and a number of injuries. The governor, Magda Lyle, 36, is in intensive care and fighting for her life after crashing her car outside the prison gates in what is believed to have been a deliberate and selfless act of bravery that foiled the escape bid.

It is understood Ms Lyle was kidnapped by armed and masked raiders at her home near Tintern early yesterday morning and forced at gunpoint to drive her own car to the prison five miles away in the Forest of Dean, where a riot and fire were already raging as part of a pre-arranged plot. An unmarked van driven by one of the kidnappers followed Ms Lyle's Skoda. As they approached the prison she is thought to have braked her car at high speed with the deliberate intention of causing a collision with the pursuing van. Both vehicles were wrecked and the unidentified driver of the van was killed. Ms Lyle and her masked passenger

47

suffered life-threatening injuries and had to be cut from the wreckage by fire officers. They were flown by helicopter to Gloucester Royal Hospital and are in intensive care.

The circumstances of the riot inside the prison have been pieced together from phone and social media messages sent out by prisoners. The disturbance started in C Wing. At least two prison officers came to unlock in the morning and were attacked, tied up and held inside cells. Their keys were used to gain access to other areas of the prison. The CCTV system was disabled and up to a hundred inmates rampaged through the building, arming themselves with anything that came to hand. A stairwell was set on fire. Flames were seen at the windows of C Wing and several prisoners got on to the roof and hurled tiles. The riot lasted more than six hours.

An elite Tornado unit – officers specially trained and equipped to suppress serious disturbances – was sent in early in the afternoon and succeeded in freeing the prison officers and restoring order. A number of prisoners were treated for minor injuries.

HMP Bream is an isolated Victorian building housing up to 780 Category B prisoners deemed to be in the second rank of risk 'for whom escape needs to be made very difficult', including murderers and many serving terms of ten years or more for violence, arson and terrorism. Over recent years disturbances and other incidents including several suicides have been reported there.

A prison spokesman said, 'The disturbance was brought to an end by trained officers at 2.45pm. The events inside the prison seem to have been coordinated with the kidnap of the governor and we are working on the assumption that this was a conspiracy by people in the prison and outside to create a major disturbance to allow certain prisoners to escape. If so, it failed. A number of offenders are being moved to other prisons while the damaged sections of the building are repaired and restored to normal. An investigation will take place and those responsible may expect to have their sentences increased substantially. A statement about the incident is likely to be made in Parliament in the next few days by the Prisons Minister. The condition of the injured governor, Miss Lyle, is said to be critical. Her brave action almost certainly averted a mass escape and we are deeply indebted to her.'

8

Ben Brace shocked Caroline Irving at the 2018 New Year's Eve Ball by asking her to marry him.

Destroyed her night out.

She wasn't up for this, regardless that she loved Ben to bits. Okay, they were living together in some style in the Georgian house her father had bought her in Camden Crescent, Bath, but marriage was a no-no.

The band had finished playing 'Auld Lang Syne'. Sky rockets were shooting into the night sky and cascading over the city. People were shrieking and cheering. Difficult to tell what else was happening around her in the Assembly Rooms because Ben had grabbed her and kissed her passionately the second the new year dawned. And as their lips parted he spoke the words. He was hugging her as if she was the last upright object in a force-twelve hurricane. Clearly he'd planned this. He wasn't an impulsive man.

Big romantic moment.

The blast in Caroline's brain was bigger than any of the thunder flashes exploding outside.

'Lost for words?' Ben said, smiling. 'This isn't like you.'

Supremely confident. In truth, slightly patronising, he was so sure of himself, but she could forgive him that.

She was going to hate hurting him.

'You can nod if you want.'

Terrified of giving the wrong signal, she braced her neck and stared ahead like a guardsman on parade.

'I know,' he said, misreading the signs and taking her silence for rapture. 'Caught you by surprise, didn't I? Take a moment to think it over, like five seconds.'

They'd never spoken of marriage. Love, yes. Unreserved love, the best, the tops. All their friends thought of them as the ideal couple, made for each other. Ben had been so over the moon when she'd invited him to move in with her that there was no nonsense about tying the knot. Sharing had been the only decision. Caroline's house in Camden Crescent was much bigger and more comfortable than his modest flat in Walcot.

The bride thing appealed, of course. Like most girls she'd dreamed since she was five of the big white wedding, planned the dress, the flowers, the bridesmaids, the horse and carriage, the guest list, the reception, the string quartet and the honeymoon. No expense spared. Money had never been a problem.

Money wasn't the issue.

'That's at least fifteen seconds,' Ben said.

'I love you,' Caroline managed to say.

'So?'

How to handle this: she was at a loss.

He said, 'I thought this was how you'd like it done, the new year and all that. Want me to kneel? Slightly embarrassing, but if that's your wish, love of my life, I'm up for it.'

'Oh, Ben!' She shook her head. 'Shall we go outside? It's so noisy here.'

He released her from the embrace. Still holding her hand, he pushed through animated revellers towards the exit. Caroline, racking her brain for something plausible to say, was pulled after him.

A sharp breeze was blowing in from Bennett Street. 'We

don't need to go right outside,' she told him, so they stood next to a sedan chair in the crossing point between rooms where it was less noisy.

'You're not going to tell me you're married already?' he said in a jovial way that didn't exclude a small concern that she might be.

'You've got a bloody nerve.'

He reddened. 'Sorry.'

Her sharp reaction had stopped him in his tracks. Her chance to explain why she couldn't accept. She'd need to be tactful, but clear. 'Don't get me wrong, Ben. I truly appreciate being asked. The thing is, a wedding isn't just about the couple getting hitched. It's about a lot of other things.'

'Tell me about it. I've been best man twice.'

'I'm not talking about the way it's done.'

'Religion? It doesn't have to be in a church.'

'Not that.'

'Friends and family?'

'In a way, yes.'

'I didn't think you were all that close to your family,' he said. 'The few times I've mentioned them, you change the subject somehow.'

'Am I that obvious?' She took a deeper breath. 'Actually I'm not too proud of my lot, but I love them. Blood ties and all that.'

'Would they object to me?'

'How could they? They haven't even met you.'

'To my family?'

'They don't know them either.' She was in denial. Every fibre of her body was tensed for the car crash she saw coming.

'My dad being in the police?' he said. But his father wasn't just 'in the police'. He was one of the highest-ranking officers in Avon and Somerset, Deputy Chief Constable George Brace.

'That's never been mentioned.'

'But it is the problem, isn't it? I can see it in your eyes. Listen, Carrie, my love, Dad's all right. First impressions can be so misleading. He's got this high-powered job and he has to act the part, but that isn't the man I know at home. Get him out of uniform and he's a teddy bear, really, I promise you.'

'You don't have to,' Caroline said. 'I liked him. He was really sweet to me and so was your mum.' Ben had introduced her to his parents in November after the Remembrance Day parade and service, and they'd all gone back to Camden Crescent for sandwiches and a drink. The solemn rituals in the Abbey may not have been the ideal preparation for a relaxed first meeting but, to his credit, Deputy Chief Constable Brace had taken off his silver-trimmed tunic and loosened his tie and helped in the kitchen, talking warmly to her. If he was uncomfortable about his son being in a relationship, he didn't show it at all.

'Where did we go wrong, then?' Ben asked.

'Nobody went wrong, as you put it. You and I are living together. Can't we leave it at that? I'm just not ready for marriage.' She was about to add that she would never be ready, but she'd already said enough to ruin the start of their year. He didn't deserve the full let-down, poor guy.

He wasn't giving up. 'Can't you tell me why? You seemed to be saying just now it was about family, yet I got the feeling you didn't mind mine that much.'

'Aren't you listening? I *liked* them, Ben. They're lovely people. Can we leave it now?'

'I've really goofed, haven't I? Idiot.'

He'd gone pale. A worse thought took root in Caroline's head. Had he already bought the ring? 'Please, Ben.'

'I can't think how I got you so wrong,' he said. 'I was sure you'd say yes.'

This was getting harder by the second. She sensed a real danger of her stand becoming such an issue that he'd end the relationship, and how could she blame him if he did? She was the one in the wrong, unwilling to say why it was impossible. 'It's me,' she said, ducking it again. 'I can't handle shocks. Call me immature if you like, but it's the way I am. Can we go back to the party?'

'I *shocked* you? It wasn't meant like that. I planned it as a nice surprise.'

She nodded. 'I know, and I'm sorry, Ben.' She reached for his hand and squeezed it.

'Tell me you might be persuaded if I give you time to get used to the idea.'

She shut her eyes. 'Don't push me. Please.'

'I think we ought to leave,' he said. 'Let's face it, we're neither of us in the mood for partying.'

9

Back in the house they shared, Caroline lay on her side of the bed clutching the duvet to her chin and agonising over whether she really needed to tell Ben the reason she couldn't marry him. She couldn't keep it to herself indefinitely. He was hurt, deeply hurt, and her heart went out to him. After they'd walked back from the Assembly Rooms without holding hands or making any kind of contact, he'd said he would shower and go straight to bed. He'd blown her a kiss – more painful to take than if he'd ignored her altogether. She'd made hot cocoa and drunk it alone in the kitchen. How pathetic was that?

She'd crept upstairs, collected a nightie from the airing cupboard and undressed in the bathroom.

When she finally got to bed, Ben was lying with his face to the wall. She knew he wasn't asleep yet, however regular his breathing sounded. They'd fallen out a few times before – of course they had – and always found a way to make up before they slept. Some of the best sex they'd shared had started with them forgiving each other, putting injured feelings into passionate lovemaking. The heady mix of guilt and blame worked like an aphrodisiac – *you're a selfish, ignorant punk and I can't get enough of you. Treat me like the tart I am and don't even think about saying you're tired.*

But this falling out was in another class. Nothing so trivial as a thoughtless remark. Her rejection of his proposal was a threat to their relationship and the fault was entirely hers because she'd avoided saying what she should have come out with at the beginning. Right now it was screamingly obvious to her that Ben needed to be told what was behind the rebuff. In his own eyes he'd made a fool of himself, psyching up to make the big romantic proposal only to have it treated like a bad smell. There was no way of getting over that, short of rolling over and saying I was wrong, my love, I want to be your bride and let's name the day.

She couldn't do that.

Outside, the fireworks had finished. Determined party people would stay dancing and drinking until dawn, but most would have decided the best way to celebrate was in bed with a partner of their choice.

Even if she plucked up the courage to tell him the truth, she couldn't see how it would change anything.

She may have drifted into a shallow sleep when Ben spoke. She had no idea what time it was.

'You still awake?'

'Mm.'

'I won't sleep at all unless we talk.'

'Same with me.' But her heart raced.

He didn't exactly sigh. More like a heavy breath to release pent-up emotion. 'Tonight came as a shock to me. I didn't expect—'

'I know,' she said, to help him. 'My fault. I was caught by surprise as well.'

'I've been trying to see it from your point of view. I screwed up, obviously. The timing was wrong. Should have given you some clue what I was planning.'

'That would have spoilt the surprise,' she said.

'You called it a shock.'

'The word slipped out. I'm sorry.'

'Springing it on you was my big mistake, wasn't it?'

'Not really,' she said. 'If you'd put it in writing I'd have given you the same answer.'

After a pause, Ben said, 'Listen, Caroline, if you're not ready to commit to me, I can take it. We haven't known each other all that long.'

'It's nothing like that,' she told him. 'Don't you think inviting you to live with me proves I'm committed, as you put it? You'd better believe me, I don't make a habit of shacking up with men.' Even as she was speaking she knew her words were coming out in a way that was more challenging than disarming.

'You haven't changed your mind about me?'

'Oh, Ben.'

'I could understand. I wouldn't like it. I'd hate it, but, fair enough, being with someone twenty-four-seven isn't the same as just going on dates. We could still see each other.'

He was practically offering to pack his things and leave. Wise up, woman, an inner voice told her. You're going to lose him.

He was entitled to an explanation.

Now or never.

She took an even tighter grip on the duvet. 'It's like this. I can't even think about marrying you because of who I am. My dad is doing time in prison. He's a professional criminal, Ben. I can't even say he went wrong once and got caught. He's a gang leader. It's a business, an empire. Other men, really bad men, work for him, breaking the law all the time.'

Ben was silent. She had no idea how he'd taken her shabby secret. She was staring into darkness, speaking at the ceiling.

'I grew up without knowing. You see, my mother drowned when I was four, so he's the only parent I've got. He brought me up, got me over the loss of Mummy and made sure I didn't grieve for long. I took it as normal having him dress me and feed me. Sometimes there were au pairs who took over when he was busy on other things, but he was the constant in my life. Looking back, he did a wonderful job as a single parent. True, we weren't hard up or anything. As I got older he put me through prep school and made sure I had ballet lessons and my own pony, all that stuff, which some of the others couldn't afford, and we had trips to Europe and America and Caribbean holidays. He was a free man in those days. Only when I got to secondary school – I was at Clifton College, with fees of over thirty thousand a year – did I discover that Daddy's income from private means, as he put it, wasn't the same as the private means most of my friends' parents lived on. I was a boarder and none of us saw much of our families. But inevitably the day came when my so-called best friend got to hear that Daddy had been arrested and was on trial for ABH – actual bodily harm – and blurted it out to the next person she saw and of course it went round the school in a matter of hours. I can't begin to tell you how my world was shattered. Thirteen years old and I find out my father's a criminal. The mockery was cruel, my holier-than-thou housemates turning on the girl who wasn't one of them any longer.'

A murmur of understanding came from Ben, but no comment.

'It was all over the media, about him being a gangland king they'd been trying to nail for years. The case came to trial and he had a top QC to defend him and still got the maximum seven years. He was released after serving about half that, I think. I didn't want to know. Daddy wouldn't have wished me to know. I spent the school holidays with a family my house matron found for me and they were lovely people, but it was like being fostered. I felt old enough to look after myself. After I finished at Clifton and went to uni, I took a student loan and tried to strike out on my own. I couldn't ignore Daddy completely. He's notorious. He was back in the news every so often. Back in jail more often than not. When they've got their man they make sure he isn't at liberty for long. People in my year would hear of it, but students aren't so bitchy as schoolgirls. I was doing my best to lead my own life, be independent, but you know how tough it is on a student loan.'

He confirmed the truth of this with a grunt. She guessed he was too shell-shocked to speak.

'I was almost forty thousand in the red when suddenly out of the blue a bank statement arrived and I was in the clear, my loan paid off. All of it. I don't know how Daddy fixed it from inside, but he did.' Caroline sighed, not proud of what she was about to admit, but needing to complete her story. 'I'm afraid I let it happen, trying not to think how he came by the funds. I worry that I may be a criminal myself, living off the proceeds of crime. I should have cut myself off from him but I never have. I can't. It isn't really about the money. He'd reached out to me, shown he cared. I don't know if you can understand this, Ben, but he's still my dad and I love him, whatever he's done.'

He said, 'I do understand.'

Hearing his voice came as a huge relief. For the last few minutes she'd been speaking into a vacuum, but Ben seemed ready to respond, so she came quickly to the point. 'He's the reason I can't face getting married. He'll insist on paying and he'll want the wedding of the year, a service in the Abbey with me in a dress like Princess Diana's, the men in morning suits, his gang members filling the pews on the bride's side. I can't bear to think of it.'

'But you said he's in prison,' Ben said.

'He'd fix that. When someone as close as your own daughter is getting married, you see the governor and ask for release on temporary licence. I might have to accept a

59

couple of prison officers walking up the aisle with us like bridesmaids. Can you imagine?'

'Are you sure about that?'

'If he isn't a risk to anyone and he's cooperated in prison they can't really refuse. Big family occasions like weddings and funerals. I'm sure he will have played his hand well, steered clear of trouble. The parole board will agree to it.'

'What's to stop us getting married without him knowing? We don't have to have a church wedding.'

'I couldn't, Ben. He's the only family I've got. It would hurt him.'

'He's hurt you.'

'Not knowingly. Besides, what are *your* parents going to make of it, your dad a senior policeman?'

'He doesn't have to know either.'

'I'm sorry, but that's wishful thinking. It's the job of the police to collect intelligence on crime barons like Daddy. If you didn't tell your father you were marrying Joe Irving's daughter one of his staff would tell him first. Then can you imagine the problems he'd face in his job? It could easily destroy his career.'

Ben had no answer to that. Caroline knew the conflict going on his head. She'd had longer to think about it and there was no solution. George Brace was a decent man who had worked his way up and was in sight of becoming a Chief Constable.

She said, 'Well, now you know what I didn't want to talk about in the Assembly Rooms. I suppose I'm in denial, desperately wanting to believe Daddy has a heart of gold when all the evidence says he's an out-and-out villain. You have a mother and a father. It's different when your dad is the only family you've got.'

'Is that why you still call him Daddy?'

'I haven't seen much of him in my adult years. Does it sound juvenile? I suppose it does.'

Ben said, 'There's a way round this. There's got to be. I don't care what your father has done with his life. It's you I want to marry.' His hand reached out to hers and found it.

She turned towards him and their lips met.

'You're cold,' Ben said, pulling her closer.

'It's the way I get when I'm scared.'

'Scared of who? Not me, I hope.'

'Scared of how you'd take it.'

'We can work something out. There's got to be a way.'

'I don't see how.'

'Now that you've told me the problem, we can sort it. New year. New beginnings. We're neither of us stupid. Tomorrow let's put our heads together and think this through.' He shifted even closer. 'Right now you need warming up.'

Not much of a chat-up line, but true.

As they were already in bed, words didn't matter much.

10

This would be a first for Caroline. She'd never visited her father in prison. The last place she'd seen him was her lodgings in Clifton and that was before she'd started university, in one of the intervals between his stretches. Her main memory of that meeting was that he'd not wanted her to get close. She'd been prepared for a hug and all she got was a rueful smile and a nod of the head. Clever with words, he'd turned every attempt to say anything personal into some sort of joke. Not a word about his prison experiences or the shameful life he was leading. He was as well guarded outside prison as in. Yet she'd sensed genuine emotion behind the forced humour. After his departure, she'd found an envelope he'd propped on a shelf in the bathroom behind her electric toothbrush. It had contained five hundred pounds in fifty-pound notes wrapped around three small photos of herself as a child with her mother on some seaside holiday. Also a postcard-sized studio picture in black and white of an austere grey-haired woman in a blouse fastened at the neck with a cameo brooch. He'd written *My Mother, aged 70* on the back. She'd convinced herself that he wasn't simply passing on unwanted clutter. Family mattered to him. These were items he'd kept for years and he wanted her to have them. She'd looked for a note explaining as much, but there wasn't one.

She'd needed to write to the prisoner location service in

Birmingham to learn where he was currently doing time. He had the option by right to withhold the information, but he hadn't, and that was a positive sign. It turned out that he was being held in Horfield, a Category B prison in Bristol for serious offenders who had escaped from other closed prisons or been involved in threats to life, arson, robbery, violence and drugs. She'd checked on the internet and learned that Horfield was notorious for over-crowding, drug use and suicides. In the league table of British prisons it was rated 116th out of 117. The only consolation for Caroline was that Bristol was a mere eleven-minute ride on the train from Bath.

The next step had been writing to the prison to request a visit. She'd had to submit details of herself and explain that she was Joe Irving's daughter. She was informed it would be up to him whether he wanted to add her to his visitor list. Visits were by appointment and the prisoners made the booking. They were allowed two one-hour visits every four weeks.

She didn't get her hopes up. If, as she'd been led to believe, he was still running a crime empire from inside, she'd be lucky to get a look-in. He'd surely want to maximise the use of visits to issue orders to his deputies.

There was a delay of almost three weeks before she heard back and she was convinced she'd been turned down. The letter arrived and she ripped it open, ready to swear.

She could visit between 9.30 and 11 a.m. on 19 February. Her birthday.

Had he realised? She was hoping so.

But it would still be a frightening visit. She and Ben had talked for hours about the difficulty of getting married without cutting themselves off from their families. The secret marriage idea was tempting, but neither wanted to pay the price of deeply wounding their parents. In the end they'd worked out a compromise. They would make it known in advance to their families that they were going to tie the knot, but in a low-key ceremony without all the hoo-ha of a traditional wedding. They'd explain their reasoning, the predicament of a major criminal's daughter getting married to the son of a top police officer. 'Can you sell that to your dad?' Ben had asked. 'After all, he's well used to doing stuff without the whole world knowing. He ought to understand, and he'll appreciate being told.'

Caroline had said she hoped so. She could see that Ben would have at least as difficult a task with his own parents. The Braces had warmed to Caroline when they'd met, but her father's identity would come as a bombshell. Ben had said he would confide in his mother first. If he could get her on side, she might help to win over his father. The Deputy Chief Constable would throw a fit when told, but he'd not want the story breaking in the media, so when he understood that they were determined to tie the knot – and here his wife could convince him – he would come to realise that a small, discreet wedding would be the way forward.

The best they could devise.

When the train pulled in to Temple Meads, heavy rain had blown in from the Bristol Channel and the sound on the glass roof was like a North Korean marchpast for the Supreme Leader. A taxi was the only option and Caroline had to queue for one. The driver rolled his eyes when she said where she wanted to go, probably because he reckoned anyone visiting the prison wouldn't tip well. Mercifully he wasn't the sort who asked questions. He spent the journey giving a commentary on the failings of other drivers. On a good day, he told her, the trip would have taken under ten minutes, but with so many idiots on the road it would take three times that, and he was right about the timing. She still had twenty-five minutes in hand before the official start of

64

visiting. She'd been advised to get there early to go through the security. She didn't want Daddy waiting while other inmates were seeing their visitors.

Her first sight of her father's current place of confinement was the twenty-foot-high redbrick wall incongruously sited among residential terraced streets. The taxi drew up in Cambridge Road near the entrance and she had a difficult conversation with the driver about arranging to be collected. She didn't want to stand in the rain when she came out, but equally he wasn't willing to sit waiting outside a prison. In the end he gave her a card with his phone number.

She approached the entrance, made herself known to the man in uniform, showed the visiting order she'd been sent, and was directed to the visitors' centre, a separate building in a corner of the staff car park.

Much to her surprise she walked into a room with a welcoming aroma of coffee and hot paninis. People were having snacks and chatting like old friends. Small children were dodging about and a baby in a pram was being admired.

'Your first time, love?' a woman asked. 'Get yourself a hot drink and then you want to pick one of them lockers and put your bag inside and empty your pockets as well. They won't let you take nothing in with you.'

She did as suggested.

'You'll soon get the hang of it,' the woman said. 'Boyfriend, is it?'

She didn't get a chance to answer because the woman went on, 'Mine's in for the long haul. Drove into a copper and broke his leg, silly arse. Wanton and furious driving, failure to stop when required to do so, assaulting a police officer in the execution of his duty and on top of that they found six hundred pounds' worth of stolen jewellery on the seat beside him. He's lucky I still bother to visit him.'

A prison officer looked in presently, ready to escort them

into the main building. He asked if anyone hadn't been photographed and had their fingerprints taken. Caroline, the only first-timer, was asked to walk at his side. Fingerprinting was a requirement, he explained on the way across the yard, but the prints weren't shared with the police or anyone else unless an offence was committed. She was already nervous of making some mistake that would keep her in here.

In the main security room she showed her passport and visiting order for checking and submitted to a pat-down search from a female prison officer. She had her fingers inked and pressed on paper and a mugshot was taken. She was given a wristband to wear. Then she was made to pass through a metal detector of the kind she'd seen at airports. As if all this wasn't enough to make her feel uncomfortable she was asked to stand in a line with the other visitors while a sniffer dog on a lead was brought in and walked along the row. Her friend from the visitors' centre was next to her and said loudly enough for everyone to hear, 'It's only window-dressing, ducky. Nobody with half a brain in their heads is going to stuff cocaine in their knickers and get caught, are they?' And sure enough, the dog got a nil return.

Finally they were allowed to enter the visit hall.

Sudden panic. She hadn't seen him in almost six years. How ghastly if she didn't recognise her own father.

Stupid. She spotted him at once. He was behind a table at the far end, dressed in a black zip-fronted jacket, watching her with those wide-spaced grey eyes that had looked into the abyss and been unimpressed. Flecks of silver in his hair she didn't remember from last time, and stress creases in his face. He greeted her with his lop-sided grin, rarely seen by the rest of the world. 'Long time no see, as the sardine said when the tin was opened.'

He must have rehearsed that corny joke for hours. Humour didn't come naturally to him.

'No sea, get it?' he added.

She couldn't stomach this for long. She seated herself opposite him. 'Yes, Daddy, I get it. Excuse me for not laughing. This is a new experience for me.'

'You don't have to tell me.'

'I always thought you'd rather not be visited here.'

'You're right about that.'

'But you agreed this time.'

'Has to be important, don't it?'

'Well, yes. I didn't want to write a letter. They get opened, don't they? I can't tell you how happy I am that you agreed to see me.'

'Don't try, then.'

And now he winked and it dawned on her that he was more nervous than she. For all his faults, he'd always been confident and it helped him survive. 'Well, Daddy, I expect you've been wondering what brought me here – and don't say a train or I'll shoot you.'

'What with?' he said.

She found herself playing his game, levelling two fingers at him.

He tilted his head as if to dodge the shot. 'Don't tell me they didn't frisk you.'

'They did. If I'm in need of a real shooter I know who to ask.' She was giving as good as she got.

He was amused and the smile spread right across his mouth. 'So why are you here?'

'I want to get married.'

His eyebrows gave a fair imitation of a level-crossing barrier lifting. 'My only daughter – married?'

'I'm twenty-five now, just.'

'Says who?'

'Daddy, you know very well it's my birthday. You picked the date for me to visit.'

'Some birthday treat, visiting me in the slammer. Who's the lucky man?'

'He's called Ben and he's living with me in the Camden Crescent house.'

'Moved in already, has he? Jumped the gun, then?'

'It's not unusual these days.'

'So you love this Ben? Is he as smitten as you are?'

'He suggested it. He proposed to me at the new year. I wasn't expecting that.'

'Hope you're not expecting, full stop.'

'Oh, Daddy. Please.'

'An old-fashioned proposal? I'm impressed. What did you say?'

'I turned him down.'

'That's my girl. And I know why. You want to send him here to do the thing proper, ask me for my daughter's hand in marriage. And I'll grill him about his prospects. Does he have prospects?'

'He's in IT.'

'A computer nerd? That's no use at all.'

'Why?'

'I need a tunnel engineer for a son-in-law. Or a locksmith.'

'Can we be serious for two minutes, Daddy? I turned him down because of you and your situation.'

Joe Irving's face darkened and she had a chilling glimpse of the hard man she knew he must be. In the blink of an eye the expression changed again and he appeared more injured than hostile. 'You didn't have to do that.'

'But I did,' she said, sensing a chance to get her main message across. 'Ben's father is a policeman, a really high-up officer in Bath.'

After a pause for thought, the really high-up criminal said, 'Tricky.'

'Extremely.'

'Does he know about me?'

'Every policeman in the country knows about you.'

'He can pull a few strings, get me early parole.'

'I don't think that's likely.'

He changed tack and his whole face lit up. 'When are you planning the wedding? I've got to be there, walk my little daughter up the aisle.'

Caroline swallowed hard. The face-to-face across the table was unrelenting. In a normal conversation you could look away without appearing shifty. Under this penetrating scrutiny she needed courage to tell him the hard truth that she didn't want him anywhere near her wedding. 'This is what I came to tell you. We're thinking – allowing for everything – it would be best to keep it simple. These days you can get married almost anywhere. You apply for a licence—'

He interrupted. 'Hang about. This isn't what you want. It's the greatest day of your life, being a bride, and the greatest day of mine, being her proud dad. We'll do it in style, my chick.'

She'd known all along that he would react like this and she was still lost for words.

And he was unstoppable. 'Did you know I'll be out of here on probation as soon as the ninth of August? No kidding. Another 171 days and I'm a free man.'

The last thing she wanted to hear.

'I'm ashamed to say I haven't been there for you in the past, but this time I will be, and no messing.'

She tried desperately to get back on message. 'I was saying it doesn't have to be in church.' But her father hadn't finished his show of repentance.

'You must let me do this. I'm old-fashioned enough to believe the bride's father pays for the lot, so there'll be no need for the cop to reach for his wallet. We're not short of a few quid, sweetheart. You want the Abbey, we'll book it. The bishop, the bells, the choir, as many bridesmaids as you want, flowers, photographs, a cake as tall as I am and the biggest knees-up ever. Plus a honeymoon anywhere in the world.'

The speech she'd been dreading. She'd half feared he would come out with this and perhaps it was a good thing he'd got it out of his system. She stood firm. 'Daddy. I appreciate the offer, believe me, but I'm happy with a simple, dignified saying of the vows without any of those frills. Ben feels the same. I didn't know you were being released as early as August. Maybe Ben and I could have a meal with you somewhere nice to celebrate. We'll do the same for his parents.'

Bad mistake. She shouldn't have said that.

He looked disbelieving, alarmed, murderous and then – to her surprise – shattered. 'You want to keep the old lag under wraps.'

She shook her head. Words wouldn't come, but her eyes were welling up.

'You're ashamed,' he said. 'You're passing up the offer of a white wedding because of what I am.'

'No, it's my choice.'

'That's worse. That's below the belt.'

'I don't mean to hurt you. I want to make it right with you. That's why I'm here.'

'And I suppose your future husband is selling the same deal to the cop and his wife.'

'I wish you wouldn't call him that.'

'Tell me his name, then.'

'George Brace. He's the Deputy Chief Constable.'

'George Brace, eh?'

She thought there was a gleam of recognition. 'Have you met him?'

'I've met most of the local lot in the course of my chequered

career. If he's the man I think he is, he's not a total shit.'
Almost a compliment.

Caroline said, 'He was sweet to me when we met.'

'Did he know whose daughter you are?'

'Not at that time.'

'Does he know now?'

'Not yet.'

'Shit.'

'Why did you say that?'

'Slip of the tongue.'

'I'm not objecting to your language. I want to know why you said it.'

'Ben has the job of telling him, right?'

She was about to say Ben's mother but bit back the words. In a man's world, using Mrs Brace as the go-between wouldn't reflect well on Ben. 'We're trying to get both families to see it our way but I'm not succeeding very well with you.'

'What do you mean? You've made my day.'

Oh, Christ, she thought.

His eyes shone like nailheads. 'I wouldn't mind betting if you're upfront with George Brace and tell him I'm underwriting the whole shooting match he'll be there on the day for your sake and his son's, same as I will.'

'It's not a shooting match.'

'Pardon me.' He grinned again. 'Slip of the tongue. A shooting match is the very thing we don't want, right? A wedding. A family wedding.' He leaned closer across the table and held her gaze with a look of such sincerity that her own eyes watered in response. 'I won't let you down on the day, love. I know how to behave, honest – which isn't much of a guarantee, coming from me, I know.'

Now that he'd heard there was a wedding in prospect, nothing was going to keep him away. She'd underestimated the pull of family. Joe Irving was a bad, bad man, but he was still her father and able to play havoc with her emotions.

'You know I'm right,' he said. 'Deep down, you want a proper wedding.'

Against all expectations, she was starting to be swayed. Her future with Ben would be so much more secure if they both knew their two families could meet on good terms from the start. But was it realistic? 'This isn't what I came to hear,' she said.

'I know, chuck. I know. But I'd hate to be such bad news that you can't get married in a church like I did with your Ma. If she was here she'd say the same. She'd want you to enjoy the happiest day of your life.'

'Don't push it, Daddy.'

Shamelessly bringing Mummy into it. He was incorrigible. Yet what he said was right. Mummy *would* have wished for a church wedding. *Go for it, dear. He wants it. He can well afford it. Take him at his word and have the wonderful wedding you and Ben deserve.*

She said, 'It isn't only up to me.'

'If the guy loves you as much as he should, he'll go along with what you decide.'

'Maybe, but his parents deserve to be told.'

'Want me to square it with them? I can make a phone call.'

'Daddy, no!'

'Just kidding.'

To ease the pressure she steered the talk to other things, her job, friends, daily routine, even the neighbours and their dog. It was obvious he didn't want to talk about his life in prison or outside, so it had to be a monologue, but she'd never been short of words and he made a show of being interested.

People behind her were starting to leave. The prison officer nearest to them was looking up at the clock.

72

'I'll think about what you said,' she told him. 'It's a handsome offer, and I'm touched, but it's not what Ben and I were planning.'

'Have you got a date in mind?' he asked. 'September would be good.'

'Because you'll be out by then?'

'You're as sharp as your mother was. Nice soft light in September. I'm thinking of the photographs.'

She laughed. 'If I believed that, I'd believe anything. I must go. When we do fix the date, I'll let you know.'

'Not by post,' he said raising his hand. 'Like you said, the screws open everything.'

'Will it matter?'

He nodded. 'It matters. We don't want no one else knowing our movements. We keep this under wraps.'

Amused, she thought about the impossibility of the kind of wedding he'd promised being kept under wraps. She got up from the table.

'I'll call you at the weekend,' he said. 'I want to start counting the days.'

'No pressure, then?' She left with the last of the visitors.

Back in Bath, she was wondering how to tell Ben her father had run rings round her and the visit had been turned on its head. Daddy's insistence on a 'proper wedding' had been expressed with such passion that she'd pictured it vividly and knew he was right when he'd said that deep down this was what she wanted. Against all her expectation, it was as if a burden had been lifted. Eye to eye across the table in the prison he'd made the dream achievable.

Of course it was.

Ben would be a different challenge.

He was upstairs at the computer when she got in, so she let herself in quietly and didn't disturb him. Strong coffee to get up courage? She chose vodka and tonic. Flopped into an armchair. Poured herself a chaser.

When he came down, he eyed the bottle of vodka and didn't comment, but sat across the room from her on the sofa. His first words were, 'Did it go badly?'

'Not like I expected.'

'That's a bummer,' he said when she'd finished summarising the encounter with her father.

'Excuse me,' she said, her lips tightening. 'You're talking about our wedding.'

'Which if he gets his way will go ahead with all guns blazing, am I right?'

'Poor choice of words, Ben.' She didn't tell him Daddy had called it a shooting match. 'But I do think we should reconsider.'

In the pause that followed she could have poured herself another drink and swallowed it.

'Okay, what's changed?' His voice was drained of affection and she understood why.

'Weren't you listening? He wants us to have a full church wedding like you had in mind when you proposed to me.'

'Before you told me what he is.'

That hurt.

'What do you mean – "what he is" – as if he's a werewolf, or something? He'll be out in August. He'll have served his time.'

'Paid his debt to society? Don't make me laugh. You told me yourself he's a career criminal. I've researched him on the internet. He's like the Godfather, running all these rackets, drugs, protection and almost anything else you care to mention. Anyone who crosses his path is liable to be rubbed out by one of his gang.'

'I didn't choose him for a parent,' Caroline said.

'And I didn't choose mine, but you can see the situation my old man will be in. Impossible.'

'Daddy doesn't think it's impossible. He's willing to bet that if we go ahead your father will be there on the day.'

'He might, out of a sense of duty, but I can't foist this on him. He's the innocent party here.'

'Are you suggesting Daddy is making trouble? That's the stupidest thing you've ever said to me. He's offered to host the wedding and pay for everything, remember.'

'From the proceeds of crime. Makes it worse.'

'You're so bloody negative,' she said. 'You haven't even met my father and you're slagging him off. He's big enough to welcome you as a son-in-law and he knows almost nothing about you.' She hadn't mentioned Daddy's tongue-in-cheek offer to question Ben about his prospects.

'It sounds like your mind is made up,' he said. 'You want the white wedding, regardless.'

'Right,' she said, deciding he might as well be told now. 'Dead right. I've changed my mind and that's what I want.'

Ben released a long, laboured breath. The issues here were stretching nerves to the limit. Seconds passed before he said, 'I wasn't sure how certain you were.'

'Now you know.'

'Too true, I do.'

'If the whole thing is a step too far, you'd better say at once.'

'Oh, God help us.' He sat back on the sofa and stared at the ceiling.

A make-or-break moment.

'All right,' he said finally. 'I don't know how I'm going to sell it to my parents, but if that's what you want, I'll try.'

Caroline got up from the armchair, crossed the room and sat beside the man she would marry.

11

Most tourists visit Bath in summer. Unfortunately the air in summer can be so humid that some vow never to return. The waspish poet Alexander Pope once described the city centre as a sulphurous pit and Hester Thrale, the diarist, likened it to a stew-pot. Even so, both were regular visitors.

Peter Diamond, the city's senior detective, had put up with the place for so long that he scarcely noticed. He didn't often remove his jacket, even when his staff were in short sleeves and using battery-operated fans. But on this sweltering June afternoon even he sensed it was harder to breathe down here in front of the Abbey than in the rarefied air of Emersons Green where the CID had its office. He was supposed to be meeting his immediate boss, the Assistant Chief Constable, Georgina Dallymore, and he couldn't understand why she hadn't chosen to see him at the office. The likeliest explanation was that she was combining police business with a shopping trip.

Conspicuous in his dark suit and trilby among the lightly clad tourists taking selfies, he strolled about looking for a large woman in police uniform carrying several of those jumbo-sized bags that dress shops supply. She ought to have been obvious.

She surprised him. Her voice came from behind.

'I hope you haven't been waiting long, Peter.'

He turned and saw that for once she wasn't in the black serge and silver trimmings, but a print dress. No shopping bags. And she wasn't alone.

The man's face was familiar.

'You know Deputy Chief Constable Brace, of course.'

The DCC, no less. Knew him by sight and reputation. They'd passed each other often in the corridors of Concorde House and exchanged nods, smiles and the occasional word, so it wasn't necessary to shake hands. George Brace outranked everyone in Avon and Somerset except the Chief Constable. Managing to be friendly and dignified as well, he was a high flyer originally from the Gloucestershire Police who, like Georgina, was rarely seen in civilian clothes. Today was the exception. Tall, fit-looking and probably still in his forties, he was wearing a peaked golf cap, pink shirt and slim-fit tartan trousers as if he was ready for a round of the course at Sham Castle.

'I suggest we go inside, gentlemen,' Georgina said. 'Cooler and more quiet, one hopes.'

Being called a gentleman by Georgina ought to have been something to savour, but Diamond was under no illusion. The refinement was meant for DCC Brace.

The Abbey was a strange place for a briefing, if that was what this was about. The great West Door with its heraldic carvings is kept closed except for special occasions, so they entered through the smaller arched door on the left, Brace first removing his golf cap and Diamond his trilby. After the sunshine the interior seemed unnaturally dark until they emerged from the entrance passage and experienced the splendour of the building.

Cooler, for sure, and lighter inside than most great churches because of the vast windows stretching from end to end. The air was spiced with the pungent smells of lime-stone and hymnbooks. No service was in progress, but someone was repeatedly producing a single heavy bass note from the organ, as if an ocean liner was leaving harbour.

Georgina bestowed a queenly smile on the steward in the official blue gown. 'We're not visitors,' she explained and swanned past the donations box. To the others, she said, 'It's all right. They know me in this place. I'm a regular worshipper, Matins every Sunday and sometimes Evensong as well.'

Diamond's religion was rugby and real ale.

When Georgina reached the main aisle she faced the altar and made a deep genuflection, leaving no doubt that this was her second home. She turned to the others. 'I suggest we head for the south transept. We won't hear ourselves speak if we're under the organ.'

A short way up the south aisle a tall silver-haired man in a black cassock headed towards them in a meaningful way. Georgina said in an aside to her two companions, 'This is the head verger,' and stepped ahead to greet him, but he veered to her left and gave her only a cursory nod as he passed by. Instead he stopped in front of Diamond and said, 'What's going on, Mr Diamond? This isn't your usual day.'

Profoundly wishing he'd been ignored, Diamond muttered, 'I know.'

Georgina was glaring as if someone had broken wind.

'Or am I mistaken?' the verger said.

'No,' Diamond said. 'My day is Friday. These are colleagues of mine. We're looking to find some peace and quiet.'

'Peace goes without saying in this place,' the verger said, 'but we'll only get quiet when the tuner has finished. I'm sorry it's so distracting.'

'No problem,' Diamond told him. 'It's needed doing for some time.'

'Absolutely,' Brace added. 'You want the notes to be true.'

'Indeed,' Georgina said, but she sounded awfully depleted.

After the verger had left them, Diamond expected the inquisition and it started at once.

'You're a dark horse,' Georgina said. 'You didn't tell me you worshipped here. I've never seen you.'

'You wouldn't on a Sunday, ma'am.'

'Right. He said something about your usual day.'

'Friday after work.'

'He even knows your name.'

'Yes.'

'I've never thought of you as a church member.'

'I wouldn't want you to, ma'am. It has nothing to do with policing and we have more important matters to deal with than my boring habits. Shall we move on?'

For the present, the matter was shelved, but Georgina was unlikely to let it rest there.

They had the south transept to themselves apart from an old couple wearing headphones and gazing up at the stained-glass window known as the Jesse. The pictorial panels trace Christ's descent from King David's father, so there was plenty for them to take in.

'This will do nicely over here, don't you think?' Georgina stepped across to a wall crowded with memorial tablets and turned to Brace. 'Would you like me to explain what this is about, sir?'

The Deputy Chief Constable took a long look at the elderly tourists. They seemed to be engrossed. 'Keep your voice down, then.'

'I don't think they're listening.' She stepped close to Diamond, uncomfortably close, pinning him against a relief of the Good Samaritan. 'What you're about to be told is strictly in confidence. No one else must hear of it, not even close colleagues. Understood?'

Georgina was carrying on as if she was bidding to be the next M in the Bond films.

'DCC Brace—' she started to say and was interrupted by Brace himself.

'We can dispense with rank. It's George.'

She blinked rapidly about five times. 'If you say so, sir.'

'George, Georgina and Peter, all right?'

Diamond nodded. It was all right with him.

Thrown by such familiarity, Georgina swallowed hard and mustered a smile. 'By all means. You may not be aware, Peter, that, em, George has a son, a delightful young man called Ben and he's getting married on September the eighth to a young lady by the name of Caroline. They've booked the Abbey for the wedding.'

'Nice.' Diamond tried making eye contact with George, who seemed to have taken a sudden interest in the Abbey's famous fan vaulting.

'There is a complication, however,' Georgina went on. 'Some time after the arrangements were set in train, George learned that although Caroline is a charming young woman living in a beautiful house in Camden Crescent, there are serious question marks about her father. Putting it bluntly, he's known to us in another connection.'

'That isn't blunt,' George Brace said. 'He's a gang leader with a record as long as your bloody arm.'

Even the tough-talking head of CID was surprised by that. He was at a loss as to what to say next.

'You'll know all about him,' Brace added. 'He's Joe Irving.'

'Really?' Diamond's toes curled at the name. 'I thought Joe Irving was doing time.'

'He is, but he'll be out by August and he's going to be here, walking his daughter up the aisle. Do you see the hole I'm in?'

'I do, but . . .' He didn't complete the sentence.

'You want to know how I got in this pickle? I was ambushed, Peter. Are you married?'

'I was.'

'You'll understand, then. I'm a busy man, as you'll appreciate, forced to leave the domestic stuff largely to my wife to take care of. I take an interest, of course I do. I knew my son was getting serious about this young woman – moved in with her, in point of fact. I first met her last November and decided she was just right for Ben. It was obvious they were well suited. When my wife said they were getting engaged and wanted to name the day, I gave them my full support.'

'As you would,' Georgina put in.

'I'm happily married myself and I'll do all I can to make sure Ben is as fortunate as I am. I didn't ask about the girl's people at that stage. They were obviously not short of money because they'd bought the Camden Crescent house for Caroline.'

'The entire house,' Georgina stressed in case Diamond didn't know that most of them were divided into expensive flats.

The DCC was intent on telling the story. 'It turns out that she has only the one parent, her father, and he's absolutely set on giving her a wonderful white wedding. He's the driving force behind all this and is insisting on paying the lot and no expense spared. They booked the Abbey and the reception is going to be in the Roman Baths. The young couple got on with the arrangements, organised the dress, the cars, the catering, had the invitations printed and drew up the guest list. In my innocence I didn't question any of it.'

'Did your wife know Irving is a convict?' Diamond asked.

'Peter, you've put your finger on it. Mothers and sons. Ben told Leticia at an early stage but they didn't tell me. She's very protective of him, always was. He isn't a bad lad, but he got into scrapes when he was growing up, as boys do, and I would only hear about the damage when it couldn't

81

be hidden from me and I had to foot the bill for a broken window, or removing graffiti, or some such. Leticia always softened the blow.'

Georgina said, 'I can understand that.'

Brace went on as if she hadn't spoken. 'By the time I got to hear the truth about my son's future father-in-law, the whole shebang was set in stone. I saw red, of course, hit the bloody roof.'

'As anyone would,' Georgina said, gazing at her superior as if he was a martyred saint.

He ignored her. 'I told my wife and son what a scurvy trick they'd played on me. My own marriage was at risk, I was so mad. My marriage, my career, my son's happiness. When I calmed down enough to take stock, I realised I was hamstrung. Couldn't cancel the wedding without it back-firing. Everyone in my family would hate me, not to mention Caroline's lot. And there were all the contractors who stood to lose money over it. Someone was sure to go public and we'd be sunk as soon as it was known Ben was already living with a criminal's daughter in a house bought with ill-gotten gains. The damage was done. The end result would be the same as if they married, d'you see?'

Up to a point, Diamond thought, but why tell me? This didn't bode well. Standing so close to the Good Samaritan, he was mentally with the priest and the Levite who walked by.

'In the end,' Brace said, 'I decided the only option was to let the wedding go ahead as planned. It may still end in my resignation through no fault of my own, but I'll have done the right thing by the young couple.'

Georgina fluttered her eyes. 'Typically unselfish.'

'Her family are investing serious money. They'll want it to be a success. With goodwill on all sides, we can make a go of this.'

The 'we' was ominous. 'Makes sense,' Diamond said, beginning to sound like Georgina, he was so uneasy.

'Have you met the guy?' Brace asked.

Difficult to know which way to jump. Either was dangerous. Diamond chose to be truthful. 'Joe Irving? Personally, no.'

'Good. We thought not.'

Georgina lavished a told-you-so smile on Brace, who was far too wound up to notice.

'You probably think I'm a mug, Peter.'

'Not at all, George. I'd be the same.'

Endearingly, George Brace's face took on the rosy hue of a prophet's cloak in the Jesse window. 'Good man, because I need you on side, batting for me. You're used to plain clothes.'

'None plainer,' Georgina murmured.

'And blending in with the crowd. No disrespect, but you look a bit more senior than the average CID fellow. Ideal for this.'

'For what?'

'It will all be unofficial, I have to say.'

'What will?'

'I want you there on the day as a guest of my family, making sure nothing goes wrong.'

Diamond couldn't go on pretending he didn't understand. He was done up like a kipper and he didn't care for it one bit. 'Are you expecting trouble, sir?'

Georgina said, 'God forbid.'

'George,' Brace reminded him. 'I told you it's George.'

'Sorry.'

'Trouble?' Brace looked up at the ceiling again as if the trouble was a fault in the structure and the whole south transept would crash down at any second. He said without shifting his upward gaze, 'Having you on hand is a sensible precaution when I've got a crime baron across the aisle. He'll have enemies for sure.'

'Sid Felix, for one,' Diamond said, thinking the way to play this was to show it was too fraught with danger to be left under his control. Felix was a gang leader almost as notorious in Bath as Irving, and a deadly rival for the pickings to be had from crime right across Somerset. The Felix gang had taken clear advantage from Joe's recent absence from the scene.

The Deputy Chief Constable blanched at the name. The muscles either side of his mouth tensed and he lowered his head to lock eyes with Diamond. 'Do you know something I don't?'

'I know about the feuding that goes on. Every crook worthy of the name has heard Joe Irving is due for parole this year.'

'But do you have inside information?'

Diamond shook his head. 'I don't keep tabs on the gang culture. That's Zephyr's job, isn't it?' Zephyr was the regional team responsible for monitoring organised crime in the West Country.

'What made you pick on Felix, of all people?'

He shrugged. 'Isn't he the obvious one? He sprang to mind first.'

'You've put your finger on it, Peter. The man is a real and present threat. You know what happened to John Howard?'

He'd be a poor detective if he didn't know. Howard, a rising star in the Bristol crime scene, had specialised in 'cuckooing', taking over the homes of vulnerable people in return for drugs. He had been gunned down in the street outside the Dolman Hall on a February night in 2017. His death had allowed the Felix gang to extend control of drugs and prostitution in the red-light district from St Paul's to Fishponds. 'The Zephyr lads nabbed the hitman pretty fast, if I recall.'

'But they didn't get the top dog who put out the contract.

The poor sap currently in jail for life is terrified of fingering Sid Felix. He wouldn't survive another hour if he did.'

Georgina uttered another of her preachy comments. 'That's what our prisons have come to.'

'But do you know the background to the shooting?' Brace said. 'Normally these big-name crooks stay hidden and well guarded. John Howard's son is a boxer. That night at Dolman Hall he was due to fight in one of the supporting bouts. Naturally the proud father wanted to see his son in action. The hitman sussed this and was waiting at the entrance. He fired three shots as Howard stepped out of his car.'

'Vicious,' Georgina said.

'Do you see where I'm coming from?' Brace demanded of Diamond. 'Family loyalty forces the victim into the open, a particular place at a prearranged time.'

'Like here? Inside the Abbey?'

Georgina gasped and said, 'Perish the thought.'

Brace was grim-faced. 'Or at the reception in the Roman Baths.'

The parallels were all too obvious: proud father steps out of the shadows and puts himself at risk of death for his son's sake. But the remedy being suggested was out of order.

'You want me to act as a bodyguard for Joe Irving?' Diamond said in disbelief. 'He'll bring his own if he's got any sense.'

A resigned sigh from Brace. 'I daresay he will.'

'And they'll be armed,' Diamond said.

Georgina said, 'Keep your voice down, Peter.'

'We can't do body searches at the Abbey door.'

'Lord, no,' Brace said. 'I'm not suggesting that. A shoot-out is the worst possible scenario.'

'If he brings bodyguards they won't be using water-pistols. You need armed police, not me. Have you told Zephyr?'

There was a pained look from Brace.

Georgina clicked her tongue in disapproval.

'They'd stand out a mile,' Brace said. 'It's my son's wedding, a family celebration. Whatever precautions we take must be discreet. This is why we've chosen you. Are you an AFO?'

His blind spot. Georgina came to the rescue. 'Authorised Firearms Officer.'

Embarrassing. 'Not my thing, guns. I did a course at one time. Don't know how they passed me. I'm way out of date by now.'

'Go for a refresher, Peter. There's plenty of time.' Brace made it sound like the offer of a drink.

Georgina said, 'I'll make sure he does.' No question where her loyalties lay.

'The Tri-Force Centre at Black Rock is a great day out,' Brace said. 'I'm a regular there. State-of-the-art facilities.'

Diamond was still looking for a get-out. 'There must be others with firearms training.'

'No use to me. I need you – a wise head to advise me exactly as you're doing. Georgina tells me your experience is second to none.' Brace placed his hand on Diamond's shoulder and gripped him firmly. 'Oh, yes, you must be there. I'm encouraged by everything I've heard from you.'

12

They wasted no time. A large envelope marked *PRIVATE AND CONFIDENTIAL* and labelled *Detective Superintendent Peter Diamond* was propped against his computer screen when he got to the office next morning. He ripped it open and took out the wedding invitation, a textured pink card with the wording inside a floral frame.

Mr Joseph Irving requests the pleasure of your company
at the marriage of his daughter Caroline to
Benjamin Harold Brace in Bath Abbey
on Saturday 8 September at 2pm and at the reception in
the Roman Baths at 7.30pm.
RSVP Minerva House, Camden Crescent, Bath BA1 5HY

A handsome invitation to his shittiest assignment ever. He stared at it with distaste. He'd been well and truly fitted up. Being recruited to watch the back of a serial lawbreaker had to be the low point of his career. He'd not crossed swords with Joe Irving, but everyone in CID knew of this hardhead's reputation. The man had a stake in most of the organised crime in Bath and Bristol. Over the years he'd done a few stretches in prison, never for anything that would put him away for life. He was more slippery than a cowshed floor.

The job didn't sit well at all, but Diamond understood why he'd been chosen. George Brace wanted absolute discretion, a senior detective capable of mingling with the guests and alert to every suspicious incident at the wedding. He might well be right in assuming Sid Felix or some other villain would see it as the perfect opportunity to take a shot at Joe Irving. And if they did, what could anyone do to stop it?

Even if the wedding passed off without so much as a dropped hymnbook, George Brace was baying at the moon if he thought his career could be saved. He was obviously an intelligent man. In his heart of hearts, poor sap, he knew the truth about his daughter-in-law's family was sure to get out. You can't bury a news story as big as that. He was papering over the cracks for the young couple's sake.

And what of Diamond's reputation? Once Brace was forced to resign, questions were sure to be asked about the man who conspired with him to keep the whole thing under wraps. Georgina would look away and say nothing.

He needed to wriggle out of this.

The door opened. The caller hadn't knocked so she had to be Georgina, belligerent in the black and silver today, another presence altogether than yesterday's schmoozer in the summer frock.

'I found this on my desk,' Diamond told her.

'I know,' she said. 'I put it there.'

'I worked that out, ma'am. What's the point of giving me this? I thought I was supposed to be going undercover.'

'The invitation *is* your cover, Peter. You're a wedding guest. There's no need to reply. Your presence is taken for granted.'

'Too bloody true.'

'Come now.'

'I don't have a choice.'

'That's no way to deal with this. The Deputy Chief

Constable picks you out for a special assignment. Anyone else in this place would sell their birthright for such an opportunity.'

'Will you be there?'

'At the wedding? I don't expect so. It's a family occasion and there's a limit to the number they can seat in the Roman Baths.' She wasn't selling her birthright, for sure.

'You're welcome to take my place.'

'That isn't amusing, Peter.'

'A family occasion, you say. We know what family means to men like Irving. He'll dredge up most of the pond life in the city. Some of them are sure to recognise me.'

Georgina was quick to spot that escape route and block it. 'Highly unlikely. Joe Irving won't want his criminal friends witnessing his daughter marrying into a police family. To them it would be supping with the devil.'

Made sense. 'His enemies, then. Sid Felix.'

'If any of them turn up, they won't be guests.'

'You mean they'll stand out?'

'I suggest you get hold of a guest list and make sure you can recognise everyone who is invited.'

'Some hope!'

'Don't be so negative. This won't be one of those huge weddings. I told you a moment ago there's limited seating.'

'At the reception?'

'They'll be using that gallery overlooking the Great Bath. I've been to functions there. You can't seat more than eighty, maximum.'

'And I'm supposed to know who they are? Eighty strangers?'

'Most of them will be the DCC's people. You can ask him for photos of them all. He'll have family albums or images from the internet. I'm already thinking you should offer your services as an usher.'

He was open-mouthed.

'Meeting and greeting the guests as they arrive at the Abbey and handing them the order of service,' she went on.

'I know what an usher does, ma'am.'

'It's a splendid way to vet them,' she said, pleased with her own suggestion. 'You could have their pictures on your phone and check them one by one.'

'I'd rather be inconspicuous.'

She let out a sharp, petulant breath and shook her head. 'Do it your way, then. I was trying to be helpful.'

'You were saying most of the guests will be from the bridegroom's side?'

'That's my understanding. The bride will have her own friends, no doubt, but I don't think there's much family.'

'If they're worried about security why are they using the Abbey and the Roman Baths? It's not exactly keeping the wedding under wraps.'

'These are people of status in their different ways, Peter. Irving is a very big wheel in the dubious world he moves in. His only daughter is getting married and he wants the best for her. She'll want it, too, as any bride would. Daddy can well afford it. And of course the DCC is one of Bath's elite. They can't possibly go to some backstreet pub.'

'They could do it abroad, the Bahamas or somewhere.'

Georgina's tongue clicked in irritation. 'Get with it. Joe Irving can't go abroad. He'll be fresh out of prison and on parole.'

'Hadn't thought of that.'

'Your mind isn't on the job. You're too busy trying to worm your way out of it.'

Just like you, he thought, but didn't say so. 'As I said to George at the time—'

'You mean the DCC?'

90

'George is what he told us to call him.' He added, straight-faced, 'I thought it was George, Georgina and Peter from now on. As I said to George, there could be shooting.'

'Thank you for reminding me,' she said. 'Get yourself a priority booking on the firearms course.'

No mercy.

'And another thing. I don't care to be addressed by my first name except when we're with the DCC. Understood?'

He shrugged.

'Do you have a better suit than the one you're wearing?'

'I have another, yes.'

'That brown one? I've seen it. A better one, I said.'

'Why? For the wedding? Can I get one on expenses?'

She rolled her eyes.

He added, 'I don't suppose I'll earn any overtime for this job.'

'You'll earn the lifelong gratitude of the Deputy Chief Constable.'

'Won't buy me a new suit, will it?'

'You're such a curmudgeon, Peter. Can't you be joyful in the Lord, like any other church-goer?'

She meant to harp on about the church-going until she prised out every detail. Well, he thought, harp all you want, Georgina. My personal life is exactly that: personal. 'I don't know about the Lord. It's hard to be joyful in the job.'

She softened a little. 'You may not want to hear it, but I'm going to give you some advice. Stop resisting and go with the flow. Talk to the DCC and his son and prepare a plan of action. Check the arrangements and each name on the guest list. Do a recce of the Abbey and the baths. My firm expectation is that nothing will go wrong, but be prepared. Sign up for the firearms course. Make sure you're armed on the day and ready to use your weapon if needed. Put Sid Felix under surveillance and any other would-be assassin you know of. Carry a phone to get back-up in an emergency. I recommended you for this because you're brilliant under pressure. Time and again you manage tough situations. The DCC is in a spot, Peter. He needs a strong, cool-headed man and no one else will do.'

Compliments from Georgina had to be cherished.

'And if I pull a sickie on the day?'

'I'll make sure you really suffer.'

Normal service was resumed.

He passed the rest of the morning being strong and cool-headed and much of the afternoon collecting data on Joe Irving. There was no shortage. The National Crime Agency had an extensive file. Irving's record on the Police National Computer showed he'd been involved at some level in kidnap and extortion, bribery and corruption, drugs, money laundering, illegal firearms and profiting from prostitution. The best that could be said for him was that he didn't go in for art theft or forgery. Nobody could accuse him of being artistic.

The prison service had its own dossier on the man, his Prison National Offender Management Scheme file. He'd seen the insides of a large number of jails and had been regularly moved, not for bad behaviour or his own safety, but because of the control he had over other offenders. Typically on arrival he would let it be known that he intended to rule the wing. His reputation went before him and there was no shortage of volunteer heavies keen to make sure he succeeded. They carried out the beatings. Nothing was ever traced back to Uncle Joe, as he was known. Even governors and prison officers respected him and made sure he was given special treatment, a cell to himself in a good position, clothes that fitted, food that was edible, almost no cell searches and certainly no body searches.

The list of prisons he'd honoured with his presence read like a gazetteer of England: Albany, Bedford, Birmingham, Bream, Bristol, Chelmsford, Doncaster, Durham, Exeter, Gartree, Leeds, Norwich, Parkhurst, Pentonville, Thameside, Wandsworth and Wormwood Scrubs. All Category B and none for more than a year and a half. He must have spent a significant proportion of his detention on the road, quite likely in comfort. A few years ago a story had broken in the press about prisoners being transported in stretch limousines when vans weren't available. If there was a candidate for the stretch limo it had to be Joe Irving.

And now he was about to be released from Bristol and the police service were pulling out all the stops to make sure his daughter's wedding passed off without a hitch. First-class treatment outside prison as well as in.

But Diamond knew that a powerful man like Irving makes enemies like Felix along the way, rivals for the top spot watching for any sign of weakness, ambitious newcomers and people who had been punished by his thugs or sidelined on his orders. There are no rules of engagement in gangland. You're constantly under threat.

By the end of the day he knew more than anyone would wish to know about Irving and he'd come around to thinking there was no avoiding this thankless duty. Tomorrow, being Saturday, he'd take his suit to the cleaners and buy a new shirt.

He said goodnight to Sergeant Ingeborg Smith and Inspector John Leaman, the two in his team remaining in the CID room, went out to his car and drove the route that never ceased to bug him, sixteen dreary miles from Concorde House to Bath, where he'd been based until the powers-that-be decided on an out-of-town location. From Keynsham onwards it was nose to tail as usual on a Friday. His blood pressure had risen several millimetres by the time he parked in Manvers Street next to his former workplace. The new owners, the University of Bath, had given it a 4.5-million-pound refit and renamed it the Virgil Building. Virgil was some Roman poet who'd never set foot in Bath. The least they could have done was called it Cop House, after all the fine men who had graced it for more than fifty years.

He didn't look inside the Virgil Building. Too infuriating. Instead he headed in the other direction, up Pierrepont Street and across Orange Grove towards the Abbey.

There was still plenty of activity in the flagged space in front of the West Door. Parties of tourists meeting up after free time wandering the streets. Shop workers beelining towards the buses and the station.

The quiet when he entered the Abbey church was a total contrast. An immediate calm.

Not many were inside at this end of the day, yet it was one of the best times to be here. Late afternoon sunlight streamed through the stained glass, sending multicoloured beams across the stonework. His mood had altered. He stepped slowly to the right and up the south aisle where he'd come the previous day with Georgina and George Brace. They weren't in his thoughts now. His mind was wholly on somebody else. He made this personal pilgrimage each Friday after work. Even though he wasn't a believer, his late wife, Stephanie, had been. He missed her as much as ever. She would come here often for communion and her funeral had been held here. This was his way of honouring her memory.

He approached one of the candle stations, dropped in some coins, held a wick to the flame, placed the candle with the others, stepped back and stood in quiet contemplation.

Of Steph.

A private moment no one else needed to know about, or ever would.

13

Jack Peace was a killer in the making. Murder had been on his mind for the past three years, the one treat in prospect that had kept him from topping himself. When you're banged up, you can easily go under if you haven't got a reason to carry on and his purpose was stronger than most: common justice. He'd promised himself he would act when the opportunity came, and now the time was approaching. He knew when it had to happen. He knew where. He knew how. All that remained was to execute it perfectly.

'How much?' he asked the woman in the Abbey shop.

'Eight pounds, sir.'

Some chance. He'd already evaded the people inside the door wanting a four-pound voluntary donation. 'I'm on benefits.' His shabby clothes suggested as much. Even his T-shirt was torn at the armpits.

'I'm afraid there are no concessions.'

'I don't have eight pounds on me.' His look of disappointment verging on desperation would have touched anyone's heart. 'Can I pay later? I can get it tomorrow.'

She shook her head. Evidently trading in promises wasn't encouraged by the Abbey treasurer.

'How long are you open?' he asked. 'I might be able to get it this afternoon. People are generous in this town.'

'The last tour starts at five.'

'Five.' He lifted his arm and looked at the space on his wrist where a watch should have been. His hand was chapped and dirty as if he was a rough sleeper. 'That's not long.'

He could read the question running through her do-good head. How long does it take to collect eight pounds in a paper cup?

'You came here specially, didn't you?'

Peace knew when to up the ante. He was a peerless liar. 'I was baptised here. My mum, may she rest in peace, always said she wanted me to see the view from the top. She went up there once and she was talking about it for the rest of her life. Is it true there's a space in the ceiling and you can look right down to the floor?'

She nodded. 'There are several. For ventilation.'

'My old mum was right, then.'

She looked right and left, definitely checking to make sure no one else was within earshot. 'Here.' She touched the button on the point-of-sale printer, handed the ticket across and made a fluttering gesture with her hand as if to show she wasn't insisting on cash. 'It starts on the hour and takes fifty minutes.'

'You're a Christian lady,' he said.

'I'm not sure of that.' She'd just robbed the Lord of eight pounds and her cheeks were inflamed with guilt. 'Can you manage stairs?'

'I'm not a pensioner.'

'I only mentioned it because there are two hundred and twelve, but there are stops on the way up.'

'No problem.'

'The people over there are waiting for the guide to appear.' She reddened again.

Jack grinned at that. She'd made a routine situation sound like a miracle about to happen. He had that effect on certain women, unnerving them with eyes full of dark intent and as implacable as the flagstone floor.

Next, she'd think he was going up the tower to throw himself off.

If she'd known what was really on his mind she would have been even more disturbed.

'Does everyone speak English?' the guide asked when they were seated in front of him in a pew. He looked like a student. Ponytail, jeans, worn trainers.

Stupid question: does everyone speak English? If any of them didn't, they wouldn't answer. Eight were on the tour, including Jack Peace. Two looked Japanese and they seemed to understand what had been said.

'I must check your tickets first.'

Jack had his complimentary one ready.

'They should have explained when you bought your tickets that it's a lot of steps. Access is up a spiral staircase and some of the steps are uneven.'

Another daft statement. You could quickly tire of this young guy. If you were doing the fucking tower tour you'd expect steps. Old churches didn't have lifts.

'The first climb is a hundred and twenty steps, but that's the most you'll be asked to do and there's a chance to sit down at the top. We'll go up now and our first stop will be the ringing chamber. Keep to the right where the steps are widest and hold the rope with your left hand. Take your time and watch your heads. We don't want an accident.'

Definitely not, Jack thought. He believed in being deliberate. Before going up, he wanted a close look at the lock on the bell-tower door, so he stood aside to let the others go first.

Next time he went up the tower he'd be alone and he needed to know how to break in.

The lock wouldn't be a problem.

He mounted those stairs quickly to catch up. Above him, excited voices echoed off the stonework.

97

Having climbed all those steps, the tour group emerged heavy-legged but triumphant in the open air and found themselves behind a stone parapet at roof level above the nave. The guide informed them that they'd reached the Bishop's Balcony. Between gaps in the stonework were glimpses of Orange Grove and the old Empire Hotel.

Jack didn't bother with the view. Another lock wanted checking. Same type. Easy.

'Something interesting about the door?' the guide asked him.

'No, mate.'

'Watch your head as you go in.'

'Can't be done.'

'What?'

'Watching your head. Can't be done without a mirror.'

'Ha ha. Got you.'

Stupid prick.

Inside was a large room with a wood floor. Bell ropes with fluffy striped hand grips hanging from spaces in the ceiling. The group were expected to sit on benches around the sides for a lecture on bell-ringing that didn't interest Jack one bit.

While the guide was chuntering on about the ropes, a youth across the room was taking pictures with his mobile. The pesky teenager pointed the thing directly at Jack.

Out of order, kiddo. Nobody takes pictures of Jack Peace, and least of all when he's on a job.

'Feeling strong, everybody?' the guide said. 'We're about to move again.'

'Thank Christ for that,' Jack muttered.

'Did you have a question, sir?'

'No, mate.'

They were led along a narrow wooden walkway to sit in a cramped space behind some enormous clock that Jack knew with a sinking heart was sure to be discussed at length.

You could make out the Roman numerals in reverse against the daylight through the glass segments.

'We're now above the north transept,' their guide told them. 'This is the Abbey clock you see from outside when you're standing in the High Street, where they had an open market formerly, so everyone could look up and check the time. It replaced an earlier clock originally fixed to the north face of the tower. This one dates from 1888 and has a six-foot diameter and was designed by Lord Grimthorpe.'

As if anyone cared, least of all Jack.

The minute hand moved seven minutes before everything that needed to be said about the clock was gone through. And then – would you believe it? – the guide started up about something else.

But this time he had Jack's total attention.

'When you first came into the Abbey this afternoon, you can't have failed to notice, seventy-eight feet above you, the famous fan vaulting extending across the entire building and thought by many to be the finest architectural feature of the Abbey. Although it looks as if it was constructed all at one time in history, it wasn't. The work was started in the reign of Elizabeth I and only completed in 1873. Right now, we're above the oldest section. You'll get an opportunity presently to see something people below us are totally unaware of.'

'Gaps in the ceiling?' Jack couldn't stop himself saying. He was like a kid on Christmas Day. He'd come here specially for this. Been thinking about it ever since he'd nicked the Abbey guidebook from a bookshop over a week ago.

'Hey – someone's done his homework. Yes, the holes are meant to be for ventilation, but many of our visitors find them fascinating for another reason. You'll each have a chance to look through and see people moving about below – and they've no idea we're watching them. Sneaky, but there's a bit of the Peeping Tom in all of us and this is always a highlight of the tour. So let's retrace our steps and you will see for yourselves.'

Jack didn't reach the spyhole first. One of the Japanese girls pushed ahead of him and her companion wasn't far behind.

'Fucking hell.' He was incensed.

'Be patient and you'll all get a turn,' the guide said. 'In the meantime, I'll tell you how a fan-vaulted ceiling is constructed.'

When Jack's turn came, he was devastated. The vent wasn't a decent-sized gap in the stonework, as he'd expected. It was a hole no bigger than a beermat. You might get a gun barrel through, but that was all. You couldn't shoot with any accuracy because you wouldn't be able to see. You could end up shooting the bishop by mistake.

Mission aborted.

Jack decided to quit the tour. He was about to make some excuse when he remembered the sonofabitch who had taken the pictures.

Lecture over, everyone got up to start the next ascent of the spiral staircase, to the bell chamber itself. Jack made sure he was right behind the teenage photographer and waited until they were some way up before reaching forward and lifting the phone from the kid's back pocket.

'Sorry, mate. Lost balance for a moment.'

The teenager checked his pocket. 'My phone's gone,' he said in panic.

Jack spread his hands to show they were empty. The mobile was already clattering down the steps. 'I thought I heard something fall. I'll fetch it for you.' Made sense. He was the lowest on the stairs.

He found the phone about ten steps down. Just to be sure it was damaged beyond use he crunched the screen with his heel. Then he moved on down the stairs.

14

The DCC was a busy man with responsibilities ranging beyond the city of Bath. Peter Diamond had to wait ten days before getting to see him, but that was a useful interval giving him the chance to get the bizarre assignment in perspective. He'd concluded after much reflection that there was no wriggling out. He was the only possible choice. George Brace needed someone senior, responsible and experienced in undercover work. He couldn't ask anyone of lower rank. That was how the cookie had crumbled.

Diamond wasn't without sympathy for George. When family life gets entangled with the job, you need all the help you can get. George hadn't made any mystery of it. His situation was dire and not just on the day of the wedding, but for the rest of his career – if he had one. At least he'd realised what a favour he was asking. He'd had the decency to get on first-name terms from the start. Diamond approved of that.

The two met in the staff car park, but not by accident. Diamond had been waiting in his car, knowing George was due in about eleven. He got out as the black Volvo drove into the reserved space marked DCC.

Brace lowered the window. 'Peter – a man I planned to see today.'

'And here I am.'

'You're free right now?'

'If you are, George.'

'Well, why not? Why don't we do this somewhere else? You look like a man who knows a good pub.'

Good call, Diamond thought. 'Personally, I like the Folly. They do real ale and there's a nice garden.'

'The Folly, did you say? Sums up my situation. Hop in the car and tell me the way.'

They could have walked there, it was so near, but Brace looked like a man who drove everywhere.

In sunshine on the patio, with tankards of Old Thumper on the table and the Folly brook babbling somewhere in a wooded area across the lawn, Diamond felt he could get a taste for policing at executive level. Better than sitting in front of a screen in Concorde House, for sure.

'How are the preparations going?' he asked.

'For the wedding? You'll need to ask my future daughter-in-law. She's running the show. I don't say that unkindly. Caroline is better at organising than anyone in my family. She's learned to fend for herself, I suppose, with her father being in the slammer most of her life.'

'He's an organiser, too, in his own way.'

'Yes, but I doubt if organised crime takes in floral arrangements and bridesmaids' dresses. Cheers, Peter.'

They sampled the Old Thumper and agreed that it was good.

'I prefer sitting outside,' Brace said. 'One can talk without being overheard.'

'That's true.' They were the only drinkers out there.

'And I can smoke.' He produced a pipe and a pouch of tobacco, an unusual sight in 2018. 'Calms the nerves.' He went through the performance of lighting up. 'You must meet Caroline.'

'Really? I thought I was going undercover.'

'The bride needs to know who you are and so does her father.'

Diamond almost threw up the ale he'd just swallowed. 'Him, too?'

'Absolutely. Best if he knows why you're there. Don't want any misunderstandings, do we?' He puffed out smoke.

'I guess not.'

'It may discourage him from bringing in some heavies of his own.'

'I'm the official heavy, am I?'

Brace's smile was slow in coming and far from convincing. 'Nothing personal. I can arrange for you to meet Irving after he's released from Horfield.'

Diamond was making more rapid adjustments than a Hong Kong tailor. 'That'll be good.'

'You'll want to know precisely who is coming.'

'Georgina suggested I ask you for pictures of your family members.' He was about to add, 'So I don't shoot them,' but Brace wasn't fully in tune with his humour.

'Sensible. I'll see that you get them. Caroline will supply pictures of her friends and so will Ben. That generation are forever snapping away with their phones.' Brace tore open a bag of crisps and offered them. He was evidently a seasoned smoker because he'd mastered the trick of speaking with the pipe in his mouth. 'You're giving me confidence, Peter. I'm feeling better about this nightmare wedding already. Will you be checking the Abbey ahead of the ceremony?'

'Certainly will, George.'

'And the Roman Baths?'

'You bet.'

'You know both locations pretty well?'

'Well enough. I'm more concerned about what happens outside.'

'Oh?' He put the pipe on the table and reached for the beer.

'If anyone wants to take a shot at Joe Irving, it would be easiest when he arrives at the West Door with his daughter.'

Now it was George Brace who gagged on the drink. 'You're right. As father of the bride he's got to be there.'

'An open area where a hitman has escape routes. The big space in front of the Abbey is a huge concern. Will there be photographs when they come out? Everyone lined up?'

'Dear God, yes.' He jammed the pipe back in his mouth.

'A killer couldn't ask for better. Pick them off as they stand there.'

Brace had gone as pale as moonlight. 'What can we do? We can't close the whole area to the public.'

'If you don't mind them being in on the act, I can get some of my CID team to mingle.'

'Will they be armed?'

'They'll need to be.'

Brace sighed. 'Guns at a wedding. It doesn't seem right.'

'You said you wanted me armed. You encouraged me to do a refresher at the firearms course.'

'True.'

Brace sat back and vibrated his lips. Even here in this idyllic setting he was feeling the stress. He'd be a lot more stressed if he knew Diamond hadn't pulled a trigger in twenty years.

'Have you been yet?'

'Been where, George?'

'Black Rock. The firearms training centre.'

'Finding the time is my problem.' He outlined the measures he'd taken to get up to speed on Irving and his history of crime and punishment. 'Normally I'd delegate this stuff, but it's all down to me. I'm researching the Felix gang as well.'

'I managed to fit in the weapons course, and so can you. It will look good on your CV.'

Diamond wasn't going to get out of this. 'I'll get booked in, then. Better be sure than sorry.'

'Perish the thought, Peter.'

With uncanny timing a bang went off somewhere behind the trees.

Brace jerked forward and slopped some of his drink on the table. 'What's that?'

'Someone shooting at rabbits, I expect.'

'Bloody Irving hasn't been released yet and already I'm jumpy.'

'He'll be more jumpy than you on the day,' Diamond said by way of reassurance.

'Why is that?'

'As father of the bride he has to make a speech. Isn't that the custom?'

'My God – I hadn't thought of that.' With something new to worry over, Brace raked his hand through his hair. 'What on earth will he say?'

15

No way could Diamond duck out of the firearms training. His new friend George Brace was renowned for efficiency and would be sure to check the attendance register. George was proud of the Tri-Force centre, so-called because the Gloucestershire and Wiltshire police forces also used the facility. Quite a coup for Avon and Somerset.

The training was done in a former stone quarry at Black Rock, near Police Headquarters at Portishead, and was so state-of-the-art that it had been opened by Theresa May when she was Home Secretary, in January 2016. Firing ranges, fake houses, interactive target systems and even an abseil training area.

It seemed to Diamond that everything about Black Rock was designed to make the average copper feel like PC Plod. Macho young men in Kevlar strutted about the ranges as if they were auditioning for the next Terminator movie. He refused to be intimidated. He knew something about Black Rock that wasn't spoken about. The grand opening should have been two years earlier than it was. In August 2013, an anarchist group calling themselves ACAB – All Coppers Are Bastards – beat the security and started a fire that destroyed the newly constructed main building.

He felt better for knowing that.

Herb, his handgun instructor, turned out to be salt-of-the-earth when they dropped the formalities, friendly, straight-talking and good at his job, the kind of man you'd want at your side in a crisis situation.

'Why are you doing this?' Herb asked after Diamond missed the target altogether for the umpteenth time. The only element he had passed so far was the draw from holster and that hadn't been quick.

'Order from on high,' the big detective said.

'Personal protection officer, are you?'

'Not really.'

'Because I wouldn't want you protecting me or anyone I know.'

'Thanks for that, Herb.'

'In fact, I'm glad I'm wearing bulletproof clothes.'

'Would you sign me off if I promise not to shoot anyone?'

'That's not the way things are done here. Want to try your luck at abseiling instead?'

'Do you really want to know? I'll stick to what I do best. Give me another twenty rounds, would you?'

'How's your vision?' Herb asked, after that set of bullets had gone astray.

'Twenty-twenty last time it was checked.'

'How long ago was that?'

'Let's keep trying. It's about hand-eye coordination in my case. I'm getting the idea of steadying the aim.'

Herb was silent for a while. He seemed to be checking who else was on the short range with them.

'Maybe you could take the gun yourself and give me another demonstration,' Diamond said, seeding an idea with Herb. He was subtle enough to say this without giving a wink.

'Not allowed,' Herb said.

Diamond unclipped the magazine to reload. 'I'm okay at this bit.' He dropped two bullets on the ground. 'Ha, getting overconfident.'

107

Herb glanced right and left again. 'Give it to me,' he said through his teeth. But he didn't fire at the target. He dipped into his pocket and found an attachment and clipped it to the pistol's accessory rail.

'What's that?' Diamond asked.

Herb held the gun as if he was about to demonstrate. 'Watch the target.'

A small red dot appeared on the still unmarked centre mass target.

'Can you see that?' Herb said. 'It's a laser. When you get it on the bull, you squeeze the trigger.'

'Smart.'

Diamond took over again. The laser dot hovered about a lot, but he got his timing right and scored his first hit.

'Keep going,' Herb said.

'Magic,' Diamond said.

'Keep your voice down.'

Persistence and the laser sight attachment paid off. Herb removed the gadget from the gun and pocketed it before they went to see the chief examiner, who said, 'Well done. The best cluster I've seen all week. You could get a job here.' They signed Diamond off. That was on the short range. Herb decided not to try anything more ambitious.

Diamond left Black Rock thinking he would form a group called NACAB. Not all coppers are bastards.

16

The next challenge was meeting the young couple who were due to get married. George insisted that this was necessary and made a lunch date in August at the house in Camden Crescent. His son would be cooking, he explained. Young Ben liked to have a change from sitting at the computer. There was no need to bring a bottle of wine or flowers for Caroline. They preferred to keep the whole thing low-key. 'We don't want you going to any expense at all. And don't come in a suit, for heaven's sake. They'll be very casual.'

Difficult. Diamond rarely wore anything except a suit. He was forced to go to Marks and Spencer for jeans and a polo shirt and he got some startled looks in Concorde House when he turned up one morning dressed like that.

'Change of image, guv?' Ingeborg Smith enquired.

'Sort of. Do I look cool? Be honest.'

'Cool?' She weighed her words before answering. 'Different, for sure.'

'You mean ridiculous, don't you? People with a shape like mine shouldn't wear jeans. Come casual, I was told, and I bought these things. I don't want them to look brand new so I'm getting some use out of them.'

'What's the gig?'

'Come again.'

'The occasion.'

'A lunch date.'

'Nice. Anyone I know?'

'Not that kind of date. This is a working lunch at some-body's house. What else could I wear except this?'

'It looks okay. Really.'

'The jeans smell of chemicals. Mothballs or something.'

'That'll go in time. You could try a pinch of baking soda in the wash if you want to get rid of it. That absorbs the smell.'

'I dare not wash them in case they shrink. I had enough trouble getting into them. This is a one-off, anyway. I won't ever wear them again.'

'You'll be fine, just fine.' But anyone could see she was straining every muscle to keep a straight face.

Bath's building boom at the end of the eighteenth century started with Camden Crescent, said to have the finest of all views across the city. A law of nature states that a good view always means a stiff climb. Diamond planned to use the car until George phoned to suggest it was such a fine summer morning that they should meet at the top of Broad Street and walk up. Not good news when you're gravitationally challenged.

The DCC was waiting by the traffic lights, suave in a pink button-down shirt, purple cravat and chinos. From Christopher Barry or John Anthony, Diamond decided. A Deputy Chief Constable could afford to shop at classy places.

Diamond was in the problematical jeans. Keith Halliwell, his second-in-command, had suggested 'distressing' them by ripping holes in them. Diamond took this as poking fun. Making a fashion statement can bring out the worst in people you ought to be able to trust.

As they toiled up Lansdown Road, the start of the northern slopes, George said, 'It gets steeper higher up. Will you be okay?'

110

A bit bloody late to ask, Diamond thought. He said he would be fine.

'Did you know the course of English history almost changed up there? Queen Anne was leaving the city after one of her visits and the gradient was so steep that her coach started rolling back. She could have been killed. Fortunately some of the Bathonians lining the route saw what was happening and rushed to hold it steady. The place where it happened is a footpath now. They rerouted the road after that.'

'The only thing I can tell you about Camden Crescent,' Diamond said, 'is that Bath's most notorious murderer, John Straffen, abducted a child from there and strangled her in 1951. She was the first of several child victims. He escaped from Broadmoor and killed another. They decided after that to keep him in maximum security prisons. He was locked up for fifty-five years.'

'Better not tell Caroline that story. She's blissfully proud of her address.' George cleared his throat. 'I'm glad you agreed to walk up the hill with me. I wanted a quiet word before we show up at the house. When we discuss your role at the wedding it might not be a good idea to mention to the young couple that you'll be armed on the day. As far as they're concerned, you'll be there to lend confidence to the occasion, prepared to step forward only if anything untoward happens.'

'Okay,' Diamond said, feeling most unlike a confidence-giver.

'You and I know you're fresh from Black Rock and equipped to take on anyone who draws a weapon, but nobody else needs to be told. I hear you had all nine in the target with the handgun. Works wonders for my morale, Peter, knowing I can rely on you.'

Diamond stared ahead and stayed silent.

George chatted on, as if to lift the mood after the talk of

111

a queen in peril and children murdered. 'They're full of excitement about the wedding. We'll have to put up with some toe-curling stuff about hen parties and stag nights, but you and I have been there before.'

'Been where?' Diamond's mood wasn't lifted one bit. An alarming thought had popped into his head: was he about to be drafted into Caroline's hen night as well?

'We both got wed. You said you were married once.'

'That's right.' He'd heard that the only men allowed into these girlie events were male strippers. The hell with that. There was only so much he'd do to keep his job.

'White wedding?' George asked. 'The full works?'

'Only what we could afford.' Be serious, he thought. No one would want me to take my kit off.

'You weren't in uniform?'

'No.' Maybe I should say so now.

'Morning suit and grey topper?'

'It wasn't that kind of wedding.' Get real. It will never happen.

They finally reached Camden Crescent, built on a slope so steep that parts of the planned structure collapsed at an early stage in the construction and were abandoned, leaving ten houses to the left of the Corinthian columns at the projected centre and only four to the right. It is still a glorious sight from Hedgemead Park, just below, where another 175 properties collapsed in a landslip in 1881. Reader, if you ever think of moving to the northern slopes, hire a surveyor.

The door was opened by a young man wearing a striped apron. 'Dad? Are you early or am I running late?'

George laughed. 'We can go away and walk around for a bit if you like.'

'Don't be like that.' He swung the door wider. Ben Brace was tall, with bleached, slicked-back hair. His smile was exactly

like his father's. 'You must be Superintendent Diamond.'
He wiped his hand on the apron before holding it out.

'Peter.'

'Peter it is.'

The interior was distinctly more modern than the Georgian
formality of the front had suggested. Glass stair panels,
sunken lighting, Mondrian-inspired artwork.

A smiling woman in a pale blue dress came down the stairs.

'My wife, Leticia,' George said, and spoke to Leticia, 'So
this is the superhero I told you about, my dear.'

Diamond, uncomfortable already, didn't need that intro-
duction, but Leticia pressed his hand between both of hers
and said, 'The man himself. I'm thrilled to meet our top
detective.' Straight away he felt two inches taller. He was
intrigued to meet the woman who had kept the Joe Irving
connection a secret from her husband for so long. Already
he could tell she was a smart lady. It didn't need detective
work.

'Slight change of plan, people,' Ben said when he'd shown
them into a large sitting room with a Persian carpet and
white leather sofas. 'Caroline isn't here.'

'You haven't had a falling out?' George said.

'Christ, no. I'd rather be dead. It's like this. She had a
call from her father late yesterday to say he's coming out
a day early.' He turned to Diamond. 'You know my future
father-in-law's situation, don't you?'

George said, 'It's why Peter is here.'

'Well, Carrie left early for the prison. She's going to bring
him here.'

George said after an intake of breath, 'Here?'

Diamond said, 'Today?' The hairs stirred on the back of
his neck. He hadn't bargained for a face-to-face with Joe
Irving.

'They'll go to his house in Sion Hill Place first, so he can shower and smarten up. We don't know how long they'll take, so we'll eat now.'

'We don't mind waiting,' George offered. 'We don't want him thinking we're not civilised.'

'The food can't wait. It's ready. They'll get the second sitting.'

'Does he know about me?' Diamond asked, thinking fast. 'Maybe I should leave. This is more of a family occasion.'

Ben said, 'Not at all. He'll expect to meet you. Carrie will have told him all about you.'

Diamond heard this with disquiet. What exactly had Caroline told her crime baron father to justify having an undercover cop at the wedding?

'It'll be the first time Mum and Dad have met him,' Ben added.

Leticia placed her hand lightly on Diamond's arm. She was unusually tactile considering they'd only just met. She said in a tone only he could hear, 'Please don't abandon us. George doesn't show it, but he needs your support. He's on pins.'

Ben said, 'Excuse me, or we'll be eating burnt quiche.' He returned to the kitchen and his mother followed.

'Sorry about this, Peter. Not in the script,' George said, clearly under stress, yet managing to sound like a brave British officer in a film about the war. 'I knew we'd have to meet the sonofabitch at some stage before the wedding, but this isn't the way I imagined.'

'Do you think they planned it all along? Get all the medicine down in one go?'

'I'm sure they didn't. This early release comes out of the blue. Someone pulling some strings to make sure there is minimum publicity.'

'They could have told us.'

'The fact is, they didn't. I'm bloody glad you're here, though, and so is Leticia.'

They were called into another expensively furnished room for lunch. Silver cutlery and bone china plates on a large round table with a lace cloth. All funded, no doubt, from the proceeds of crime.

'Are you a wine man, Peter?' Ben asked.

'He'll drink whatever you put in front of him,' George said before Diamond could answer. 'He blends in with his surroundings.'

'Which is more than you do, my darling,' Leticia said. 'I told you the cravat was OTT and you wouldn't listen.'

There was a choice of quiches and they seemed to have been home-made. Diamond helped himself to two slices, with a spoonful of new potatoes. His blending-in didn't extend to sampling any of the exotic-looking salads.

'You're not a salad man, Peter?' Leticia said. 'You'd better have more quiche.' And she heaped another slice on to Diamond's plate.

With the four seated at the table, Leticia to Diamond's left, the talk got on to the wedding. Ben told the others that his best man was a university friend called Kevin and that Caroline had chosen her three bridesmaids, all aged under eleven, from a cousin's family on her late mother's side. Most of the family guests would be Braces. Caroline – the organiser – had drawn up a list she'd hand Diamond later.

'The wedding's at two in the afternoon, right?' Diamond said.

'That's my understanding,' Ben said.

'You'd better be one hundred per cent certain, son,' George said. 'A bride can be late, but never a groom.'

Diamond was trying to make a point and he wasn't being deflected. 'And the reception is seven-thirty.'

'That's because we have to wait for the Roman Baths to close to the public. We thought about having what they call a sunset wedding in there, but Caroline wanted the service in the Abbey and that's the slot we've got.'

'That's what Caroline decided and that's the way it's gonna be,' Leticia said with a smile.

'Do you see where I'm going with this?' Diamond persisted. 'The wedding takes about an hour, followed by photographs for say another half-hour. Where are your guests supposed to go for the next four hours?'

Ben was unfazed. 'It shouldn't be a problem. Some who live locally will go home and change into something less formal for the evening. Any staying overnight at hotels can do the same. And we'll have an open house here for anyone else.'

George said, 'Peter's thinking about security.'

'You mean for Mr Irving? He's got his house in Bath. He'll chill out there, I expect.'

'So am I expected to chill out with him?' Diamond asked.

'Not at all,' George told him. 'We want you mingling with the crowd. We can vet the guests, but not the passers-by. That's where a security issue could arise.'

'Dad, it's highly unlikely,' Ben said.

'Son, you don't know this man's reputation. Peter and I do. He has a fan club of one, and that's Caroline. Everyone else is a potential enemy.'

Leticia spoke George's name in a tone that told him to shut up. Turning to Diamond, she said, 'Empty plate. Have another slice of quiche.'

Soon after, Ben took a text message from Caroline. He looked up and said, 'I'd better bang some things in the oven. They'll be here in ten minutes.'

They were all in the sitting room when the sound of the front door opening stopped the conversation. Leticia said in a low voice, 'Imagine how he's going to feel, poor guy, coming

from where he has and meeting all of us for the first time.'
She got up and crossed the room.

The men stood. George motioned to Ben to be at the
door to greet his future father-in-law. Caroline came in first,
slim, sprightly and determined to take the heat out of the
moment. 'Hi, guys, meet my daddy.'

Daddy filled most of the doorway. He'd used enough
aftershave to launch a spacecraft. He was entirely in black:
Lacoste T-shirt, chinos and loafers. A chunky gold chain
showed up against the shirt. His forearms were so densely
tattooed that they matched the rest of the outfit.

Caroline named everyone in the room and Joe Irving
nodded to each. He didn't go in for hand-shakes, it seemed,
he didn't smile and he wasn't much of a talker either.

Leticia said, 'You must be ready for a good lunch, Joe.'
And then, sensing that this innocent remark might be taken
amiss by a man fresh out of prison, she added, 'I hope you
don't mind. We were told to have ours earlier.'

George said, 'And it was good, very good.'

Diamond said, 'I'll vouch for that.'

Joe Irving didn't say a word.

This would be more of an ordeal than anyone had
imagined.

Caroline said. 'Ben, my love, I told Daddy what a great
cook you are.'

'Better let him make up his own mind,' Ben said, apeing
the stiff upper lip of his father. He had more need than
anyone to get on sociable terms with the crook, but how
can you deal with such indifference? He was banking on the
lunch to do the trick. 'It's about ready. Why don't the rest
of you enjoy yourselves in here while I look after the new
arrivals?'

'Good idea, son,' George said and spoke for everyone.

*　　*　　*

Maybe the wine had helped. When Joe came back with Caroline, he was showing the suggestion of a grin. The others had agreed to make the next session less of a confrontation and were playing with a Newton's cradle Leticia had moved from the mantelpiece to a low table close to Diamond's chair. She was kneeling on the carpet. 'Have you seen one of these, Joe?' she asked, striking two silver balls against the others to produce a reaction from the ones at the end. 'There's some law of physics involved, but I just enjoy playing with it.'

Joe's expression didn't change.

Caroline said, 'You'll all enjoy this more.' She stooped and released a black and white kitten she'd brought in.

The perfect icebreaker.

'Ooh, how adorable – when did you get him?' Leticia asked.

'Last weekend.'

The kitten was investigating Diamond's shoes.

'Are you comfortable with cats, Peter?' Caroline asked.

'Got one of my own,' he said. 'That's why this one is interested. What's its name?'

'Claude.'

'That figures.' Already Claude was testing his claws on the new jeans.

Caroline stepped closer to prevent any damage, but Diamond held up his hand to stop her. 'Let him enjoy himself. I was told jeans need distressing.'

Then Joe spoke for the first time. 'Will he come to me?'

'Daddy, I'm sure he will if you take a seat,' Caroline said, eager to encourage more. She told the others, 'When I was growing up we had two tabbies living in the grounds, brothers that had gone quite feral. Daddy put out food for them and called them Reggie and Ronnie.'

'Little perishers. I think of them sometimes,' Joe said

118

unexpectedly. 'I took them to the vet and had them neutered and then returned them to the wild. It's what you're supposed to do. They didn't hold it against me. Kept coming back to feed.'

Caroline said, 'Our larder was stuffed with cans of gourmet ocean delicacies. Nothing but the best.'

'Why not?' Joe said. 'I've roughed it myself from time to time. Doesn't mean I don't enjoy good grub when I can get it . . . like your partner's quiches.'

Unsolicited praise. Relief all round.

Ben grinned his appreciation.

'No pets allowed where I was for the past few years,' Joe said. Now that his tongue was loosened he was threatening to take over. He'd planted himself on the sofa and, as if on cue, Claude abandoned Diamond and went to inspect this new attraction. In a second, the kitten jumped up and climbed on to Joe's lap to play with the gold chain.

The crime lord couldn't have looked happier if he'd just walked out of the Tower of London with the Crown Jewels. The kitten hooked its claws through the T-shirt. Joe didn't flinch.

'What will you do with him when you go on honeymoon?' he asked. 'He's too young for a cattery.'

'Oh, shoot! We haven't discussed it,' Caroline said. 'We've had so much else to think of.'

'He can come to me.'

'Really? That's brilliant, Daddy.'

'Bleeding obvious, I'd call it.' At this stage Claude had made it to Joe's shoulder and was nuzzling the bristles on his neck.

'Listen to him purring,' Leticia said.

'Claude or Daddy?' Caroline said. 'So now that we're together, shall we discuss the wedding?'

*　　*　　*

119

While this charming scene was being played out, Jack Peace was making wedding preparations of his own. He was in Abbey Church Yard, the square in front of the Abbey's West Door, deciding where to make the kill. The wedding party would emerge to be photographed after the ceremony. This was the obvious place, with everyone lined up for a series of group photos – no different from a firing squad set-up.

Only it wasn't so simple. Right now, mid-afternoon, was when the bride and groom would appear, followed by all the rest. And right now was one of the busiest times. People used the open space as an assembly point. The area was thronged with tour groups, schoolkids and their teachers as well as sightseers gawping at the Abbey front. A wedding would be a magnet, everyone elbow to elbow. You couldn't use a handgun with confidence that you'd get away.

There had to be a better plan.

From higher up?

Jack was as competent with a rifle as he was with a handgun.

He turned, looked higher, blinked and liked what he saw. He was staring at exactly what he needed – a balustrade along a curved corner of the Roman Baths building. The classic design in creamy Bath stone on a sturdy plinth, balusters like a long row of over-large skittles topped with a solid rail.

That balustrade was a thing of beauty.

It seemed to have been put there with a sniper in mind, on a level only one storey high and within thirty feet of the West Door. At either end, and at intervals between the balusters, were piers the size of filing cabinets. Get behind one of those, Jack, my lad, and you've got it made. Closeness, cover and the element of surprise.

He crossed the square for a better look.

The balustrade was built over what looked like a room,

going by the windows underneath. Was there access from inside?

There was a way to find out. Like any tourist he walked up to the Roman Baths entrance and went in. He didn't intend to buy a ticket. If anyone asked, he'd say he was planning to meet a friend who hadn't turned up and he wanted to check if they were waiting inside.

He found himself in a vast, ridiculously grand entrance hall under a spectacular decorated dome with a glazed centrepiece and half-domes at either end. Marble pillars, a high Venetian window, chandelier, polished woodblock flooring. Ahead of him people were joining a line to buy tickets for the Baths and being diverted along a system of barriers that eventually brought them to a counter in the centre where blue-shirted officials were in control.

Jack didn't need to go anywhere near the ticket people. When he got his bearings, he saw the bit that interested him, up a corridor immediately to the left. Less overblown than the entrance hall, it still had black and white marble flooring, pillars and statuary.

Good thing he'd taken the trouble to check. The windows he'd seen from outside weren't, after all, part of a room. They were built above a staircase that followed the curve of the wall down to a lower level.

He'd seen enough to know there would be no easy access to the roof. He stepped closer to check for alarms on the windows.

Mistake.

A man was coming up the stairs. He wasn't in uniform, but he might as well have had SECURITY tattooed on his forehead. Jack knew the type.

'Can I help you, sir?'

'No, mate. I'm okay.'

'You won't be going down here. It's staff only.'

'Isn't this the toilet?'

'The other way, my friend. I can show you. You must have walked straight past the signs near the entrance.'

'Right you are.'

'If you're wanting to look round, you need to buy a ticket.'

Fucking cheek. He thought Jack had been trying to sneak in.

Not today, Jack thought. He allowed the guy to show him the toilet and humoured him by going inside. Then he left the building.

Out in the open he stood looking up at the balustrade.

Better than beautiful.

Heaven-sent.

There was space behind where he could crouch out of sight. There didn't seem to be any CCTV. Could have been made with him in mind. All he had to figure out was a way to get up there with an assault rifle.

17

With the guest list in his pocket and the schedule for the wedding in his head, Diamond left the house in Camden Crescent feeling as unhappy as ever about this godawful job. Joe Irving had given away nothing except his partiality for the kitten. That hadn't fooled Diamond. The man was as benign as an electric chair.

There was the small consolation that Irving hadn't rubbished the idea of Diamond protecting him. No doubt it amused a crime baron to have a senior policeman covering his ass. Little did he know. The words of Herb, the small-arms instructor at Black Rock, were lodged in Diamond's memory. *Personal protection officer, are you? Because I wouldn't want you protecting me or anyone I know.*

You could bet your life the brute was making plans of his own.

He hadn't mentioned bringing bodyguards. Everyone on the Irving side of the guest list was either a friend of Caroline's or a bridesmaid, or a parent of a bridesmaid. No mysterious uncles or distant male cousins. Didn't mean there wouldn't be armed henchmen in support.

A parking notice was stuck to Diamond's windscreen. He was twenty-five minutes over, for pity's sake. And he'd gone to the trouble of leaving the thing in the Broad Street car park. He swore, ripped it off and tossed it on the back seat.

If the police station hadn't been relocated, he wouldn't have needed to bring his car into town every time he was on a job.

Muttering strong words about the top brass and their crackpot decisions, he drove round the one-way system and parked in Orange Grove. Didn't buy a ticket. Only wanted a look at Abbey Church Yard. He knew the place like a second home, but he had never made a security assessment of it. His visits there had usually been therapeutic, an escape from the madhouse known as Manvers Street police station (secretly beloved now that he'd left it). He would sit among the tourists on the benches in the middle of the square and contemplate the West Front, the ascending and descending stone angels in various states of preservation, as good a metaphor as he could find for a fraught and fallible copper trying to cling on to the ladder. Today he had a different perspective.

He'd seen weddings here occasionally. As a spectacle they didn't excite him much, but he knew what went on. Although the square was pedestrianised, an exception would be made for the cars bringing the bride, her father and the brides-maids. The chauffeur was permitted to mount the pavement from the High Street side, move slowly around the side of the Abbey, stop at the West Door to deliver his passengers and exit by way of York Street on the south side.

Diamond crossed the flagstoned yard and stood where the car would stop for Joe Irving and Caroline to emerge and pose for a photograph before entering the Abbey.

The most dangerous moment.

With his back to the great double doors, he took a slow, panoramic view of the buildings in front of the Abbey. Which of them might a sniper choose as a vantage point? On his right, the south side, were shops and, over each of them, three floors with casement windows. Above the tourist office was a balcony with iron railings that wouldn't provide any cover. Any one of about thirty windows would be a better bet, certainly within firing distance. A gunman could crouch behind the long drapes and not be seen. But they were windows in offices and private apartments with obvious practical difficulties in using them. The sniper would need to deal with whoever occupied them.

Memo: visit each owner on the day and check for suspicious visitors.

Closer still, on the left side of the square, were the historic Roman Baths screened by the Greek-style façade and extensions. One feature caught Diamond's attention immediately: a curved corner within fifteen yards of where he was standing. It was topped by a balustrade about twenty feet high and forty yards in length that ran from the edge of the main Pump Room extension and around to link eventually with the east side of the Great Bath. Get up there behind the stonework and you'd be so close to the action that you couldn't miss. Even a gunman of Diamond's standard couldn't miss.

How the sniper got up there and down was not important. He'd manage it.

Memo: on the morning of the wedding make certain the balustrade wasn't hiding a hitman.

And there's more than one way to crack an egg. What was to stop a gunman riding in on a moped or scooter and carrying out a drive-by killing – the favoured method of murder among professionals in the twenty-first century? A guy unrecognisable in leathers and a helmet and dark visor drives up as the bride is stepping out of the car – always a slow performance. The bridesmaids are waiting and step forward to assist with the dress.

The killer ignores the bride and the bridesmaids.

The real action happens on the other side of the car.

The father of the bride steps out, a soft target. Two or three shots and the gunman speeds away.

Plausible. Horribly plausible.

So would the hit come before the ceremony or after?

Definitely before, when all the other guests are inside the Abbey. Fewer witnesses. A clean line of fire.

Leaving it till after would risk confusion. People mill around and get in the way while the official photographs are being taken. By then, the bride's father is lost in the crowd.

Troubled at how simple it would be, Diamond retraced his steps.

The drive-by killing is the way I'd do it, he thought. But how the heck can I stop it? Without help, it's impossible.

When he returned to the car, there was another parking notice. Nothing was going right.

On the drive back to his home in Weston, he pondered the hopelessness of his mission. He couldn't see himself outgunning a professional hitman. When it came to pulling the trigger he was more likely to hit one of the stone angels on the Abbey front.

The time had come to get realistic.

He needed back-up.

'What am I going to do, Raffles?' he asked his venerable tabby when he got home and opened a tin of ocean fish. This was the measure of his crisis of confidence, expecting a cat to have the answer.

Raffles was too hungry to respond. Only when the dish was empty and the last flakes of fish licked from the teeth did the veteran cat, after grooming his fur, look Diamond in the eye.

It wasn't a look that offered an opinion.

'Maybe I'll get away with it and nothing will happen on

126

the day,' Diamond said. 'What do you think? Will I get lucky?'

As if finally to make a statement – but more likely to ask for more – Raffles got off his haunches and walked over to where Diamond was standing. The usual trick was to rub his head against the trousers.

This time was different. A sniff at the fabric followed at once by the sound cats make deep in their throats that is close to a growl. Tail lashing, Raffles turned and stalked from the room.

The smell of the new jeans?

The lingering scent of the kitten?

Or of Joe Irving?

Will I get lucky? No chance.

18

'Peter, we're stuffed.'

In one smooth movement Diamond zapped the rugby match he was streaming on his computer and rested his chin on his knuckles like Rodin's *The Thinker*. 'How come?'

'The news of the wedding has leaked,' George Brace said. He'd stepped into the office without knocking, in full uniform and as pale as a peeled potato. 'On my way in this morning my own driver congratulated me. I was gobsmacked.'

'You would be.'

'I couldn't even pretend to look pleased.'

'Did he say where he heard about it?'

'She. My driver is female. She's over the moon. Women love a wedding. No, she didn't say who told her.' He'd taken off his peaked, silver-edged hat and was tapping it like a tambourine. 'It's going to be public knowledge, Peter, all over Avon and Somerset.'

If it isn't already, Diamond thought. And no bad thing. The story had been bound to break at some stage and George's misfortune could be his salvation. 'It didn't come from me. My lips were sealed.'

'Hadn't even crossed my mind,' George said. 'I trust you like one of my own.'

'Thanks.'

'Do you think she knows who the bride's father is?'

'Not if she congratulated you.'

George nodded. 'Good point. But someone will find out. It won't be a secret much longer.'

'Got to agree with you there, George.'

The stricken Deputy Chief Constable moved towards the armchair in the corner. 'Do you mind?' He lifted off a couple of newspapers and a cushion and dropped them on the floor, sank into the upholstery and loosened his collar and tie. 'Okay if I light up?'

Diamond shrugged. Smoking was banned in Concorde House, but how could anyone stop the second most senior officer in Avon and Somerset? 'Be my guest.'

The pipe, pouch of tobacco and Zippo were produced from inside the jacket. 'Filthy habit,' George said. 'Deplorable.'

What could Diamond say to that? He studied the back of his hand.

George added, 'Stopped fifteen years ago and took it up again recently.' After some tamping and a burst of flame, he got the thing going. 'Stress.'

An understanding nod from Diamond.

George went on, 'I was in a fool's paradise thinking a wedding in the Abbey could be kept quiet.'

A sympathetic murmur.

'People are going to be shocked.'

Some will, Diamond reflected. And some will think it's hilarious. 'Maybe it's for the best, George.'

'How's that?'

'Well, if it really is common knowledge, we can police the day properly, get some uniforms on the streets.'

George looked startled. He hadn't thought this through. 'I don't know about that. What's Joe Irving going to say?'

He almost said, 'Fuck Irving.' Instead he remembered who he was talking to. 'I've no idea, but he'll be safer than he would with me as the only back-up.'

'You're not planning to pull out?'

129

'Lord, no. I wouldn't miss it for the world.'

A strong declaration of support. Too strong. George sucked on his pipe and puffed out smoke. 'You're not taking any pleasure from this, I hope.'

'Me?' Diamond put on a deeply pained expression. 'I'm as shocked as you are.'

'I invested a lot of trust in you, Peter. You gave me confidence that we'd get through unscathed.'

A boost to that confidence was wanted here. Diamond spoke with the certainty of an evangelist. 'We can and we will. I'm not suggesting we cancel all leave and fill the city with bobbies.'

'God, no!'

'We can police the wedding discreetly. A patrol car in Orange Grove and another in York Street. Some of my CID in plain clothes mingling with the crowd.'

'I'll need to think about this.'

'Naturally.' He let a few seconds pass while George chewed on his pipe. 'Let's not forget your family and friends coming to the wedding in all innocence deserve to be protected as well.'

The eyes expanded like bubble-gum. 'You think they're at risk?'

'A hitman doesn't fire a single round. He fires several to make sure. Bullets spraying everywhere . . .'

'Don't.'

'You get my point?'

'But you'd close him down, Peter.'

'And what if there's more than one?'

'Oh, my sainted aunt! We do need back-up.'

A victory for Diamond. 'Reluctantly, yes.'

He did feel genuine sympathy for a man whose stellar career would be shot to bits whatever happened at the wedding. At George's age – he probably hadn't hit fifty yet

130

– he could have made Chief Constable without any doubt, but it wasn't going to happen now. It was likely he'd be put out to grass, some boring admin job like strategic planning, hidden away in headquarters chanting his business-speak until he retired.

George seemed to be thinking the same. 'I worked my butt off getting to DCC,' he confided. 'Had some early successes and learned how to work the system, who to impress and how to rise up the ranks.'

There was no way Diamond would have picked a high-flying career man as a friend, but he was starting to warm to this hapless guy. With George there was no pulling rank. They talked on level terms and had from the start. He liked that. It wasn't any fault of George's that his son had fallen in love with a top criminal's daughter and his wife had conspired to make the wedding unstoppable.

'I had graduate entry, which helped. Soon got to inspector rank and got a name at headquarters for volunteering. Made sure I was never overlooked when it came to serving on key committees. If you're savvy like me, you also get a line into the Ministry of Justice and when some crime gets beyond the scope of any single police authority and needs investigating, like the phone hacking or the sexual abuse, your name is high on the list. Do it well and next thing you find you're picked to lead an inquiry and they bump you up to chief superintendent. I don't mind telling you I pushed the boundaries, took a few short cuts to reach the level I am now. You should be more like that, Peter. Ambitious.'

Diamond didn't take the last comment personally. He knew George was talking about himself.

George softened his last remark. 'I have enormous respect for genuine guys like you who get the real work done.'

'I've had my moments,' Diamond said, always uncomfortable with praise. 'I'm not proud of what happened in the

131

Met when I was young. And I got in trouble soon after arriving here. Threw up the job and returned to London.'

'I know,' George said and exhaled a cloud the size of Texas. 'I looked at your personal file.'

'Really?' A sharp reminder of the pecking order.

'You'd expect me to, wouldn't you, when I'm putting my fate in your hands? No one could call you a smooth operator, but you're a damned fine detective. After you resigned and we needed you back, you answered the call.'

'Is that still on my file?' He'd done enough soul-baring and he switched abruptly to the here and now. 'I'd like to get my team involved and plan a strategy for the day.'

'Your team?' The colour drained from George's face.

'It can't be a one-man show any more.'

'You already said. But how many?'

'Three or four at this stage. We don't have to bring in reinforcements until nearer the day.'

'In plain clothes?'

'Mostly. We'll need those two patrol cars north and south of the Abbey as a deterrent. My senior CID people will bring their own ideas to the table.' He was starting to fall in with George's way of speech. 'You're welcome to sit in if you wish.'

George removed the pipe and shook his head. 'I'd find that too embarrassing.'

'Understood, but are you happy for me to go ahead?'

'"Happy" isn't the word I'd choose, but I'll go along with whatever you suggest.'

'A handgun is no use to me,' Jack Peace told the man in the pub. 'What I need is an AK-63 and two forty-round boxes of ammo.'

'You think I have AKs?' the man said.

'I know you do.'

'Yeah?'

'Yeah. I know everything about your business, squire. I know the people you supply. I know your stock and where it comes from.' Jack's unblinking gaze spoke as surely as the words.

'Clever bugger, are you?'

'Clever enough to close you down if you don't play ball.'

'That's been tried before. Didn't work.'

'This time it will. I was inside with Joe Irving.'

A twitch. Enough said.

'He's out now. Did you know?'

'I heard he is. You think because you mention that monster I'm going to fall on my knees and beg for mercy. Are you trying to tell me you're buying for Joe Irving?'

'Did I say buying?'

'What else?' A pause for thought. 'Ah, I get you. You want to hire.'

'Borrow.'

'Is there a difference?' The man reflected on his own question. 'Oh, no. I'm not a charity, my friend. This will cost you.'

'No,' Jack said, amenable as a moray eel, 'it comes free.'

'No chance.'

'Don't fuck me about. You took delivery three weeks ago of seven AK-63s liberated from the Hungarian military, broken down into components, transported overland and smuggled here in a consignment of machine tools. Do you want to see my copy of the paperwork?'

'Where did you pick up that piece of knowledge – University of Wormwood Scrubs?'

'No.'

'Somewhere similar, I bet.'

In reality, Jack had called in a favour from the arms dealer's gay partner whom he'd once protected from a homophobic bully in Strangeways.

'I'll collect the AK and the slugs Thursday night. You'll

133

get the gun back Sunday or Monday. Oh, and I will take the handgun after all.'

'And what do I get out of this arrangement – apart from a hot weapon I can't sell?'

'The freedom to stay in business.'

'Bollocks.'

Jack took that as the high five that sealed the deal.

19

'Have a good time?' Ben asked.

'Is that a question or an offer?' Caroline released herself from the backpack and let it fall and gave him a hug and a kiss. She'd just returned to the house from Bristol Airport. 'It was all right, but I'd rather have gone with you.'

'Tea? Coffee?'

'Just water. Hello, rascal.' She picked up Claude the kitten.

They moved into the kitchen where something that tickled the taste buds was simmering in the slow cooker. Ben opened the fridge and handed her a bottle. 'Did they behave themselves? No nasty surprises?'

'Nothing I'd call nasty. Actually they spent most of the time on their phones trying to check what their boyfriends were up to. But Dublin is so cool. Live music everywhere and the Guinness is awesome.'

'Nobody pinned an L-plate on you?'

'Per-lease!' She let the kitten run free and drank most of the water. 'What's been happening here?'

'Very little. It's spooky. We get married on Saturday and it's all gone quiet. A few more cards and the gas bill.'

'What's the weather going to do?'

'Hurricane Caroline is due to hit Bath at two o'clock Saturday, but apart from that . . .'

'Be serious, Ben. Have you checked?'

He took out his phone. 'Sunny intervals with the chance of showers. It's been like that all week.'

'You haven't heard anything from Daddy?'

He shook his head. 'My mum, fussing over flowers, that's all.'

'I had a call. He's still insisting I spend the night before at his place, so he and I can leave together for the Abbey. He's so last century about the way things are done. Everyone knows you and I are already an item, for Christ's sake.'

'What did you say?'

'I was like you've got to think this through, Daddy, because you'll also have three hyped-up bridesmaids running riot in your home on Saturday morning, but he's not bothered.'

'You'll go?'

'Got to keep him on side, haven't we? He'll be picking up the tab. I mustn't forget to take the kitten and his things.'

'You'll remember the kitten and forget your wedding dress.'

'That's well possible. Has that policeman been in touch?'

'Peter Diamond? No.'

'What do you make of him?' she asked.

'He's just another plod, like my dad. He'll do his job on the day and get a good tip. You and I don't have to worry about him.'

'I don't think he likes Daddy.'

'He wouldn't, would he? They're poles apart. He's only coming for my dad's peace of mind.'

'Your mum made sure his plate was well filled. I think she fancies him.'

'She's like that with everyone. She'll organise us all on the day.'

Caroline's eyes flashed defiance. 'She'd better not try. It's my day . . . and yours. We'll do things my way.'

Ben sighed. 'I'm thinking this wedding is going to test everyone's tolerance.'

'Stop thinking it, then, misery guts. Man up. You'll be the happiest guy alive on Saturday.'

20

Jack marched up Manvers Street looking no different from a tourist who'd arrived for the weekend on a late train and was making his way to a hotel to pass the night. The black case he was carrying appeared innocuous enough, but instead of overnight things contained the assault rifle and ammunition he'd collected from the arms dealer. Stripped down, the gun parts fitted snugly into compartments in the case. He'd have the whole night and the morning to assemble it.

Hidden under his long black T-shirt was a gun belt. Having a back-up handgun was common sense and gave him confidence. The Glock semi-automatic was loaded, but unlikely to be used except in an emergency. He also had a bedroll attached to a backpack containing a balaclava mask, duct tape, a kitchen knife, toilet paper, a pack of sandwiches, water and a flask of brandy. He would be sleeping out tonight, on the flat roof behind the balustrade of the Roman Baths. His long-held plan was in its final phase.

The Abbey precincts are quiet after 10 p.m., even on a Friday. The city doesn't close down completely, but such night life as Bath can boast about is some distance away. Even so, he needed to be careful. A stop-and-search wouldn't be welcome. The floodlighting of the ancient building makes anyone conspicuous on the wide spaces outside. He'd checked the CCTV, of course, and he wouldn't be putting himself in range of a camera. This meant approaching by way of a detour using Henry Street, New Orchard Street and Abbey Green.

Tonight the whole area seemed to have been evacuated.

Or so Jack was thinking until he raised his eyes.

Along one side of York Street at the back of the Great Bath was a balustrade identical to the one he was planning to use. Behind it, silhouetted against the moonlit sky and standing quite still, was the figure of a man.

Security guard?

Jack took a sidestep into a shop doorway and merged with the shadow, believing he hadn't been spotted.

No hurry. Best wait for the snoop to move on.

But there was no movement. The guy had his back to the street, more interested in the Roman Bath than anything down here.

Still as a statue.

After some time, Jack realised the guy *was* a statue, for fuck's sake, one of the Roman emperors positioned at intervals around the perimeter of the Great Bath. Back in the Victorian era when the Great Bath was excavated, the city fathers weren't satisfied with the discovery of an entire Roman bathing facility. They added their own superstructure topped with eight statues. Those faux Roman figures appear horribly realistic at night.

Fooled you, Jack Peace.

He grinned, more from relief than amusement, and crossed the street. Staying close to the wall, he skirted the eastern end of the baths until he came to the feature he'd already picked for the difficult part – the climb. A sturdy wooden door marked FIRE EXIT KEEP CLEAR was framed by what is technically known as a Gibbs surround, with a decoration each side of four rectangular blocks that projected about an inch and a half and formed a virtual ladder. He'd

139

liked that door frame the first time he'd noticed it and he still liked it now. The top ridges were deep enough to give him footholds and there was an ornamental lamp higher up to grab.

The only difficulty would be the heavy case containing the gun and ammunition. Even if he found the strength to hurl the thing over the balustrade he didn't want to risk damaging the contents. So he'd come prepared. He took a twenty-foot length of cord from his pocket, tied it to the handle and looped the other end over his wrist.

After one more check to be certain no one else was about, he started the ascent. Climbing the blocks was child's play thanks to the ironwork supporting the lamp. The tricky part was getting over a chunk of moulding that projected above the door. He managed that by pushing his foot against the bar holding the lamp and heaving himself upward and wriggling to the next level. Once above the moulding, he used it as a platform to reach up to the balustrade. He took a grip with his fingers, hoisted himself and scrambled over.

No sweat.

There was more space up here than he'd imagined from below, as much as twenty feet between the stone rail he'd just climbed over and the external wall of the Pump Room extension. He was standing in a narrow channel next to a pitched roof angled quite low, but sensible for drainage. The end overlooking the Abbey front was rounded. Easy to scramble over and hide on the other side if necessary.

Before exploring, he leaned over the rail and hauled up his case, taking care not to bump it against the masonry. The sense of achievement was as satisfying as anything he'd done in a long while. He squatted behind the parapet and rewarded himself with a nip of brandy.

Through the spaces he had a clear view of the West Door where everything was going to happen.

Bring it on.

Diamond's first thoughts about policing the wedding hadn't changed. Patrol cars would be parked at the points of entry and exit to the Abbey Church Yard. Each would have two armed officers inside. On the morning of the wedding a door-to-door check would be made of all the apartments and offices within firing range of the West Door. An armed officer, DC Paul Gilbert, would be positioned above ground level behind the balustrade at the east end of the Pump Room extension. At the Deputy Chief Constable's request, there would be no obvious police presence in front of the Abbey. That was a duty to be undertaken by trusted members of CID in plain clothes: Chief Inspector Keith Halliwell, Inspector John Leaman and Sergeant Ingeborg Smith. They weren't official guests, so they would be posted outside. Diamond and George Brace would be the only officers inside the Abbey.

'A gang leader like Joe Irving doesn't normally advertise his movements,' Diamond told his team at the briefing on the eve of the wedding. 'This is a rare opportunity for his enemies. They know exactly where he'll be at a given time.'

'What if someone takes a potshot while the service is going on?' Halliwell asked.

'Inside the Abbey?' Leaman piped up.

'It may be God's house, John, but that won't stop a hitman.'

'Agreed,' Diamond said, 'but this is the point. The Abbey isn't like most other big churches. It doesn't have a gallery. It's an open space. A gunman will want to be out of sight.'

'There are pillars.'

'You can't hide behind a pillar.'

'The organ loft.'

'Will be in use by the organist. He'd be noticed.'

'You seem to know a lot about it, guv.'

'I've done my homework, checked the windows, the chantry, the vestries, even the vents in the ceiling. If I thought there was a serious risk of a shooting inside, I'd have got you lot into the wedding in some way.'

'Like as members of the choir?' Halliwell said.

'No chance.'

'Bell-ringers?'

'You'd be found out there as well. The front of the Abbey has so much more to offer a hitman. Lines of fire from several angles and a choice of escape routes. Irving will be a soft target at two critical stages: when he arrives with the bride and when they come out for the photographs.'

'And before all that, when he leaves his house?' Ingeborg said.

'Good point. An unmarked patrol car will be across the street.'

Leaman was shaking his head. 'All this for a toerag like Joe Irving. Does he have any idea of the level of protection he's getting?'

'He's been told.'

'How much is it costing the taxpayer?'

'Look at it this way,' Diamond said, getting irritated. 'The Deputy Chief Constable's son is getting married to a young lady unlucky enough to be the daughter of a major criminal. We want their day to pass off peacefully, don't we?'

'Like Romeo and Juliet,' Leaman said. 'Lovers from two warring families.'

'Let's hope not,' Ingeborg said. 'Romeo and Juliet ended up dead.'

21

During a far from comfortable night on the roof, Jack had slept fitfully. He had parked his bedroll in the gully between the outer wall of the Pump Room reception hall and the pitched roof over the adjacent corridor. After six years of confinement he felt less exposed with a solid wall close by. There was just room to stretch out lengthwise. Finally, an hour or two towards dawn, his overactive brain cut him some slack and he entered a deeper sleep.

About 5.30 he sat up and wondered where he was. In truth he'd been sleeping in a generous-sized gutter. Good thing there had been no overnight rain. The air had felt sultry during the small hours, yet this morning a slight September chill had taken over. It wouldn't last much beyond dawn. The sky was as blue as any bride could wish for on her wedding day. The only vapour in view was at the far end, wraithlike wisps of steam rising from the Great Bath, hot water sourced from two miles down and forced through the earth's crust at the rate of a quarter of a million gallons a day.

He reached for the water bottle and moistened his mouth and face. After eating the last of the sandwiches, he started assembling the assault rifle. He'd not used an AK-63 for some time but it was obvious how the parts came together. This was the twenty-first-century model, the MA, used by the Hungarian army. The wooden stock and grips of the original version had been replaced with plastic components, yet the weight was still almost seven pounds. A new feature, the lower rail, could be used to attach accessories including tactical flashlights, a laser target designator and a grenade launcher.

He wouldn't need a grenade.

Just 39mm cartridges, as many as it took.

He had two magazines loaded with twenty rounds each. He'd decided if he couldn't hit the target with that many shots he would definitely use the handgun – against his own shit-for-brains head.

By 6.15 a.m., he was armed and ready, gun belt fastened, AK slung over his shoulder. Eight hours too early, but how else could he have got up here unseen?

Shortly after 7, he heard a heavy commercial vehicle being driven into the yard. He was on his feet at once. Could be simply a street-cleaning truck prettying up the yard before the tourists arrived.

Or something more sinister.

He shifted to the south end of the gully and peeked through the balustrade.

More like a van than a truck, and parked just below where he was. A large, black van with an extending ladder on top. Three men had got out and were talking in a relaxed way as if discussing how to start work. The voices didn't carry but at one point they all stared up at the balustrade.

Jack ducked out of sight.

In a moment he heard sounds of activity followed by the clang of the alloy ladder being dropped on the flagstones.

He risked another look.

Two of them were adjusting the extensions on the triple push-up ladder. The third had collected what looked like a backpack from the cab.

Alarming.

Jack resisted the urge to keep watching. He had a strong theory what this was about. Keeping his head down, he scooted back to where his things were, the bedroll, the gun case, the backpack, and scooped them up and hefted them along the gully to the corner farthest from the balustrade, right up against the outer wall of the Great Bath.

The clang of the ladder being swung and scraped against the stonework confirmed his theory. The guy with the backpack was about to be sent up here to check. He'd be over the balustrade in seconds.

Jack dragged the balaclava over his head and left the rest of his possessions in a heap. He'd use them as a lure. Hands flat to the surface he edged crab-fashion around the hip end of the roof to the other side where he wouldn't be seen. He'd wait there and see if the bait was taken.

A regular metallic clunk-clunk could only mean the guy with the backpack was mounting the ladder. One, or both, of the others would be holding it steady.

Each rung could be the toll of a funeral bell. Whose funeral?

An audible shout of, 'All right, mate?'

A shout back. Indistinct.

Then the slap of the guy's shoes hitting the surface at the same level Jack was on.

Crunch point.

'Made it,' from the top.

'Best of luck,' from below.

Jack didn't move. He was waiting for his unwanted guest to investigate and hoping to hell he looked along the gully first and spotted the bedroll and other things.

A tense interval.

Then a shout from below. 'If you're okay, we'll leave you to it.'

'No problem,' from the roof.

The scrape and rattle of the ladder being tugged away.

145

More talk and laughter between the van men and the guy above.

Jack overheard the ladder being returned to the roof rack and clamped in place. A final exchange of greetings and then the engine started and the van chugged across the yard and away.

One on one.

He weighed the options. The invader was almost certainly a cop from some elite unit. There was a good chance he'd been posted here as an observer. This roof was the perfect vantage point, as Jack had discovered. The cop would be armed and alert and primed for action, but he wouldn't yet know someone was up here with him.

The advantage of surprise. Use it to the maximum.

Observer or hunter, the cop was certain to explore the rest of his surroundings soon.

Masked and crouching in the gully between the balustrade and the roof, Jack was as still as the stonework, willing the cop to take the bait and move along the parallel gully on the other side of the roof.

Three or four minutes of silence felt like ten. Reasonable time for the cop to remove his own backpack and put his mind to choosing the position with the best view of the Abbey front. He would be in contact by radio or phone with whoever was directing the surveillance and his first duty would be to report that he was in place.

Be my guest, Jack thought. Tell them to relax.

He had learned to be patient. He waited for the crunch of shoes on grit. The felt-lined gully had collected a million small bits of weathered stone. When the cop moved, Jack would hear him.

Presently he did. And rejoiced that the approaching steps came from the other side of the roof. Heard them quicken when the cop spotted the bedroll and backpack.

146

Heard them stop.

He would be level with Jack now. Only the angle of the roof separated the two men.

Jack freed himself from the sling of the AK-63 and gripped the hand guard.

It was all in the timing now. A trained cop would hesitate over whether to open the backpack. It could be a trap, a bomb. But it could also contain vital intelligence about the owner. A dilemma.

A few seconds of total concentration on the object at the cop's feet.

He wouldn't expect to be hit from above.

The pitch of the roof was slight, simple to climb, the apex no more than four feet higher than the lowest edge. Jack launched himself forward and over. He saw the cop standing in the gully, an average-sized young guy entirely in black – baseball cap, bomber jacket and jeans. Sunglasses. The head turned and the right hand moved to the belt. Half a second too late.

Jack didn't shoot. He used the assault rifle as a club and swung the stock at the cop's skull. Caught him square above the peak of the cap and felt the force of the impact in his own hands. The cop buckled and Jack leapt on him.

They crashed heavily in the gully, but the cop still had some fight in him and thrust both hands upwards, the heel of his right hand under Jack's chin, fingernails digging into his flesh through the textile fabric of the mask, and the fingers of his left stabbing at Jack's eyes.

Painful.

Jack swayed back and whacked the cop a second time with the AK, catching him hard in the ribs.

A grunt of pain.

Anything broken? He hoped so. He needed to maim the guy. Killing him would be over and above.

It seemed that the cop was winded at the very least because the hand under Jack's chin lost all strength and slipped limply past his shoulder.

Jack slung the AK out of reach behind him, confident he could deal with the depleted cop now, sitting astride him on bent knees. As he'd suspected, the guy was armed with a self-loading pistol that Jack wrenched from the holster and tossed where the AK had gone.

'What's your name?'

Silence.

'Name?'

'Mm?' Difficult to tell whether the vagueness was down to cussedness or concussion. The eyes squinted as if they had difficulty focusing, but that may have been caused by the sunlight. The baseball hat and shades had come off in the struggle.

The face was pudgy and boyish. It's said you know you're getting old when the police look younger. Since when had they started recruiting twelve-year-olds?

Jack pulled his own handgun from the holster and let the cop feel the muzzle against his forehead. 'For the last time. Name?'

'Paul.'

'I'm ready to use this, Paul. Better do what I say.' He felt for the side of the gully with his free hand and stood up while continuing to point the gun at the cop's head. Give him a few years more than twelve. Could be twenty. 'Turn over. Face down.'

Paul the cop obeyed him.

Jack's backpack was within reach. 'The gun is still at your head.' He dragged the pack closer, pulled up the flap and felt for the roll of duct tape. 'Clasp your hands behind your back.'

He got cooperation. Good thing. It isn't easy prising tape

from a roll with one hand. The guy couldn't see behind him and wasn't taking any chances.

Heavy-duty duct tape bound tightly is as good as conventional handcuffs if used the correct way, with the wrists to the rear and anchored to the body with extra lengths around the waist. Any fool can snap the stuff if the hands can be raised above the head and forced down. Jack trussed his prisoner well and then fixed the ankles.

'You're the baby on the team, right?'

No answer.

'I'm guessing that's why you were given the seven o'clock spot. Will they send a relief?'

A shake of the head.

'Did they tell you to radio in?'

'I already did.'

'Where is it?'

'The radio? In my bag.'

'Any protocol about more calls?'

'Only if I see something suspicious.'

'You won't see jack shit from where you are. Did they give you an identity – a number or something?'

'Golf One.'

Spoken at once, without time for deception, so it could well be true. Golf was the standard word in the phonetic alphabet.

'What's your surname?'

'Gilbert.'

G for Gilbert.

Even so, Jack would only use the radio as a last resort. He tore off another strip of tape and pressed it over Paul Gilbert's mouth.

149

22

Caroline's two cousins, Angela and Ondine, arrived by 9.30 on the morning of the wedding with their daughters, Gabriella and the twins, Tonya and Trixie. The three bridesmaids were too young to be of any help getting the bride ready, so their mothers filled that role. Joe Irving's sombre house high on the northern slopes shrilled with feminine excitement.

'Where's Uncle Joe?' Angela asked.

'Still asleep,' Caroline said.

'Not for much longer. Where's his bedroom?'

'First floor.'

The bridesmaids had already started a jumping game on the stairs. 'Pipe down, will you,' Ondine called out. 'Uncle Joe's still in bed.'

Gabriella, all of ten years old, shouted, 'No he ain't. He just flushed the toilet.'

'Please!'

Gabriella's mother, Angela, a university lecturer in child psychology, said, 'I brought her up to speak the truth.'

'Can't blame the kid, then.'

'The thing that grates with me is the use of "ain't". She must have picked that up from your two.'

Caroline stepped in fast to avoid a fight. 'Such energy. They'll be worn out before the wedding at this rate.'

'This is nothing,' Ondine said. 'Wait till the twins really get started.'

'And you've got all this to look forward to,' Angela told Caroline. 'Does Ben want a family?'

'We both do.'

'I must confess I'm glad I stopped at one,' Angela said. 'Although I didn't have much choice in the matter after Gary left me for that mare from the fine art department.'

'You don't know how lucky you are,' Ondine said. 'I'm getting used to the twins now, but I'd be lying if I said it was easy. Jed wants to try for a boy, only I'm not sure that's all we'd get. Twins run in his family.'

Caroline didn't really want to hear about child-rearing on the morning of her wedding and was only spared when the doorbell rang. The flowers had arrived. Originally she'd wanted wild flowers, but in September almost all the large blooms are blue or purple and you can have too much of one colour so she'd settled mainly for shrub roses in shades of creamy pink and apricot, and they exceeded her best hopes. Her eyes welled up.

'I don't know what to say.'

Angela said, 'Don't try. Flowers are supposed to say it themselves.'

'I know, but . . . they're beautiful.'

'Presumably you chose them yourself.'

Ondine, the more spontaneous of the cousins, filled the vacuum with coos of approval.

The owner of the flower shop had delivered the flowers personally and insisted on showing Caroline how to hold her bouquet, '. . . not too high with your face looking like the blob of cream on a knickerbocker glory and not so low that people think you're protecting your virtue.'

The bridesmaids rushed to inspect their bouquets ('wicked') and insisted on trying on their floral headbands ('mega-wicked') and refusing to part with them although still dressed in tops and shorts. Joe Irving's buttonhole was two tight pink

151

rosebuds on rosemary and fern, so enchanting that Caroline decided she'd hide it from her father until just before they were due to leave.

The florist promised that the flowers in the Abbey were already being installed by her team and would look divine. The Roman Baths had to wait for the official closing at 6 p.m., and within an hour the reception area would be transformed.

Peter Diamond was in front of the Abbey by 11.30 doing the rounds of his team without making their presence too obvious. They had come on duty at ten, with the exception of Paul Gilbert, the youngest, who had needed to arrive early to climb a ladder to his viewpoint above the Pump Room extension. At that hour Diamond had still been in bed.

'All present and correct, then,' he said to Keith Halliwell, his deputy, over a large latte and a generous slab of banana and chocolate chip cake at a table outside Jacob's, the coffee house at the entrance to Abbey Church Yard. Useful tip from Peter Diamond: if you need to blend in with the crowd, make sure it's the section of the crowd who eat well.

'And a nice day for a wedding,' Halliwell said. 'If you don't mind me saying, guv, that's a sharp suit. Is it new?'

'Straight from the dry cleaner,' Diamond told him, flicking a crumb off the trousers. 'You wouldn't guess. Are you in radio contact?'

'Yes, but we're not making it obvious.'

'Armed?'

'Out of sight on my belt.'

'Mine's under my arm on a shoulder holster,' Diamond said. 'Does it show?'

Halliwell shook his head. 'You've got the figure.'

'Is that meant to be a compliment?'

'I'm agreeing it doesn't show, that's all.'

'Where's Ingeborg?'

'On the move. I saw her last in the tourist information shop.'

'And John Leaman?'

'Other side, near the Pump Room entrance.'

'Young Gilbert?'

'He's keeping his head down in the crow's nest, isn't he? He checked in early with the control room. I haven't spoken to him myself. He hates being mollycoddled, as he puts it.'

'Tell me about it,' Diamond said. 'I'd rather mollycoddle a snapping turtle.'

'I haven't seen any uniforms.'

'You won't. It's plain clothes only in the square – if my sharp suit can be described as plain.'

Halliwell stirred his coffee. 'On a gorgeous day like this it's hard to imagine anything going wrong with the wedding.'

'Don't tempt fate.'

With the cop securely pinioned with duct tape and lying in the far corner of the roof, Jack moved to the other end and checked the bag. The police-issue radio equipment was inside, along with field glasses and a body camera. Of more use to Jack were two apples, a banana, some biscuits and two bottles of water. Paul Gilbert must have been speaking the truth when he'd said no one would be taking over.

After smashing the radio with the heel of his gun, Jack put the cop out of his mind and used up some time in choosing which gap in the balustrade to fire through. He'd positioned the legs of the bipod on the base rail and worked out the most comfortable posture. Stretching out flat on his stomach didn't give him the height he would need. Squatting or sitting cross-legged didn't feel comfortable. Eventually he found that lying on his left hip and propping himself against one of the stone piers worked best.

Next he tried the telescopic sighting. The opportunity was ideal because the tourists were appearing in numbers and forever stopping in front of the West Door to pose for photographs. Each time they lined up, he took aim, put the lightest of touches on the trigger and made a firing sound from the side of his mouth.

In an hour he must have scored more than a hundred virtual hits, people of all ages and nationalities. His unknowing victims would move off and make way for the next lot. Some he'd spared – small kids, pregnant women and the disabled – and others he'd disliked on sight and wouldn't have minded gunning down for real. One large guy in a suit crossed in front of the Abbey and presented a moving target several times over. He seemed to be circling the yard. If Jack was any judge, this was a cop on patrol.

In the short intervals when nobody stopped to be photographed Jack took aim at the carvings and assassinated St Peter and St Paul several times over.

Quiet, if not calm, descended on the house just after 1.30 p.m., when the bridesmaids and their mothers got into the first car. Uncle Joe, dapper in a new Italian suit, watched from the window. He appeared surprisingly relaxed, even with the rosebud boutonniere. He told Caroline he approved of Ben's decision not to insist on morning suits. In truth, the decision had been Caroline's.

As for the bride, she looked sensational, of course, in a romantic blush-coloured sheath dress by Elie Saab that her two cousins had declared made them green with envy. The skirt was detachable for later, when she would want to dance.

'You're a picture,' Joe said. 'Pity your mum isn't here to see you. She'd be in tears.'

'Don't start me off,' Caroline said. 'The make-up took all morning.'

'Let's go, then. The Roller is waiting.'

A band of grey cloud covered the sun just before they stepped outside. The air felt sultry.

A short way up the street was another vehicle, a blue Audi with three young men inside who looked like cops. Joe eyed it indifferently and didn't mention anything to Caroline.

Inside the car she tugged his sleeve. 'Talk to me, Daddy. I'm nervous.'

'How do you think I feel?'

'You've done this before. I haven't.'

'By rights, I shouldn't be here,' he said. 'You deserved a better dad than me.'

'Oh, come on.'

'When I wasn't locked up I was up to my ears in crime. Never at home. What sort of father is that?'

'You came to a parents' evening at my school and scared the pants off Miss Meredith, the headmistress. Remember that?'

'Did I threaten her?'

'No, you just gave her a look. I was the envy of the school. From that day forward I was never given another detention.'

'If that's your best memory of me, it doesn't say much.'

'Right now will be my best memory, riding to my wedding with you at my side and being escorted up the aisle. I'm going to be so proud of you in your new suit.'

'We're not there yet.'

'There's no stopping us now.'

Joe didn't comment on that. He turned his face to the window. They'd slowed at the traffic lights at the foot of Lansdown. People were taking an interest in the wedding car, trying to see the bride. 'I'm not much good with words. I want you to know how often I thought of you when I was inside and feeling low. There wasn't much stuff in my life I

155

could be proud of. I pictured you and that helped me get through. Remember that.'

'Lighten up, Daddy. You're making it sound like a deathbed scene.'

A few fat raindrops hit the windows and rolled down.

'Oh, shit,' said the bride.

'That's my girl,' said Joe.

Their driver glanced over his shoulder and said, 'No problem. I've got umbrellas.'

'What do you mean, no problem?' Joe said in a bellow that could have caused an emergency stop. 'My only daughter is getting married. This is her big day. It's a problem, right?'

'Right, sir.'

As if to justify Joe's anger, the rain intensified and beat a tattoo on the roof of the Rolls-Royce. They'd reached the High Street and the Abbey was in sight. At the end they were supposed to slow down, mount the pavement and make their way to the West Front. Facing them was the Rebecca Fountain, the white marble statue and fountain erected in 1861 by the Bath Temperance Association. The wording on the plinth was ironic under the circumstances: WATER IS BEST. A million large beads of the stuff were bouncing on the flagstones and battering the car.

'What's the time?' Joe asked.

'Two o'clock, near enough, sir,' the driver said.

'Make a left turn and pull in. It can't go on like this for long.'

'Daddy, I don't think we should stop,' Caroline said.

Joe was insistent. 'There are spaces in front of the Empire Hotel.'

'But everyone is waiting in the Abbey.'

'Do it,' Joe told the driver.

Everything had been hunky-dory until about 1.30 p.m. – just as the wedding guests had started arriving in their smart suits and fancy hats – when charcoal smears cancelled the sun and turned the Abbey front into dark lumps and crevices, as it must have appeared before the stone-cleaning. Soon the first spots of wet struck Jack's warm flesh. A few quickly became too many. Light rain he could deal with. By 1.40 this was a summer shower and by 1.45 there was no sign it would stop any time soon.

What was a bout of rain to a single-minded man like Jack? He'd been through worse. Gun technology had moved on from the days of flintlocks and keeping your powder dry. An assault rifle is supposed to be weatherproof, so well insulated that it can fire underwater if need be. Of course, any gun needs to be held firmly. If your hands slip on the grips the recoil can kick like a bull. He'd take account of that.

But in all his planning he hadn't factored in a summer storm. The problem wasn't with the gun. What made his task a thousand times more difficult was what was happening in front of the Abbey. The whole pattern of the wedding had changed. Some early guests had gone in before the rain started. The later ones were forced to step up sharply. Umbrellas had come into play, and they weren't dinky folding things. They were the monster golf umbrellas chauffeurs used. You can't identify anyone for sure under a thing that size and even if you take the chance, you can't shoot to kill.

Almost all the guests were hidden and weren't folding the fucking umbrellas until they were at the Abbey door or inside.

The flaw in Jack's masterplan – the British weather.

From his position he had a fine view of the top of each umbrella yet couldn't see a single face. Enraged, he only avoided total meltdown by promising himself he'd have a second chance when everyone emerged after the service.

If the rain stopped.

A car with white ribbons arrived at the West Door, leaving a slipstream across the sodden yard. Helpers were ready for the bridesmaids with a canopy formed of white brollies. Two women visible from the knees downwards emerged and hurried in after the children.

Nothing was the way Jack had visualised the scene. Nobody was out there watching. There wasn't even a wedding photographer in waterproofs to record the spectacle. The entire area in front of the Abbey was deserted. Crosswinds were twisting the rain into shapes like folds of fabric. The hiss of the drops hitting the stonework grew to a drumming sound. Such was the density of the cloudburst that you could barely see your hand in front of your face.

Signs of restlessness at the West Door. The bride and her father were seriously late in arriving. Jack caught glimpses of paler colours under the shadows inside the arch. The bridesmaids were hovering nervously between the oak doors and so was the priest in his gold-embroidered cope. He stepped out once to look for the car and pulled back quicker than a cat's paw.

Peter Diamond wasn't a killjoy, yet it would be fair to say he was less devastated by the rain than any of the other wedding guests. No one would linger outside the West Door and make himself a target in these conditions. Posing for photographs simply wasn't on. In his dry spot in the coffee shop, Diamond checked the time. The wedding service would start in under five minutes. He could see people inside the Abbey poised to open umbrellas as soon as the car appeared.

He sent out an all-units radio message: *Stay on full alert. The bride and her father will arrive any second.* Of the CID people, Halliwell, Leaman and Ingeborg, the old hands, had each found a dry observation point. Anyone with half a brain would have done so.

Responses came back from each of the team except Paul Gilbert who, it had to be said, would be hard put to find any shelter where he was. By now he would be so drenched, poor lad, you could wring him out and fill a bucket. No surprise if his radio was out of action.

After transmitting the order, the head of CID made a dash across the square to the West Door under a portable umbrella that immediately buckled and broke. The suit was no longer sharp when he entered the Abbey. The jacket sagged and the trousers gripped his legs like cling film.

Bloody umbrellas. Jack had aborted his mission, at least for this part of the afternoon. Only some masochistic streak acquired through years behind bars kept him watching.

Finally, a good five minutes late for the wedding, a Rolls-Royce appeared from the left with the main players, Joe Irving and his daughter. And with cruel timing the rainfall increased to monsoon intensity, a downpour of Biblical force, thick droplets that stung the flesh. Even Noah would have thought it excessive.

Everyone waited at least half a minute before some bold soul inside the car made the decision.

The chauffeur opened his door, sprang the clip on a huge umbrella, darted around the car and ushered the bride into the Abbey. A flash of cream-coloured fabric and she was gone from view.

He returned to the car and performed the same service for Joe Irving. But for all Jack could see, it could have been Father fucking Christmas.

What a washout.

Jack stood brazenly behind the balustrade, the rifle hanging from his hand, in the sure knowledge that no one would notice him. He was saturated, of course, but so intent on what was unfolding below that only now did he discover he was ankle-deep in water.

Choked drains. Rising water.

159

The drainpipes couldn't cope with the volume.

This was the moment he remembered Paul the cop. The world would be a better place without plods, but leaving one to drown in a gutter was careless.

He swore, perched the AK on a ledge, straightened his sodden face mask, turned, crawled up the roof, grabbed the top edge and looked over.

The cop's body was all but submerged. He'd managed to wriggle closer to the corner and prop his head against the backpack to keep his face above the surface.

Jack scrambled over, grabbed the hapless guy and lifted him out of the water on to the roof. The eyes were closed and he was grey in the face so Jack ripped the strip of duct tape from his mouth.

The shock of strong adhesive being yanked off sensitive skin would have revived anyone except a corpse. The cop's eyes snapped open. He took some shallow gasps of air.

Jack trickled some bottled water into the open mouth. 'Drink up, mate. Didn't bargain for this.'

After swallowing most of it, Paul asked, 'Did you shoot him?'

'I wouldn't still be here if I had.'

'What will you do now?'

'They've got to come out, haven't they?'

'Is the rain going to stop?'

'Stupid fucking question.'

'Are you under orders to kill the bastard, or what? He's a waste of space anyway in my opinion.'

Jack ignored that obvious attempt to curry favour. 'How long does a wedding take?'

'Under an hour usually.'

'So I'll wait and so will you.' He reached for the duct tape and slammed another strip over the cop's mouth.

160

23

Seated by choice at the back, Diamond ignored his wet clothes and focused on his reason for being at a wedding on a Saturday afternoon instead of a rugby match. He started counting heads. They weren't necessarily all guests. A notice had been posted all morning about the Abbey being used for a wedding at 2 p.m., but any member of the public was entitled to wander in. After all, there's that 'declare it now' moment early in the ceremony. If you come to stop a wedding, you probably won't have been invited.

He made the tally seventy-eight, meaning that few, if any, interlopers were present. George Brace had spoken of about eighty because of a limit on numbers. Caroline's list had confirmed this.

Seventy-eight in a church that seats 1,200 left plenty of room.

Probably the storm had put off casual visitors. Whatever the reason, the modest numbers helped Diamond keep tabs. Following tradition, the bride's family were seated left of the aisle and they were so few they filled only the front row. Caroline's friends had spread themselves around the rows behind, but they amounted to about a quarter of the number on Ben's side.

George Brace was in full dress uniform as Deputy Chief Constable, bristling with silver insignia. Was the kit worn from pride or as a deterrent to ill-intentioned people?

Probably both, Diamond decided. The man was intensely proud of his status. Personally, Diamond wouldn't mind if he never had to wear uniform again – and certainly not at a social occasion.

The Trumpet Voluntary was the cue for heads to turn, phones and cameras to start snapping. Everyone except Diamond and the priest seemed to be taking pictures. The bride was radiant in her designer dress.

Big Joe would have been an easy target for a bullet. His shoulders filled most of the aisle and he was some inches taller than everyone else.

To his credit, he looked as if he was in his element. When the priest said, 'Who brings this woman to be married to this man?' Joe said as if he'd won the lottery, 'Me.' He took Caroline's hand and placed it in Ben's and returned to the pew. And when one of the bridesmaids dropped her bouquet, he stepped out, picked it up for her and put a reassuring hand on her arm. He was well in charge.

And no bullet was fired.

Try as he might to keep his mind on the job, Diamond couldn't prevent himself being moved by the words of the wedding service, words he'd heard thirty years ago when he'd stood at the front of a small London church with his beloved Steph and made the same vows, buoyed up with pride and scarcely able to believe his luck. And it was right here – in this Abbey church in 2001 – that he'd walked up the same aisle behind Steph's coffin.

Impossible not to feel a lump in his throat.

After the signing of the registers, the priest announced that the family had decided in view of the weather – he spread his hands towards the nearest window and said with a smile, 'There are certain things beyond our control' – there would be no traditional photographs outside the Abbey. Instead, they would be taken later, at the reception

162

in the Roman Baths. 'And I'm reliably informed that the disco will begin with "Here Comes the Sun".'

Outside, another heavy shower had started.

Diamond, who professed no religion, offered a word of thanks to the Almighty. The second big killing opportunity had been removed.

But another – unplanned – was about to unfold.

The new Mr and Mrs Brace and their bridesmaids walked the aisle with their families following. Somewhere above, the bells started ringing. Etiquette decreed that Diamond, at the back of the seating, should have waited for everyone else to pass him, but etiquette had never held him back and didn't now. He made a fast move to the other end of the row and was at the Abbey door in time to nod to George and Leticia as they approached.

He'd realised there would be a log-jam. Normally there's a chance after the church formalities are over for everyone to unwind in the open air, congratulate the happy couple, hug each other and throw confetti. It couldn't be done outside, so, except for the confetti, all this would happen this side of the West Door.

In that crush, anyone with murder in mind could sidle up to Joe Irving and stick a knife into him.

Diamond barrelled through. Nobody was lining up to chat with the father of the bride, so he was able to get face to face, or, more accurately, face to collar and tie. A fine ivory-coloured necktie with a pearl pin.

Joe was used to speaking without making eye contact. 'What do you want?'

'Being careful, that's all,' Diamond said.

'Speak up.'

Everyone was shouting to be heard above the bells. 'Being careful.'

'What for?'

He leaned closer. 'You know – some enemy of yours. All these people. It only wants one.'

'One what?'

Diamond made a fist to get Joe's full attention and mimed the upward thrust of a knife.

Joe barely glanced, not at all impressed. 'Bring it on. He'll have a blade in his gut before I do.'

'You're tooled up?'

Joe's eyes slid upwards. The stained-glass saints above them could not have looked more pure in heart than he did. 'Does a bear shit in the woods?'

Eventually Caroline and Ben waved to everyone, stepped into their Rolls-Royce and were driven away, but not without some confetti being thrown in spite of all the appeals from the Abbey authorities. Immediately after came the second car for the bridesmaids and their mothers. The umbrellas were up again. Joe got in beside the driver. Diamond's duty inside the Abbey was over.

He felt a hand squeeze his arm. Leticia, under a silver hat big enough to contain space invaders. 'After that you deserve a large glass of bubbly, Pete.'

George Brace, at her side, added, more in keeping with the job, 'You can stand down now.'

'Until it all kicks off again at the reception,' Diamond said.

'Will it?'

'The Roman Baths at night are about as secure as a waterhole in the jungle.'

'Now you tell me.'

'I'll try and get there in good time.'

'I saw you with Irving. I hope he appreciates the efforts we're making to keep him safe.'

'That's debatable.'

Leticia was looking through the open door. 'This must

be our car arriving. Come on, George. I've got to get spruced up for tonight.'

'Say it ain't so, Joe.' The words of the much-covered Murray Head song from the 1970s had drilled themselves into Jack's head and wouldn't budge. They were cruelly apt. Behind the balustrade in driving rain waiting for the wedding party to emerge, he had prepared the AK, set it in position, lined up the shot. He'd told himself the photo session outside the church was obligatory, whatever the weather. Evidently not.

The service was clearly over now. The bloody bells had been going for twenty minutes and no photographer was in place and no line-up, no chance to make the killing.

Finally some minders with umbrellas appeared at the door, followed by the bride and groom who ducked into the Rolls-Royce under the phalanx of white nylon and were driven away. Can you credit that? It seemed someone – probably the paymaster for this shindig, Joe Irving – had made an executive decision and cancelled the photo session. Then the bridesmaids and their mothers were ushered out followed by the man himself hotfooting it around the car under his own umbrella to the passenger seat.

Say it ain't so, Joe.

What had just happened – or failed to happen – was so unlikely that Jack kept watching in the hope that the scene would rewind and be played again with the true version.

The guests started streaming out and away in all directions. It was enough to rile a saint and Jack was no saint.

Say it ain't so, Joe.

When he'd calmed down he was forced into a drastic rethink.

The AK was no use to him any more. He dumped it along with its case and all his other stuff except the balaclava and the handgun. Dropped everything in the standing water

165

behind the balustrade. The bedroll, the backpack, the bloody lot. Nothing with his name on it, of course, and if they found any of his DNA after that drenching, science had come on a lot since he'd last checked.

The trussed-up cop wouldn't be a problem. Someone at the nick would ask why he hadn't reported in. Eventually the top dogs would tumble to the fact that their pup was missing. They knew where to come looking. And if they didn't, a night up here wouldn't kill him.

A more pressing matter, the biggest challenge yet, had to be faced right now. The wedding reception hadn't featured in his planning so far, but suddenly it was top of the agenda. His last opportunity. He needed to get back to ground level and into the Baths without being noticed. The rain had stopped and the sun had appeared – wouldn't you know it? – and tourists were already repopulating the square. They'd be there until early evening like colonies of meerkats watching every move. Anyone descending from the balustrade by the route Jack had used to get up there was sure to attract an audience. The steps in front of the fire exit with the Gibbs surround were a favourite place for tourists to sit with their ice cream.

Think.

In a little over two hours the Roman Baths would close. By then he needed to have conned his way in and found a place to hide, lie up and wait. A final chance to make the hit.

The urge to finish the job was stronger than ever.

For justice.

Not the warped justice imposed by the police and the courts. Real justice where the truly guilty were punished.

So think outside the box, man. Be inventive.

He stared down at the Abbey Church Yard where people were already buying ice creams from the shop near the tourist office. They'd make for those fucking steps below him for sure. He was trapped.

He took a deep despairing breath and it was his salvation. He was reminded of what is often called the smell of rain – the fresh, energising air that follows a heavy downpour. He filled his lungs and drew back his head for more – and his gaze fixed on the plumes of white steam rising from the Great Bath.

Got it.

Instead of going down, he'd go up. Ten feet maximum.

He'd cracked it.

Scale that pesky wall, Jack lad, and you'll be laughing. You'll be over the top and into the Roman Baths before Joe Irving and the bride and groom and all their guests arrive for the big jolly. They won't have a clue that a gunman is lying in wait.

He waded the length of the gully for a closer look and raised a clenched fist in triumph. To his right was a corner where the wall abutted the outside of the domed concert room built by the Victorians and converted last century into the imposing ticket hall he'd visited. The nineteenth-century builders hadn't stinted on detail, even up here where it would never be seen by the public. That corner was finished with stonework of the same design as the door frame he'd climbed the evening before. Large masonry blocks deeply recessed at regular intervals and – thanks, guys! – decent footholds. There was even a drainpipe to hang on to. His granny could have got up there.

Fantastic.

A change of fortune.

He couldn't start immediately while the public were inside. There would be a ninety-minute slot between closing time at 6 p.m. and the start of the wedding bash at 7.30. He'd allow an interval for the usual security check.

6.20 would be the right time to go over.

He ate the banana from the cop's backpack and had some of the water. Then he wrung the excess rainwater from the balaclava and tugged it over his head again and went to see how Paul Gilbert was looking stretched out on the roof with his face to the sun.

Tired, but drying out. Could have been worse.

'Still thirsty?'

Urgent nodding.

He removed the gag less forcefully than last time, put a hand behind the guy's shoulders to help him up and let him drink.

'Apple?'

'Thanks.'

'Don't thank me. It belongs to you. Take a large bite. I won't be hand-feeding you for long.'

'You could untie my hands.'

'No way. Take another bite.'

'There's a banana.'

'Was.'

'Is it gone, then?'

'I was hungry.'

'What have you got against Joe Irving?'

'Shut up and chew the apple.'

'The wedding is over. I heard the bells some while ago. What time is it now?'

Jack didn't answer.

Paul wasn't giving up. 'You didn't fire a single shot.'

As if he needed telling.

'That's it.' Jack took his arm away and let the smug bastard flop back on the roof. He slammed the gag against the open mouth. The duct tape was still sticky enough to do the job.

Blabbermouth could rot as far as he was concerned.

24

'False alarm, then?' Ingeborg said to Diamond.

'What do you mean – "false alarm"?' He wasn't in the best of moods after the drenching he'd got. The last time he'd tried ironing the creases out of a suit he'd ended up with the imprint of the iron on the trousers, brown on grey. Trying to dye the whole suit black hadn't been such a good idea either. The stain had become a hole.

'Nobody took a potshot at big Joe.'

He recovered his composure. 'I was never wholly convinced it would happen and I don't think Joe had many worries either, but orders are orders.'

'He could have got lucky, saved by the rain.'

They were in the back room of the Huntsman, the Georgian coffee house turned pub in Terrace Walk, conveniently close to the Roman Baths. Diamond was treating the team to a drink after their surveillance duties – except for Paul Gilbert, who hadn't yet arrived.

'So will you be going to the reception, guv?' John Leaman asked.

'I have to, don't I? I'm on the guest list. And so is bloody Irving. I'm on duty until it's all over and he's safe in bed tonight.'

'And you don't think he's worried?'

'Joe? He doesn't turn a hair. It's George who is bricking it.'

'George?'

'The DCC.'

'You're on first-name terms now?'

Diamond shrugged.

'A knees-up in the Roman Baths should be fun,' Keith Halliwell said.

'If that's your idea of fun, I don't share it.'

'Will you be doing a sweep of the site in case someone is hiding?'

'Sorted. The place closes at six and they routinely make a check in case anyone is left in there. Tonight the security guys will be joined by two armed police officers.'

'Will anyone be on the door when the guests arrive?'

'Are you volunteering, Keith?'

Ingeborg laughed. 'Walked into that, didn't you?'

'Actually,' Diamond said, 'they'll have a receiving line as we go in. Joe Irving, George Brace and his wife and the new Mr and Mrs Brace. I can't see any dodgy character running that gauntlet.'

'Are you hoping they'll let you in, guv?'

'And why shouldn't they?'

'The suit.'

'What's wrong with the suit?'

'All the wrinkles. It dried out badly.'

He frowned. 'Do you mind? I went home and changed. This is my second-best suit.'

Nobody commented.

He shook his head, uncertain if he was being sent up. 'What time is it? The thing starts at seven thirty.'

'You've got a couple of hours. Time for a few more rounds.'

'Where's young Paul?'

'We were wondering,' Halliwell said. 'He had some trouble making contact. Personal radio on the blink, I reckon.'

'The rain?'

'Could be.'

A general pause for thought.

Ingeborg said, 'Is it possible he's still on that roof, do you think?'

A couple of them giggled at the thought.

'Can't be. He'll have seen them drive away, same as we did.'

'How did he get up there?'

'A ladder,' Diamond said. 'Before any of us were up and about.'

'Did anyone send a ladder to bring him down?' She put her hand to her mouth and stared at each of the others. It was cruel, but they couldn't help seeing the funny side.

Waiting for 6.20 was worse than being in the slammer, but Jack wasn't going to blow his last chance by going too early, before the crowds had left. He used the time checking the handgun several times over.

Precisely on schedule he replaced the Glock in its holster, pulled on the balaclava and stepped up to the wall.

Easy. The drainpipe acted like a handrail.

Using the footholds in the masonry he climbed to the top and looked over.

He was leaning on a raked Roman-style roof with faded interlocking terracotta tiles growing a coat of moss. Ahead, a large paved promenade around a rectangular space that gave views of the Great Bath about thirty feet below. The same stone emperor Jack had taken for a real person the evening before was mounted on the balustrade of this walkway and so were seven others on plinths ranged around its length. The stonework up here had weathered, but it wasn't old, not as old as it pretended to be. Everything at the top level, including the emperors, was fake Roman. The genuine stuff, the Great Bath and its surrounds, was at basement level.

No one appeared to be about, so he heaved himself up and shuffled and crawled along the top rows of tiles to the end, where the roof linked to a square building. Using the wall as a support he made a cautious descent down the slippery tiles. Then with the help of another drainpipe he lowered himself to the terrace itself.

He was in.

First reaction: check that the gun was still in its holster.

Second: look for somewhere to hide in case anyone appeared.

Forget it. This place was as exposed as a prison landing. There was nothing on the terrace to shelter behind except the emperors. Worse still, the entire area was overlooked from a corridor behind huge arched windows along the side he'd climbed over. Lights were on and people were in there arranging flowers or something.

All that he could see of the terrace was bordered by that balustrade. Yes, another bloody balustrade. He was becoming a balustrade phobic.

He peered over. To avoid being spotted he needed to get down to the excavated level. The Victorians had built a colonnade around the edge of the Great Bath. The columns supported the terrace and everything up here. Of more immediate interest to Jack were the real Roman remains, the chunks of masonry, broken columns and recesses. Useful as cover.

Fortunately he didn't need to do more steeplejack stuff. He could use the stairs.

Still alert for security people, he headed to the far end. Stepped down to the lower level. Paused a second. From the bottom stair he could see a layer of steam rising in wisps from the greenish water in front of him, the whole reason for the city's identity, hot water from two and a half miles down forced through the earth's crust.

He stepped out on to flagstones laid by the Romans almost two thousand years ago.

And froze.

An armed cop stood facing the bath no more than five yards away. Ultra-short assault rifle. Body armour. Belt bristling with pouches and holsters. Handcuffs, baton, radio, Streamlight torch. And a back-up handgun.

Jack's hand automatically felt for the gun on his belt. He could shoot first. He had the advantage. He'd floor the guy, even in the ballistic-plated vest. But sanity prevailed and an inner voice told him he wasn't here to take on some anonymous cop.

With extreme care, alert for the slightest twitch, he took a step backwards.

And another.

Two more and he was back in the shadows.

The sound of footsteps from the opposite side of the bath, brisk and business-like. For crying out loud. Another armed cop was facing him from across the water. Fortunately Jack had merged with his surroundings now. The cop wouldn't see him if he stayed still.

How many more armed police were in the building? Anyone would think there was a terror alert.

'How are you doing?' from the second cop.

'Done this side,' from the first.

'Move on, then. I'll check here.'

'Okay.'

Jack drew his gun. This could be curtains if the cop decided to use the staircase.

Thank Christ the fucker turned right and stepped towards an arched exit at the other end.

Huge, grateful breath.

173

The second guy started a slow search of the south side, using his torch to explore the shadowy alcoves.

Stay still and keep cool.

More testing minutes passed before the inspection was completed and the second cop left the same way the first had gone.

So what was it about, all this police activity? An extra level of security because the bridegroom happened to be the top cop's son – or had they arrived in response to an emergency call? To Jack's knowledge, he'd given no clue about his presence here. He'd left the young cop bound up like King Tut. He'd made sure he destroyed his radio.

Get a grip, Jack. It can't be anything to do with you.

But would they remain on duty for the whole shindig, or was it only a check before the guests arrived? Surely no bride and groom would want their wedding breakfast patrolled by armed police?

Tough it out, man.

He was about to move on when – shit a brick – two more people, a man and a woman, appeared from the same end the cops had used. This was getting farcical.

He backed fast into the shadow, hoping to God he hadn't been seen.

Panic stations? No. He was bloody angry. They had no right to be there. The place had closed half an hour ago. The fact that *he* had no right to be there didn't cross his mind.

These two were acting as if they owned the bloody bath. The man, wearing what looked like a black velvet jacket, was gesturing in an exaggerated way with both hands and the woman seemed to be taking him seriously. She was holding some gadget in her right hand that Jack now recognised as a light meter.

Photography, then.

But what kind of saddo uses light meters in the digital age?

Jack had read about this while he was inside. Modern technology was wonderful, but there was a fad for retro things like old cameras with their fiddly controls for shutter speeds, apertures and the rest. Some people said you got better results using film, probably the same people who insisted music sounded better on vinyl. Snobbery typical of Bath.

No prize for guessing this was the wedding photographer getting ready for the session that should have happened outside the Abbey.

Too fucking late for Jack.

Joe Irving with all his money had no doubt paid top dollar for this prick in velvet planning the shoot with his assistant. All uncertainty was removed when the squeeze picked a tripod off the ground and stood it up. Seemed they were planning to line up everyone on the opposite side of the Great Bath and shoot their pictures from across the water. So arty.

Their set-up was no help to Jack, who had his own shoot to think of. He'd need to get nearer to his target to be certain of the kill. He didn't have the AK any more. The Glock is designed for close combat. He hadn't gone to all this trouble to total someone else in error.

He would pick his moment. And when it came, he wasn't going to miss.

After they'd fetched a ladder and Halliwell had gone up and was horrified to discover Paul Gilbert stretched out on the roof, bound hand and foot and gagged, Diamond, who wasn't built for ladder work, decided he'd better make the effort and see for himself.

To say that he was gobsmacked is an understatement. A

short while ago he'd been smugly celebrating his prediction that the wedding would pass off without incident.

His first duty was to make sure Gilbert's attacker wasn't still about. No one else was visible either side of the roof. There wasn't anywhere to hide.

The young detective constable was in a sorry state, blood smeared on his forehead and seeping from a wound in his matted hair, but if he expected sympathy, he didn't get much.

'How the hell did this happen?' Diamond asked after the gag was ripped off and the duct tape cut.

Gilbert needed water first. Halliwell massaged his legs to restore circulation. He groaned.

'Am I hurting you?' Halliwell asked.

'It's not you. It's my ribs.'

His account, when they got it, posed more questions than it answered.

'Description?'

'I can't say.'

'What do you mean, you can't say? You get clobbered and tied up and you can't even tell me what your assailant looked like?'

'He had one of those masks you pull over your head. Holes for eyes and mouth.'

'Balaclava.'

'Yeah. Bala . . .' He couldn't get his mouth around the word. He was still in a state of shock or concussion.

'Height?'

'Don't know, guv. Average, I suppose.'

'Clothes?'

'Black. All black.'

'Leather? Tracksuit?'

'T-shirt and jeans.'

'Any accent?'

'Nothing I noticed.'

176

'You said he hit you with a rifle butt?'

'Yes.' He felt for the injury.

'What sort of rifle? Fully automatic? Magazine-fed?'

'I didn't get much chance to see it.'

'After you were felled, did he threaten you with it?'

'He hit me with it.'

'You told us that already. I'm asking if he threatened to shoot you.'

'Pulled a handgun on me.'

'His, or yours?'

'His, I think. He grabbed mine when he was taping me up and slung it away.'

Halliwell interrupted. 'Guv, that looks like one of our Glocks behind you in the gutter.' He was pointing along the roof to what appeared to be a police-issue weapon.

'Fetch it, then.'

A slight, respectful pause. 'Better leave it, hadn't we? Prints. This is a crime scene now.'

'What?'

'Assaulting a police officer.'

'Mm.'

Halliwell was right, of course. Diamond's mind wasn't on the legalities of what had happened. Who was more befuddled by what had happened, Gilbert or his boss?

He turned back to Gilbert. 'Did you get him to talk?'

'In the end, I did, but he didn't give anything away except he was really pissed off about the rain. It was like a mon . . . mon . . .'

'Monsoon. We know. We were there.' He chose not to add that 'there' had been mainly inside the coffee shop. After all, he'd made the dash for the Abbey and ruined his best suit.

'I could have drowned,' Gilbert said. 'I was lying in six inches of water.'

'He didn't help you?'

'He was round the other side, trying to line up a shot, I suppose. He came back finally after the wedding was over – I know it was over 'cos the bells were going – and he dragged me up here.'

'At any point did he tell you why he was here?'

'Like I say, guv, he wasn't a talker. I'm sure he meant to use the rifle. From where I was, I couldn't see anything, but I don't think he fired a single shot. Nobody was hit, were they?'

'No thanks to you, getting ambushed as soon as you got up here. Where's your bag?'

'He took it away, but he shared some of the water with me and let me take bites at an apple.'

'Decent of him.' Diamond asked Halliwell to go the other side of the roof and check for the bag.

Paul Gilbert was looking bereft, as if the enormity of events had caught up with him. 'I'm sorry, guv. I messed up badly.'

Diamond softened a little. 'And paid for it. He gave you a kicking in the ribs, did he?'

'That wasn't a kick. That was with the end of the gun.'

'After he'd knocked you down?'

'Should have been on my guard. The day hadn't started when I first got up here. Didn't cross my mind someone else could be here already.'

'You've been tied up for how long? At least ten hours.'

'I don't like to think.'

From the other side of the roof came Halliwell's voice. 'Better come and look at this, guv.'

'Stay sitting here,' Diamond told Gilbert. 'We don't want you keeling over.' He took the long way around the end of the raked roof.

At once he saw why Halliwell had called him. The narrow gully between the roofing and the balustrade was cluttered

178

with discarded objects, among them a smashed personal radio, two backpacks, a bedroll, several empty water bottles and a banana skin. And an assault rifle.

'He left the gun behind?' Diamond remarked. 'Strange.'

Halliwell shook his head. 'They're not easy to come by. Why did he do that?'

'Got a theory?'

'He left in a hurry?'

'I don't think so. He spent some time with young Gilbert.' Diamond rubbed the back of his neck, trying to put himself into the mind of the unknown gunman. 'He had no more use for the rifle, so he sacrificed it. He didn't want to be seen with a bloody great weapon in broad daylight.'

'You don't think he's done a runner?'

'Do you?'

'Well, he's not here any more.'

'What's that wall at the end? The Roman Baths are on the other side.' His eyes widened. 'He could be in there now.' He reached in his back pocket and pulled out his phone.

25

The second-best suit hadn't been improved by Diamond's going up the ladder and along gutters. Ingeborg, bless her, had liberated a red rosebud from a flower arrangement in the pub for her boss to wear as a buttonhole, telling him it would divert attention from the wrinkles.

Brazen it out, then.

Shoulders back, chin up, he made sure he was first along the receiving line before the official start. He had a different greeting for each of the main players.

For the groom: a firm handshake and, 'Congratulations, young man.'

For the bride: a polite brush of cheeks, more congratulations and, 'Make sure he treats you well.'

For the bride's father: a meeting of eyes, a nod and a cool, 'Good to see you.' To which he might have added the words, 'still breathing'.

For the groom's mother: 'Leticia, how nice,' and an attempt at a social kiss which she transformed into a collision of lips and a hug that would have snapped the ribcage of a lesser man.

For the groom's father after that: a raised thumb that said he had survived the embrace and Bath CID was on the case.

Encouragement was never more needed. George Brace had taken the phone call about Paul Gilbert badly. He may have been expecting trouble, but to have it confirmed that a gunman had overpowered one of the team and beaten him about the head and body with an assault rifle was deeply alarming. If he'd said, 'Oh my God,' once, he'd said it ten times over.

Diamond, for all his swagger, was actually more shaken than an astronaut on re-entry. He'd never wholly believed George's theory about a murder attempt at the wedding. Now he was chastened: finding young Gilbert trussed up and injured had been a personal blow. Seeing the AK-63 for himself removed all doubts how deadly the intent was. He was shamed by the miscalculation he'd made. Far worse could have happened, like a bullet to Paul Gilbert's head. He'd put the young man in harm's way. Should have posted someone more experienced on the roof. Because a drive-by shooting had seemed more likely than a sniper's shots, he'd considered the balustrade as no more than an observation point, the safe option. How stupid was that?

But this wasn't the time for beating himself up. An armed man was roaming free and meant to kill. He had to be found and stopped. Get on the case, Diamond, or you'll regret this day for the rest of your life.

With a wedding reception in full flow.

They were under the coffered dome in the reception hall, as grand a setting as Bath could rise to, certainly grander than the Pump Room, the Assembly Rooms or any other public building. A string quartet was playing 'What a Wonderful World'. The contrast between the jollity of the occasion and the imminent threat couldn't be more stark.

No penny-pinching at this wedding. Vintage Perrier Jouet was on offer, courtesy of Joe Irving. Any high-principled policeman would have sucked on a lemon rather than take a sip. Diamond wasn't high-principled, and wouldn't normally allow anything to get in the way of a good drink, but mixing it after the beer session with the team wouldn't be clever, so he carried his glass to the side and tipped most of his into a giant floor vase containing a flower arrangement. From behind the clusters of white hydrangeas he would have a view of everyone coming in. And no one would notice the suit.

In truth, it was unlikely that the gunman would enter the same way as the official guests. Going by young Gilbert's memory of a black T-shirt, jeans and balaclava, the guy was unsuitably dressed for a wedding. If he hadn't given in and gone away, he'd be inside the building already, hiding up and waiting for a chance to get close without being noticed.

Or was that another mistaken assumption?

'Excuse me, sir.'

He tensed.

The hand on his sleeve was a young woman's. She had crept up from nowhere. If she'd been the gunman, he'd have been dead meat.

His hand snaked inside his jacket and gripped the handgun.

She had a disarming smile. 'Sorry if I startled you.'

'Not at all.'

'Are you with the bride or the groom?'

'The groom, I suppose.'

Small talk wasn't his forte at the best of times. Here and now it was asking for a miracle.

'Would you mind joining the group over here? We're working against time, you see.'

He didn't see. And she didn't look as if she was working, dressed as she was in a quivering ostrich-feather fascinator and a close-fitting peacock blue dress from which much of her appeared eager to escape.

Who did she think she was, ordering people about?

'Not now,' he said, taking his phone out instead of the

gun. 'I'm about to get a picture of the bride.' A smart detective always has a cover story.

'She'll still be here, believe me,' she said. 'This won't take more than a couple of minutes. I'm with Maurice, the official photographer – Dixie is my name, did I say? – and Maurice has been asked to get shots of everyone informally before we do the group photos.'

The word 'shots' was unfortunate. 'Where is he?'

'Maurice? Over there by the musicians.'

Maurice didn't have the look of a killer. He was in a velvet jacket, frilly shirt and bow tie. Two professional-looking cameras were dangling from his neck.

'He wants to take one of me?'

Dixie shook her head. 'Solo shots are a no-no. They won't look good in the album. We want to show the guests enjoying each other's company. Why don't you join these charming ladies to our left and I'll call Maurice over to take a threesome.' She spoke loudly enough for the charming ladies to look across and make an assessment of Diamond. They were wearing hats he recognised. They'd sat in the front pew with Irving during the service. The bride's cousins.

'I haven't met them,' he told Dixie.

'That's the whole point,' she said. She wasn't going to be denied. 'It's about circulating at this stage. Shall we get your glass topped up for the picture?'

He stood his ground, but Dixie waved to the charming ladies and they came over. 'Did someone mention a threesome?' one said. 'We're up for it, aren't we, Angie?'

It must have been the champagne talking.

Dixie said, 'I only meant a group photo.'

'No problem,' the bold one said. 'Get the action on video if you like, as long as we get our cut of the profits.'

Diamond's toes curled. He couldn't escape from these two without making a scene.

183

'I'm Ondine, and this is my cousin Angie.'

'I wish you wouldn't call me that,' Angie said. 'My name is Angela.'

'Have it your way, then,' Ondine said. 'Call me what you want. I'll answer to anything. We're the bridesmaids' mums, for our sins.'

'I'm Peter,' Diamond said, resigned to this, his eyes trying to do the impossible and watch the entire room at the same time. This situation, with people moving from group to group, could have been choreographed for a close-up killing. The gunman was armed with a pistol.

And probably a knife.

Dixie said, 'If you lovely ladies stand either side of Peter it will make a sensational one for the album. Don't move from this spot while I fetch Maurice.'

In their heels, they were taller than Diamond.

'All that talk about a threesome and she only wants a wedding picture,' Ondine said with a pretend pout. 'Shame. But that doesn't stop us getting to know each other better. What do you say, Peter?'

He didn't say anything. Neither did Angela.

'By yourself, are you?' Ondine asked, getting closer than he liked.

'Today I am,' he said.

'Friend or family?'

'Friend.' He needed to switch the attention away from himself. 'So your daughters were the bridesmaids. Charming, I thought. I suppose they're at home and in bed now.'

'If only,' Angela said. She was definitely the more reserved of the pair, and when she did speak it was usually sharp-tongued. He wasn't sure which cousin he found harder to take.

'What time is it?' Ondine said and checked. 'Gone eight-thirty already. You're right, Peter, if it weren't for all that

184

rain we had, they'd be off our hands and we could roam free. Lordy, they're needed for the group photos. Got to have the bridesmaids in the picture.'

'So where are they?' As if he truly wanted to know. He took another long look around the room, but not for children in frilly dresses.

'Round and about, driving someone bloody mad, I expect. You can't expect kids of their age to stand still for long. They're in a rare old state. I hope it doesn't all end in tears.'

'It will,' Angela said.

Spoken with the certainty of one who knew. Quite a conversation-stopper because it seemed to convey much more than the fragile emotions of three small girls.

'Let's hope not, today of all days,' Diamond said with yet another glance towards Irving. He hadn't been eviscerated yet. 'Where are you ladies from?'

'Birmingham, in my case,' Ondine said, 'and Angie is from Broadstairs.'

'Long journeys.'

'Yes, we're staying overnight at Uncle Joe's. Posh house in Sion Hill Place.'

'More of a tomb, if you ask me,' Angela said.

'Be fair,' Ondine said. 'He hasn't lived there for yonks. All it needs is a woman's touch to make it more homely.'

'Unlikely.'

'Don't count on it. I think there may be a lady in his life.'

'Really? Tell me more.' For the first time, Angela showed some interest in what was going on.

Suddenly this was women's talk that Diamond had no part in.

'The one who called this afternoon when he was out.'

'You didn't tell me. Who was that?'

'You were busy with the girls' hair. No one else was bothering to answer the bloody doorbell, so I had to go.'

185

'What was she like?'

'Stropped off when she saw me, I can tell you. Freaked out, in fact.'

'Why?'

'I was in my silk dressing gown, wasn't I?'

Angela started laughing.

'Straight out the shower.'

'Oh, Ondine! What did she say?'

'She said sod all at first.'

How did I get trapped here? Diamond asked himself. Why am I listening to this stuff?

'Then she asked if he was at home, called him Mr Irving – Mister Irving, all very hoity-toity – treating me like I was some slapper off the streets.'

'Fair comment.'

'Mean.'

'Because of the way you were dressed, or undressed. What did you say to her?'

'I told her he wasn't at home and I could see she didn't believe me. She must have thought he was upstairs buck naked and panicking in case I let her in. I said I'd tell him she'd called and I asked for her name, but she wouldn't give it. She said something about' – she mimicked the pretentious voice – '"coming back at a more convenient time" and then she was off.'

'What age was she?'

'Mid to late thirties.'

'Young for Uncle Joe.'

'Try telling him that. I wouldn't dare.'

'I expect she's stalking him,' Angela said. 'Did you think of that? With all his money he's quite a catch. He was expecting her to call and that's why he went out all afternoon.'

'I don't think so. The truth is he needed a bloody break from a house full of females.' Ondine turned to Diamond.

'Girl talk. Best ignore it. We don't often meet as a family. Are you married, Peter?'

'Not any more.'

'Tough. It's usually the woman who is left, for one reason or another, ain't that the grim truth, Angela?'

Angela didn't answer.

'Here comes the guy with the camera,' Ondine said. 'Dishy. Do you think they're an item?'

Angela shook her head. 'If they are, he's a cradle-snatcher.'

'Or she's found her father figure.'

Diamond was near screaming point. He wasn't remotely interested in what Dixie and Maurice got up to unless it was killing crime barons.

'This won't take a minute, people,' Dixie told them. 'Stand exactly where you are and show you're enjoying yourselves. Didn't you get your glass topped up, Peter? An empty one won't look good.'

'I'll put it out of sight.'

'No, no. You hold it up to the camera. That's the whole idea. I'll grab one off the tray for you.'

She was off again, leaving them facing the photographer, who didn't have anything to say. He was peering into his viewfinder.

And something about Maurice was familiar. I've seen you before, my friend, Diamond decided. But where?

When Maurice made eye contact, there was a flicker of something that might have been recognition.

In a long police career you're forever meeting people and assessing them as trustworthy or otherwise. Thousands, for sure, without all the others you come across in your personal life. Dark brown hair, eyes darker still, pale, long face that wasn't used to smiling. Difficult to place.

'How do you want us?' Diamond asked Maurice to see if the voice gave a clue.

'You're fine as you are, my pet.' But the response came from Dixie, back with a filled glass of champagne that she handed across. 'Get in closer, ladies. Peter won't bite.'

Don't count on it, the way I feel.

The picture was taken, Dixie said it was gorgeous and the photographers moved on to corral someone else.

'That was cool,' Ondine said. 'Maybe we'll get lucky and share a table at the meal. And if we do, Angela is a dab hand at rearranging the place cards to make sure who she's sitting next to.'

Angela gave her the point of her elbow and said, 'Do you mind?'

The cousins tottered off.

There was barely time to dispose of the champagne before the best man invited everyone to move through to the Great Bath for the group photograph.

A new challenge.

It would be dark down there. Evening had closed in.

Mental image of all the guests lined up along the edge, in high spirits. One tips forward into the water and everyone cheers, not knowing he is fatally wounded. Hilarity turns to horror.

26

Diamond moved fast and made sure he was close behind Joe Irving when the exodus from the reception hall began.

'You again?' Irving said, glaring over his shoulder.

'Doing my job,' Diamond said.

'Good thing I know who you are, ain't it?'

They passed through the gallery overlooking the Great Bath. Lavishly decorated tables were already in place for the wedding breakfast.

'Straight on and down the stairs,' the best man called out.

Flaming torches in sconces lit up the scene and were reflected in the water, so atmospheric that you might have believed you were back in Roman Britain if it were not for the instructions being issued from the opposite side where Maurice the photographer had his camera and tripod set up.

'Pass along the side, please, and go carefully. The footing is uneven in places. I need the bride and groom and bridesmaids and principal guests between the centre columns.' The voice was Dixie's, through a portable megaphone.

Eighty tipsy guests shuffling along the water's edge by torchlight was crying out for a mishap, whether accidental or deliberate. For Diamond, the minder, the big risk wasn't some idiot falling in. It was the opportunity for killing at close quarters. Along each side of the bath were relics of the Romans, broken columns, chunks of masonry and arched alcoves where the killer could be lurking. The only way to protect the intended victim was to act as a human shield.

'That's wonderful,' Dixie broadcast over the water. She had the megaphone in one hand and a flashlight in the other. The beam travelled along the line-up. 'Can we have the three bridesmaids on the lowest step, but carefully? Someone give them a hand down. You're looking gorgeous, girls. Bouquets upwards please, so we can see the flowers. Perfecto. This won't take long. I know it's getting cooler by the minute and you aren't dressed for outdoors, but we're doing this for the happy couple, aren't we?'

Everyone was facing one way except Diamond.

He had his back to the bath, his hand on the gun under his jacket and he was peering into the shadowy extremities. He could have used that flashlight.

'Someone is being bashful,' Dixie announced. 'There's always one, isn't there? Who's that skulking behind the father of the bride?'

Heads turned.

Leticia said in a piercing voice, 'Peter, we're ready!'

He turned to face her. 'They don't need me.'

'Did I hear the name Peter?' Dixie's voice echoed off the stonework. 'I met you, didn't I? Come out. I know who you are.'

He refused to make conversation across the bath.

'You're not showing yourself, Peter.'

Lewd laughter travelled along the water's edge.

'Yes, I could have phrased that better,' Dixie said. 'Peter, would you show your face?'

What's the worst that can happen on an undercover mission? Being loud-hailed by a megaphone must come close.

No way would he raise his hand and say, 'Here I am.'

Dixie was losing her cool. 'Peter, if you stand behind Mr Irving we won't see anything of you, big as you are. Would you move to the side? You're not actually one of the principal guests, are you?'

Someone along the ranks shouted, 'Get on with it, love. We're getting cold.'

'Do as she bloody says,' big Joe rasped.

'I'm on duty,' Diamond said.

'Sod that. You're not needed.'

'Tell her I'm ill.'

Joe shouted across to Dixie, 'He just threw up. Take the picture without him.'

With that settled, the photography at last got under way. Several takes of the entire company, after which the majority were free to return upstairs. Then the inevitable group pictures of the principals in various combinations.

Diamond watched from the shadows like Harry Lime in his all-time favourite film.

Mercifully, the only shots were with the camera. If the gunman was inside the building he'd missed his best opportunity of killing Joe.

Upstairs in the covered gallery, mutiny was being discussed to the strains of the string quartet. People don't like to be kept waiting when they're hungry, but you can't start before the bride and groom arrive. It was well past 9 p.m. Most of the guests had been seated on chairs with white covers and pink sashes for almost half an hour and not even a bread roll had been served. Candles had been lit at each of the round tables and were in danger of burning out. The applause when the young couple and their VIP guests finally arrived from their photo session was more about the prospect of food than anything else.

Diamond slipped in behind George Brace and Leticia. He already knew where he would be seated. The efficient

Caroline had made the seating plan and promised to make sure he was on the next table to her father. But being so close came at a price. He was with the bridesmaids and their mothers.

'Yoohoo,' Ondine said, waving. 'You're with us.'

'Here, between Ondine and me,' Angela said.

'Don't ask,' Ondine said.

They introduced their small daughters, Ondine's twins, Tonya and Trixie, and Angela's Gabriella. The bridesmaids didn't look up. They had already untied the ribbons on their special packs of food and were making short work of the popcorn.

'And that's my meal ticket, Jed,' Ondine said of the tired-looking man across the table. 'He's had a skinful already. We see too bloody much of each other all the time, so I don't need to sit next to him.'

Jed rolled his eyes upwards. He looked as if he needed the break.

To be sure of his bearings, Diamond glanced at the next table where the bride and groom, their parents and the best man were already being served with their starters. Irving didn't look happy and pushed aside his mango and brie parcel. He could be forgiven. He'd be making the first speech.

'Mummy, I hate chicken nuggets,' one of the twins said.

'Eat the sausage and the carrot sticks, then,' Ondine told her. 'You've got loads to choose from.'

'Why can't we have pizza?'

'You have what's put in front of you and you bloody enjoy it.'

'Can we play?' Gabriella said.

Her mother Angela said, 'If you do, the box may be gone when you come back.'

'Don't want any more. It's rabbit food.'

'Shush. Aunt Caroline may be listening.'

'She ain't.'

Angela winced at the word.

Ondine said, 'It won't hurt for them to leave the table. There are speeches to come.'

'Please,' the girls said as one.

'Very well,' Angela said, 'but act responsibly.'

Ondine said, 'Don't go anywhere near the water. Don't do nothing we wouldn't do,' and then muttered, 'As if they listen to me.'

The bridesmaids had already run off, at peril to a waitress bringing the starters.

'They can't get up to much,' Ondine said. 'All the Roman stuff is closed, isn't it?'

'Except the Great Bath.'

'Crimbo – they're not that daft, are they?'

The girls were soon forgotten. Ondine got the giggles when Angela asked Diamond if he would like a roll. He didn't rise to the joke. The next hour would be a trial.

Among the guests, the starter had banished the hunger pangs and all thoughts of mutiny. Before the main course, the best man stood up and said, 'Ladies and gentlemen, please put your hands together for our host, the father of the bride.'

Mr Big's big moment.

Diamond didn't put his hands together. He put his right hand inside his jacket and around the handle of the gun and his left across his chest to cup his chin as if concentrating on the speech.

Joe Irving standing to speak was heaven-sent for a gunman. Being so tall and wide, he was an easier hit than one of the paper targets on the range at the Tri-Force Centre. While being applauded, he drained his glass and looked around for a waiter.

He struck a confident note from the start and he wasn't reading from a script. 'Someone fill me up again. Here we are, then. Bit of a comedown for me, this is. As most of you know, a couple of weeks ago I was a guest of Her Majesty, but all good things come to an end and I don't mind slumming it with you lot for my one and only daughter, Caroline. As well as being pretty, she's as smart as a smacked bottom. Remember that, Ben. Don't ever mess Carrie about. She's sitting here beside me looking like butter wouldn't melt, but, let's face it, she made me write the cheques for this bender, and that's not easy. I've known hard men who'd rather put a gun to their heads than tap me for a fiver.'

He was delivering this as if he did it every day and getting laughs and he looked set to continue some time, regardless of the danger he was in, with no concern that his minder's nerves were as strung out as the festoon lights above him.

'It's no secret that I haven't been much of a father. I wish I'd been there for you more often, Carrie, my love, but stuff happens, as they say. Now you're grown up I hope you can forgive me and remember the good times. You've had a special place in my heart since the day you were born and now I've learned to respect you as one very smart lady. You organised all this and got yourself hitched to the son of one of the top cops in town. Who would have thought it? Deputy Chief Constable Brace and serial offender Irving sharing a table at their kids' wedding.'

Who would have thought it and who was having to deal with it? Peter Diamond, desperate for this sentimental drivel to dry up. He glanced across at George Brace and saw that he, too, was suffering, tearing his paper napkin into shreds and no doubt wishing he'd come in a humble suit instead of the black serge and silver emblems of rank.

Still with his audience lapping up each word, Joe took

another swig of champagne and launched into the next phase. 'I'm supposed to tell you a joke before I sit down, so here goes. Sorry, George, it's a cop joke, but, Carrie, you can relax, because it's a clean one. This geezer is out late in his car, about two a.m., when a cop stops him and asks where he's going. He says, "I'm on my way to a lecture about alcohol abuse." And the cop says, "At this time of night? Who's the lecturer?" And he says, "My wife."'

Enough drink had been consumed for this to get some genuine laughter. The speech had gone well so far. No shots had been fired.

Quit while you're ahead, Diamond longed to tell him.

'Tell you another funny thing. I don't know why, but I have a bit of a reputation. My lawyer is always saying I never hurt a fly. A few flies might tell you different, but they're not talking no more.'

Pause for laughter.

Joe stopped grinning and lowered his voice and you couldn't doubt that he was a hard man. 'I'll tell you this for nothing. It's people who disappoint me, people who don't do as I say. So I'm telling you lot right now there might be a knock on your door tonight' – he looked around the room and there was a frisson of unease before he gave a playful smile and said – 'unless you stand up sharp and drink to the success of this marriage. Good health and happiness to the bride and groom, Caroline and Ben.'

It was over.

Cries of 'Caroline and Ben'. Thunderous applause. No shots. Joe sat down and basked in the glory.

Strange. All the obvious opportunities had passed by. It was becoming possible to believe that this ill-omened wedding would end without incident. Diamond removed his hand from the gun and drank some of the wine. His thoughts even turned to the main course being served

195

already to the top table. It looked like a roast of some kind. He wouldn't object to that.

'He's a lad, our uncle Joe,' Ondine said. 'I never thought he'd make such a good speech. Lovely, what he said about Caroline.'

'"Smart as a smacked bottom"?' Angela said with a curl of the lip.

'That was for a laugh. I mean about having a special place in his heart since she was a baby. When he came out with that, I welled up, I really did. What did you think of it, Peter?'

'Better than I could do.'

The plates arrived before he needed to say more.

'What is it, beef?' Ondine asked.

The waiter said, 'Venison, ma'am.'

'That's got to be a first at one of our family weddings,' Angela said.

'Smells nice,' Ondine said. 'How does it cut?'

'With a knife, dear.'

'You crease me up.'

The venison was good, even if the vegetables were judged by the cousins to be undercooked.

'Make the dinner last, people,' Ondine said. 'We're in for another speech when we clear our plates.'

'Who from?'

'The groom. Poor lad, having to follow Uncle Joe. He's not enjoying his venison. Look at him.'

'He'll be all right.'

'You bet he went to a good school and learned to talk proper. He's got a lot to think of, thanking Uncle Joe for the nice things he said, and then praising up Caroline. And he mustn't forget to propose a toast to the bridesmaids.' She clapped a hand to her mouth. 'Oh, Christ, where are they, the little demons? They've got to be in here for the toast. Jed, we've got to round up the girls.'

'Leave 'em be,' Jed said from across the table. 'They don't want to listen to speeches.'

'Didn't you hear me? They're going to be toasted.'

'Serve 'em bloody right.'

'He doesn't get it,' Ondine said. 'He's half pissed. I'm going to have to go looking.'

'I'll come,' Angela said.

But they were saved the trouble. The three girls came running from the far end of the room.

'Mummy, Mummy.'

'Look at the state of you,' Ondine said. 'How did you get like that?'

All three had black smears on their pink dresses. Their hands and faces, too, were marked with dirt.

'Mummy, guess what we found.'

'You're a bloody disgrace, all three of you.'

'A dead body,' Gabriella said.

Both twins nodded and gave triumphant smiles. 'We found a dead body.'

27

'For God's sake, keep your voices down.'

'But it's *true*, Mummy,' Gabriella said.

Diamond checked his watch.

10.20 p.m.

'Don't be so daft.' Ondine turned to Angela. 'What are they on about?'

'I haven't the faintest idea.' Angela asked the twins, 'Where were you – somewhere near the water?'

'No,' Trixie said. 'Mummy said to stay away from the water, so we did.'

'How did your clothes get in such a state, then, if it wasn't round the bath?'

'We had to climb over the wall. Gabbie helped us.'

'*Climb over a wall?* Where was this?'

'Downstairs where the body is.'

'Shhhh! If Aunt Caroline hears you say such things it will ruin her wedding.'

'You asked, so I told you,' Tonya said.

'Speak quietly, then. You climbed over a wall. Where?'

'It wasn't a real wall. We could see through it.'

'You've lost me now.'

Diamond, who was all ears, said, 'They must be talking about the barriers around the museum exhibits. Some of them are clear plastic.' He asked Gabriella, 'Is this a statue you're talking about?'

'No.' Tossing back her hair, her left hand on her hip and her right unfolding in front of her, the image of a little drama queen, she said, 'It's a dead person.'

'Where exactly is it?'

'In a big place with stepping stones.'

'Is that why you climbed over, to play on the stepping stones?'

A sigh and a head shake. Grown-ups can be so dense and grown-up men are the densest of all. 'We wanted to see the body. Anyway, the stones were much too high to play on, high as this table. They were in rows, like bricks on top of each other.'

He'd lived in Bath long enough to know what the child meant. 'I think she means the hypocaust, the underfloor heating system. Have you been down there?'

Ondine shook her head. 'Hypo what? Never heard of it. We came for the wedding, not the tourist stuff.'

The tourist stuff was what she now got. 'The Romans had furnaces that sent hot air through this underground chamber she's talking about and heated the floor of the sweat-room above. What's left are stacks of tiles that once supported the flooring, at least a hundred and fifty of them.'

'Whatever it is, their dresses are ruined,' Angela said, as uninterested as her cousin in the history of the place.

Trixie started chanting, 'We found a body, we found a body . . .' and the others chimed in.

'Girls!'

The force of one word from Angela silenced them and caused heads to turn on the next table. She turned to the others. 'Generally I believe in free expression, especially from children. Nobody wants talk of death at a wedding.'

'So right they don't, giving everyone the creeps,' Ondine said. 'Simmer down, girls. There's a speech coming up and he's going to say some nice things about you.'

'Be patient, and you might get a present from your new uncle,' Angela added.

Children are easily distracted. The twins eyed each other excitedly and Gabriella asked, 'What sort of present?'

'Like a thank-you for being well-behaved bridesmaids.'

'Yes, but what is it?'

'How would I know?'

Ondine added, 'You'll have to wait and see and behave yourselves in case he changes his mind.'

Diamond wasn't sure what to think. The parents disbelieved their own children and the kids themselves weren't acting as if they'd truly seen a corpse, in spite of what they claimed. Wouldn't they be shocked or sickened? Not having offspring of his own, he wasn't sure how young brains worked, particularly modern young brains desensitised by television images. Kids got high on horror these days.

They'd seen something that excited them, obviously, and they'd talked of what could only be the stone piles in the hypocaust, so there was an element of truth for sure. He would have liked to check for himself, but his duty kept him here.

'When do we get our presents?' Gabriella asked.

'It could be soon, I think he's getting ready to stand up.'

'I can't see no presents.'

'It might be something small, from his pocket.'

'Like what?'

'Wait and see. But first we're all going to button our lips and listen to the speech.'

'Boring.'

Truth to tell, boring was an understatement. Ben needed a better scriptwriter. Probably Caroline enjoyed the compliments he paid her but most of the audience were relieved that the ordeal didn't last long. At least Ben did the right thing and proposed a toast to the bridesmaids at the end.

Then he reached behind him and produced three promising-looking parcels. Each bridesmaid stepped up to receive one and swiftly unwrapped it.

Personalised white bathrobes.

'Awesome,' Ondine said. 'Try them on, girls, and cover up your mucky dresses.'

The robes were a good fit and for a few seconds the girls had the attention of everyone in the room and milked it by parading between the tables with the steps and swirls of fashion models.

'Now you can give Aunt Caroline a kiss,' Ondine told them when they returned to the table.

'Do we have to?'

'Don't argue. Do as I bloody say.'

'After that, can we go off and have another look at the body?' Gabriella asked.

'I wish you'd shut up about the body. And don't you dare mention it to Caroline.'

They did as they were told and the bride hugged each of them in turn and Maurice the photographer got some cute pictures.

'Can we go now, Mummy?'

'That wouldn't be polite and we don't want you ruining these lovely robes,' Angela said. 'Sit down and listen to the next speech. It's the best man and he's sure to be funny.'

If he was, it was lost on three-quarters of the room, including the bridesmaids. His in-jokes were a hit with some of the groom's friends and that was all. Irving appeared bored and George embarrassed by what was being said about his son.

'Did you follow any of that?' Angela asked when the young man eventually sat down.

'Went over my head, darling,' Ondine said. 'That's the last of the speeches, isn't it? How long have we been sat here?

I've got a pain in the bum – and for once I don't mean Jed.
Bring on the disco, I say.'

She must have spotted the string quartet packing up their
instruments.

The best man was on his feet again.

'Jesus save us,' Ondine said. 'Not another speech?'

It was an announcement that the disco would be starting
in five minutes in the reception hall where the receiving
line had been.

At the mention of a disco the bridesmaids decided
they'd stay. Suddenly the body in the hypocaust had lost
its pulling power. Their mothers led the way, followed by
Jed, who looked in no shape for dancing. Diamond
lingered, waiting for Irving to make a move. When it
happened, he got close behind, alert for an attack. But
they made it safely to the disco.

The transformation of the reception hall was dramatic. The
DJ had set up his work station at one end where the tickets
were issued. The main lights were replaced by colours
streaking all over the room. Tables had been put around a
smallish dance floor. Two were reserved for the bride and
groom and their close families.

'Coo-ee!' Ondine hailed Diamond. 'We kept a place for you.'

His heart sank. There was no escape.

The DJ announced himself and said he'd get a great
evening under way with the only possible track, Neil
Diamond's 'Sweet Caroline'.

'I can dance to that,' Gabriella piped up.

'So can I,' said each of the twins.

'No you bloody don't,' Ondine told them. 'Everyone waits
for the bride and groom to start it off.'

'Why?'

'It's what happens at weddings, that's why. I'll tell you when you can join in.'

This new location posed a bigger security risk. Had the gunman been waiting all this time to make the kill when the strobe lights were on? Diamond could see Joe intermittently because he knew where he was seated, but checking for anyone approaching was next to impossible. Guests were moving between tables, keen to stretch their limbs now that the formal part of the evening had ended.

And then it occurred to him that there was nothing to stop him doing the same. He got up and moved to the main table. The bride and groom had already taken to the dance floor and the best man had left his seat, so there was an empty chair beside George Brace, who turned and asked, 'Something the matter?'

'Could be nothing. I heard it from the bridesmaids. Don't know what to make of it.'

Joe Irving across the table also leaned forward and cupped his ear. Wouldn't hurt for him to know as well. Nobody else was left to listen in. The chatty Leticia had moved away to speak to other guests.

Diamond repeated the melodramatic claim he'd heard from Gabriella and the twins. 'Their mothers seem to think it's best forgotten, some tall tale the kids made up.'

Irving had heard enough to want to be in on the discussion. He moved round and planted himself in his daughter's chair, next to Diamond. 'The kids found a stiff – is that what you said?'

'What *they* said.'

'I'll go and look.'

'Can't countenance that,' George said at once. 'It's a job for the police. Your safety is paramount.'

'My choice, right?'

'No,' Diamond said in support of George. 'Our call, not yours.'

'Get away. Who paid for this party?'

'You could easily walk into a trap.'

'Kids setting me up?' Joe said. 'Give me a break.'

'I'm your protection officer and I must insist you remain here.'

'I never asked for a fucking minder.'

'But you're still breathing.'

The crime king wasn't used to being defied, but he smirked. 'Thanks to you, copper, is that what you're saying?'

'The day isn't over yet.'

George took out his phone. 'I'm calling for assistance. It wouldn't be wise for any of us three to go looking for this body, or whatever it may be. My best guess is that some drunk came in from the rain and found a dry place to sleep it off.'

'While you're doing that, I need a slash,' Joe said, getting up. 'And I don't need no witness.'

'You're getting one,' Diamond said at once. 'I'm coming with you.' He would make sure the evil jerk didn't go wandering and visit the hypocaust.

The toilets were close by, in the corridor near the entrance. They fell in step with Maurice the photographer, evidently on the same mission, cameras still dangling from his neck.

'Do I know you?' he asked Diamond. 'Maurice Ableman. I have a feeling we met before.'

'Snap,' Diamond said, 'But I can't remember when. I'm Peter Diamond.'

Irving said, 'Better tell him you're fuzz. He might not want to know you.'

'That's it,' Maurice said. 'The police. Before I went free-lance I worked with a crime scene unit. Three years ago. The Somerset sniper.'

Diamond remembered now. At any major incident the

CSI people came and went and there was rarely much said to the photographer.

'Are you still serving?' Maurice asked.

'They never give up,' Irving said.

Diamond nodded and left it at that. He was pleased to have one mystery explained.

When they returned to the disco, the small dance space was filled with wedding guests of all ages executing a variety of jerky movements that passed for dancing. The exhausted bridesmaids and their parents had left. They had a key to Uncle Joe's house. No more had been said about the corpse.

George was still at the table and Leticia was with him. 'Here you are,' she said. 'I was starting to think you guys had jumped ship.'

'No way,' Irving said. 'This is the fun part of the evening.'

'Let's put that to the test, Joe. Before you sit down, you and I must take to the floor.'

'And dance, you mean?' Panic passed across Irving's features.

'It's your treat as the father of the bride. You get to dance with the groom's mum. And don't look like that or I'll speak to Caroline.'

The ultimate threat.

Leticia was used to getting her way. She didn't exactly drag Joe towards the dancing, but she grasped his arm as if she'd made a citizen's arrest.

Left alone at the table, Diamond asked George whether he'd got through to headquarters.

'Late Saturday night,' he said. 'Ongoing incidents all over. Multiple vehicle crash in the Wells Road and some kind of knife fight in Kingsmead Square. Our call is grade two. They'll let me know when they can get a patrol car here. Let's hope it's not for nothing.'

Diamond's thoughts were elsewhere, in the hypocaust, as he tried to watch the dancers with the strobe lights flashing over them, creating freeze-frame effects, Leticia making the movements of a knife-throwing act with Joe the petrified assistant hoping the blades would miss. 'Do we know what time this ends?'

'Last orders at midnight,' George said. 'We must all be out by twelve thirty. A bloody long day. I appreciate your efforts, Peter.'

'Do you think Irving will stick it out to the end?'

'That depends on Leticia. Now she's got him on the floor, he won't escape until her legs give way. But at least he's not been attacked by anyone apart from my good lady. We're coming out of this better than I dared hope.'

'And you?'

'Me?' George said.

'Your reputation. Did the press get hold of the story? I haven't seen anything.'

'It could still happen. People taking pictures with their phones. It only needs one of me sitting with you-know-who. Minutes later it's all over social media.'

Diamond knew about that from personal experience.

'One good thing,' George added. 'I don't have any worries with the official photographer. Maurice used to work with the police.'

'I remember now.'

'Too much to hope today's blast will pass unnoticed, but we can be thankful the story didn't break before the wedding and ruin the day for Ben and Caroline. They'll have nice memories, thank God.' He pulled out his phone again. 'Or am I tempting fate? There's a voice message.' He listened. 'The patrol car is here. They found a body.'

28

Two flood lamps on stands. Several figures at work in white protective suits under the cones of light on the far side of the otherwise murky hypocaust. One of them spotted Diamond and waved.

'Hi, guv.'

Ingeborg Smith's voice – and no apology for sounding so cheerful at this hour of the night.

'What do you have?' he called back.

'Gunshot to the head. Male. Weapon beside him. You'll need to wear the kit if you come down.'

It was 12.40 a.m. and one day on duty had morphed inexorably into another. The cops called to search the hypocaust had confirmed the truth of the bridesmaids' story. The senior people in CID had been contacted and learned that their night off was cancelled. On arrival, they had sealed the crime scene before the last guests had left the disco upstairs.

Diamond was kicking himself for not taking the small girls more seriously. His attention had been so taken up with Irving that he could scarcely comprehend a different killing in the same building. This new development called for a whole rethink.

Joe Irving had detained his minder until the disco finished. The father of the bride had stayed the course for the last hour and a half. When Leticia had called time, he had danced with

Caroline. This full-on wedding had been his show, as much a celebration of his release as the joining of bride and groom. Finally, with a look of contentment on his spent face, he had sunk into the back seat of a car and been driven home.

Duty done for Diamond. He should have been pleased. The old lag's survival was something to celebrate. Against all expectation, he had come to tolerate the man a little, if not actually to like him. Psychologists have identified a phenomenon known as Stockholm syndrome, a process by which hostages form a bond with their captors over time. Given longer together – perish the thought – Diamond might have regarded Joe as a twin soul. In reality, the mood in that last ninety minutes hadn't been fraternal. Diamond had been impatient to go down into the hypocaust. When the DJ finally called time on the disco and the lights were turned up and the farewells exchanged, there was no more than a nod between the father of the bride and his minder.

As for George Brace, he'd been hit by a new emergency.

'I need to get Leticia home. She's had a few drinks too many and she doesn't want the party to end. She's talking about forming a conga line of all the people who are left here and dancing through the entire museum.'

'She's serious?'

'You've met her, Peter, and some of the others are up for it. If I don't stop her, she'll lead everyone blithely into the hypocaust.'

'Not a good idea.'

'So we're leaving as of now. Are you game to carry on?'

'My job, isn't it, see what's down there?'

'Good man. I want to know, too. I'll be in touch early Sunday morning.'

The fact that Sunday morning had already begun seemed to have escaped George.

Taxis had been laid on for the last of the revellers. Diamond had watched them off the premises and hurried down to find out the truth.

A box of forensic gear had been left this side of the viewing barrier. He stepped into the suit, tugged it over the ample contours of his body and zipped it, pulled the hood over his head and put on the latex gloves and mask, and climbed over the barrier, thinking of the overcurious bridesmaids and their exploration earlier. Just getting over and letting themselves down among the stacked tiles must have needed a team effort.

The stacks of terracotta tiles stood hip-high, in parallel rows, like blocks of high-rise buildings in a miniature city devastated by bombing. Many had taken damage and been reconstructed. Some were stunted and even the tallest looked ready to topple on contact, so he threaded his way through with caution. He was notoriously clumsy and stumbled at one point. Fortunately, the nearest column supported his weight. Destroying sixteen centuries of history wouldn't have helped his reputation.

Another of the masked and suited figures spoke. 'Had a few drinks, guv?'

Keith Halliwell's voice echoed off the stonework.

'Hardly any. I was on duty.'

'How was the reception?'

'Don't ask.'

'No aggro?'

'Only in my head.'

Forensic tape had been draped over the stacks that enclosed the body, leaving one narrow access for the professionals to use. Under the glare of the floodlight the deceased lay on his back, arms angled against the nearest stacks, hips twisted awkwardly. A bullet wound in the left temple. Some seepage of blood below the head on the other side where the exit wound must have been. The corpse was clothed in T-shirt, jeans and trainers, entirely in black.

'What's that on the ground by his head?' He pointed to what looked like a piece of black cloth.

'A balaclava. He was wearing it. The police surgeon removed it to examine him.'

He had little doubt who the dead man was – the gunman who had dominated his thoughts in all the hours since they had found Paul Gilbert. The description matched. Gilbert had talked about a masked man in black who had pulled a handgun on him.

'So the doc's been by?'

'Came and went. She confirmed that life was extinct – which we all knew – and that was all, really.'

'You said the weapon was beside him.'

Ingeborg spoke up again. 'To the left between the stacks of tiles. You can't see it from where you are. A Glock semi-automatic, gen five.'

'Have a heart, Inge.'

'Generation five, the latest model.'

'How can you tell?'

'Have a look for yourself. It could be important.'

He wouldn't know a generation five from a blunderbuss, but he took a step sideways and peered between the stacks at what was basically an automatic pistol of the sort he'd tried to master at the firearms course.

Ingeborg said, 'This one differs from pre-2017 models in several details, and the most obvious is the protruding lip on the floorplate of the magazine which improves the grip and the reloading.'

'Where did you pick up that bit of technobabble?'

'Black Rock, last winter.'

'I was there last month. I noticed my instructor's protruding lip. Can't remember much about the gun.'

'You passed?'

'They offered me a job on the staff.' He didn't add that

210

he'd spent most of the course trying to master the draw from holster and his success on the short range had been laser-assisted. 'We must get the gun checked for prints and DNA and test-fired by the ballistics people, see if they have it on file. There's a chance it's been fired before. Have you found bullets?'

'Only the one.'

'Are you sure?'

She said with a trace of impatience, 'That's all it takes for a suicide.'

'That's your assumption, is it?'

Ingeborg spread her hands. 'Gun held close to the head and found nearby. An empty holster attached to his belt.'

'A holster?'

'For the gun.'

'I know what a holster is. I'm wearing one myself. I'm surprised a suicide victim has one, that's all. And this is an odd choice of place to top himself, wouldn't you say?'

'Can't argue with that, guv.'

'I'm thinking we need a forensic pathologist.'

'We won't be popular this time of night if it is just a suicide.'

'They're used to night calls.'

Halliwell came to Ingeborg's aid. 'What can they tell us that we don't know already?'

'If I knew the answer to that,' Diamond said, 'I wouldn't suggest it. Make the call.' Tempers were getting frayed at this hour.

While Inge was using her phone, Diamond asked Halliwell if a search had been made of the victim's pockets.

'Nothing helpful, guv. A few coins and a packet of chewing gum. He didn't want anyone to know who he is.'

'Or his killer didn't – and removed his wallet.'

Halliwell blinked. Clearly he had some catching up to do. 'We'll be relying on DNA, no doubt.'

211

'Takes up to three days and then we need a match with some criminal already on the national database.'

'If you can think of a better way . . .'

'Okay, okay. I'm tired. We're all tired. But I'd like to get this under way tonight. They're going to want to open this place to the public in the morning, which means shifting the body out of here. If the likely prognosis is suicide, which it appears to be, I can't justify treating it as a murder scene and closing the hypocaust to visitors indefinitely.'

'Murder?' Halliwell said, frowning. 'Doesn't seem likely.'

'Suicide takes some explaining. The set-up may look like it, but why would our gunman take his own life?'

'Don't know. Because he failed to kill Joe Irving?'

'He's a professional. A hard man.'

'Hard on himself?'

'I can't see it. Has the scene been photographed?'

'We made sure of that before the mask was removed.'

'Oddly enough, the guy who photographed the wedding used to work on crime scenes.' Any significance? he asked himself. Maurice would have arrived early at the Baths to set up. He knew how crime scenes were managed. What if he and the dead man had some history?

Ingeborg pocketed her phone. 'Dr Sealy will be here within the hour.'

'Dr Sarky.'

'Sealy.'

'I heard the first time. Fair enough. If Sealy is the guy on call, we'll take him. He knows his stuff. We'll use the time making a search of the place for evidence someone else was here. Did any of you bring a torch?'

Everyone except Diamond himself. 'I'll borrow yours,' he said to one of the CSI people working under the arc-lamp. 'We can divide up the space by the rows of tiles. I'll take the three in the middle.'

He hadn't gone far when a tiny pink circle on the ground was caught in his torch-beam. 'God Almighty, how about this?'

'What is it?' Ingeborg called across.

'Confetti.'

'Who discovered the body?'

'The bridesmaids.'

'There you are, then,' she said and spiked his bubble.

Bertram Sealy arrived soon after 2.15 a.m. and insisted on being helped over the Perspex barrier. 'I'll hand you my guts bag,' he shouted to Diamond. 'And you my coffee flask,' he told Halliwell. 'And you, young lady – I can see you're splendidly robust even in the unbecoming zipper suit – can help me down.'

'You don't miss a trick, do you?' Diamond shouted back. 'Keith will help you down and Ingeborg can bring the flask.'

While they were making their way towards the pathologist through the columns they could see him squirming into a superior-looking blue forensic suit.

Sealy was more hot air than substance and Halliwell had no trouble supporting his weight.

'What have you got for me this time?' Sealy asked when he was at their level.

'I'd prefer you to tell us.'

'Thank you, young lady,' Sealy said to Ingeborg as he held out a hand for the flask. 'I need my caffeine kick. I was into my deep cycle of sleep when the phone rang. I'm sure *you* have no problems with arousal.'

For a moment Diamond thought Ingeborg would empty the flask over the annoying little man's head. She seemed to be in two minds before passing it across.

'What time was this discovered?' Sealy asked.

The smell of coffee was tantalising.

Diamond had noted when the bridesmaids had announced their find. 'About ten-twenty.'

'And you waited until the small hours to call me?'

'It was found by some children and they weren't really believed. I was upstairs myself. There was a wedding reception going on here and nobody else went to look. We didn't want to ruin their day.'

'So you ruined my night instead. Has the body been handled in any way?'

'The police surgeon removed a balaclava mask.'

'Obviously up to no good, then. The deceased, I mean, not the police surgeon. Do you know who he is?'

'Not yet. He wasn't carrying any ID.'

'Open and shut case, isn't it? He was the bride's former lover driven to desperate measures when she married another. He planned to murder the bridegroom but had a last-minute crisis of conscience and turned the gun on himself.'

'You do your job and we'll do ours,' Diamond said.

For a man plucked from his slumbers, the piddling pathologist was far too bouncy. Only the need to keep from tripping quietened him down as he followed Diamond up one of the narrow alleys between the tiles.

Inside the taped area Sealy crouched to examine the head wound. He was using a voice recorder. 'Middle-aged male. Well nourished. In need of a shave. Dark hair turning grey. Bullet wound with signs of contact discharge. The gun was held against the left temple and the bullet made a neat circular hole with an abrasion collar.' He raised the head and bent closer to see the exit wound. 'Not much doubt what killed him. So it seems the deceased was left-handed. I expect the crime scene people found some GSR on the hand and arm.' He lifted the left hand and looked at it. 'Powder particles can be very indicative, especially if you find them on the hands of the perpetrator. When did they get here?'

214

'The gunpowder particles?'

He clicked his tongue. 'The first responders.'

'The crime scene lot? Soon after midnight.'

'That's no use. You said the shooting was ten-twenty.'

'No, that's when the body was first seen.'

'Far too long, then. All residue will have dissipated inside two hours. Should have called me earlier, shouldn't you?'

'You've made that point several times over,' Diamond said. 'Can you tell me anything else?'

'Going by the state of the hands, he wasn't used to manual work, but he seems to have done some recently. There's some slight damage to the fingernails and abrasions to the soft flesh of the fingers and palms.'

'Manual work? Like climbing a stone wall?'

'That's well possible. These aren't defensive marks in my opinion. The bruising and scrape on the right forearm are consistent with the fall after he was shot. All the damage would appear to have been self-inflicted, including the fatal shot.'

'You're certain?'

Sealy wagged a finger at Diamond. 'Don't put words in my mouth. "Would appear to have been" is what I said. Is there any evidence of a second individual being here?'

'We made a search in case. Visitors are coming through by the thousand every day and there are scraps of paper, chewing gum and so forth near the viewing barrier, but nothing notable in this area.'

Sealy stood up. 'What's tomorrow? I lose track when I get woken in the night.'

'You mean today. Today is Sunday.'

'I'll inform the coroner at a civilised hour and do the autopsy on Monday. Don't expect anything sensational. You can get him moved to my mortuary as soon as you like.' He made the RUH mortuary sound like home sweet home.

29

Forensic science is a true friend of the investigator, but maddeningly unresponsive when you most need results. In the first forty-eight hours, you are on your own. Diamond had sent the corpse to the dissection table and the items collected from the hypocaust and the roof, the firearms, balaclava, backpack and other items, to the lab for DNA testing. Yet until the white coats reported their findings, he was reliant on the time-honoured process of question and answer. He complained loudly about the delay and secretly relished the chance to exercise his brain.

Although it was Sunday and the morning after an exhausting night, he was energised by the prospect of some real detective work. He never wanted to be on protection duty again. He had rallied the team for an 11 a.m. meeting. Matins without the praying, he'd called it, and was pleased to get a full congregation. The bishop himself was there, in the shape of DCC George Brace, who had asked to be kept in the loop. Even the choirboy Paul Gilbert was present, as pale as the surgical dressing on his head.

'I'm calling it a suspicious death,' Diamond told them, 'and straight away I see some eyes rolling. Hold your horses until you've heard me out. Something isn't right. A hitman on a mission to kill turns the gun on himself. I don't buy it. I wouldn't buy it if it came with all the tea in China.'

'You're a coffee-drinker,' DI John Leaman, the pedant of the team, said.

'Yes, and I told you to hold your horses and I knew you couldn't.' He switched to young Gilbert. 'Paul, you're the only one of us who met this guy. Was there anything about him that suggested he would kill himself?'

'It never crossed my mind, guv. I was too busy thinking he would kill me.'

Some of the team chuckled at that.

Diamond glared at them as if they really were in church. His main witness had suffered enough. 'You told me you tried to get him talking.'

'He wasn't saying much.'

'And neither were you with duct tape over your mouth. We get that much.'

Smiling was encouraged when Diamond made the joke.

'When he first attacked me, there wasn't much said and that was one-sided. He was questioning me and I was in shock.'

'In pain, I should think.'

'Well, yes. And a gun at my head. All I could think was to give away as little as possible. He'd overpowered me and disarmed me, I'm ashamed to say. He chucked everything out of reach.'

'What did he want to know?'

'My name. He'd guessed I was a plain-clothes officer. I couldn't stay silent. He would have shot me. All I could see was this masked face and the staring eyes behind the mask and they weren't bluffing so I said who I was.'

'Anything else?'

'He wanted to know if anyone would be coming up there to relieve me. I think I said no to that.'

'Quite right. We don't do relieving,' Diamond said. 'Anyone works for me, he's lucky if he gets the chance to relieve himself.'

Smiles all round.

'And he asked about my personal radio. I said I'd already reported in, thinking it might discourage him from keeping me prisoner for long, but it didn't. He asked for my call signal and I made something up. After that, he well and truly trussed me up.'

'And left you lying in the gutter?'

'He forgot about me. The rain came and the drains couldn't cope and I nearly drowned. I only survived by wriggling along to where my backpack was and propping my head on it. I wouldn't want to go through that again. Finally he came back and saw the state I was in. He ripped the gag off to help me breathe and dragged me out of the gutter to a higher place on the slope of the roof.'

'Did he say anything?'

'He didn't say sorry.'

Gilbert's chance to earn some laughter.

'But he gave me water.'

'The last thing you needed, I should think.'

'Actually no. With the gag on, I was dehydrated. And he talked a little. He said he hadn't bargained for the rain. I asked if he'd done what he came for and he said he wouldn't still be there if he had. This must have been after everyone had gone into the Abbey because he asked me how long a wedding service lasts and I said I thought about an hour. I tried to keep him talking and find out what he would do next. He said, "They've got to come out, haven't they?" I asked him if he was under orders to kill the bastard – trying to be chummy, like, and let him know we're no friends of Irving – but he didn't rise to that. Too obvious, I suppose. He covered my mouth again.'

'Would you say he was depressed?'

'Don't know about him. I was.'

This earned the biggest laugh of all.

'Definitely not depressed,' Gilbert added, to bring the meeting to order.

'Desperate?'

'I didn't think so. Angry is more like it, because he hadn't been able to do what he came for. He went back for another try.'

'And failed again. When did you see him next?'

'After the wedding ended. The bell-ringing had stopped for quite a long time.'

'How did he seem at that stage?'

'Calmer than before, quite a lot calmer. He took the tape off my mouth and gave me water and a few bites at the apple from my backpack. He must have already decided to go over the wall into the Roman Baths and leave me tied up and helpless, but he didn't want me dying of thirst.'

'Is that what he told you?'

'No, it's what I think.'

'Stick to what actually happened, Paul.'

'He said he wouldn't be hand-feeding me for long. I remember asking him what he'd got against Joe Irving and he told me to shut up and eat the apple.'

'Is that what you call calm?'

'In control, anyway. I tried to find out what time it was and he wouldn't say. I said I hadn't heard a shot and that really pissed him off. He pressed the tape over my mouth again and left me. That was the last I saw of him.'

'Did you see his face at any stage?'

'No, he kept the mask on.'

'But you saw the handgun.'

'Did I?'

'At the beginning.'

Paul Gilbert shut his eyes, struggling to remember. A few seconds passed. Then: 'Of course. After he bashed me with

219

the assault rifle, he put the pistol against my head.' Another pause. 'I couldn't tell you what make it was.'

More laughter.

Not from Diamond. His facial muscles tightened. 'If anyone thinks it's funny being hit about the head and body with the butt of a rifle and threatened with a bullet through your skull and then tied up and left in rising water, they don't deserve to be in the room with this young officer. You're a credit to the force, DC Gilbert. I have no more questions for you. If you want to go home and get some rest, feel free.'

'Thanks, guv. I'd rather stay.'

That storm cloud passed. Diamond leaned back in the chair and linked both hands behind his head. He was in charge here – even with George Brace outranking him – and keen to share his ideas about the death. 'Okay. Here are some reasonable assumptions. Stop me if you disagree.'

If you dare, more like.

'Our gunman was twice prevented by the rain from making the kill – both before and immediately after the wedding. All he would have seen from his viewpoint was umbrellas. He decided to have another go during the reception in the Baths. He left the assault rifle on the roof with other things he didn't need because now he was planning a close-up killing. The handgun was a more useful weapon. He will have got into the Great Bath by climbing over the dividing wall accessible only from where he was. The pathologist noticed some slight damage to his hands. The new plan was to hide up and ambush Joe Irving at the first opportunity. Are you with me so far?'

Nobody dissented, so he continued. 'Paul tells us the guy appeared to be in control when he last saw him. He'd modified his plan, but he was still committed to carrying it out. At some stage of the evening, Joe would leave the party. A trip to the toilet, a quiet smoke, an early escape. If you're using a handgun to make a clean kill, you need to get close, however good you are. This guy was a professional, that's clear enough. He will have found somewhere in the Roman ruins to hide up and wait for his opportunity.'

'Where exactly was the reception going on?' Leaman asked.

'Sorry. I should have said. It started with drinks in the entrance hall. Big room. Plenty of people milling about. Definitely a chance to get in close. I was there and I was expecting trouble, believe me.'

'He won't have been dressed for a party,' Ingeborg pointed out. 'Anyone in jeans and a T-shirt would stand out.'

'Right, he couldn't pass as a guest. I was thinking he'd step out from the side of the room, behind a plant, say. But he didn't. The guests were ushered downstairs to the Great Bath, where the photos were taken. The photography didn't happen earlier because of the rain.'

'That's an even more dangerous location,' Ingeborg said.

'A nightmare. The place is surrounded by bits of old columns and other chunks of stone from Roman times. Dead easy to hide behind. What's more, the lighting was by flaming torches. Great place for an ambush, you'd think, especially when everyone was being lined up for the camera. My thought was that the hitman would come from behind when everyone was standing along the edge of the bath facing the other side. I guarded Irving's back as well as I was able. He was a soft target there. But as you know, the hit didn't happen. They took more photos of the main guests in various groupings while everyone else went upstairs for the meal.'

'Where was that?' Halliwell asked.

'The wedding breakfast? In a glorified corridor over-looking the bath.' He caught George's frown from the back and put it more tactfully. 'No, that's too sweeping. It's bigger than that, known as the terrace. They can seat eighty people at tables along one side. That's where the meal was eaten and the speeches were given. Not so easy for an ambush. But when the formal stuff had been got through, we were told to move downstairs for the disco. Back to the reception hall, now transformed. Strobe lighting. A DJ at one end with his workstation. The main lights were off and we were sitting in the dark apart from the flashing beams. Real danger again. However, there was no shooting. Why? Because the killing had already been done downstairs in the hypocaust and the victim was the hitman.'

'When you say "victim" . . .' Leaman began.

'I used the word deliberately. I can't believe he killed himself.'

'Are you thinking Joe Irving got to him?'

'In a word, yes. There was a change in Joe at the wedding reception. He was more laidback and confident, as if he knew any danger was already over.' He brought George Brace into the discussion. 'Is that how you saw it, sir?'

'Now that you mention it, yes,' George said in support. 'He made a rather good speech, better than any of us expected.'

'The speech, yes.' Diamond raised a finger. This was a point he'd missed. 'I was surprised how confident he was.'

'He should have been, guv, with you as his minder,' Ingeborg said.

Diamond gave her a sharp look to see whether a smile had underpinned the remark, but it seemed to be meant as a genuine compliment. 'I don't think he rated me at all.'

'But there's another side of the coin, isn't there?' she said.

'What's that?'

'With you watching his back all evening it's difficult to see how he could have killed the gunman.'

'Before we come to "how", I want to deal with "when". It will help us later.' He was in his element now, dissecting a crime. 'Through no fault of my own, I spent a large part of the evening in the company of two of Joe Irving's nieces, and that's a story in itself. You'll need to know that their daughters were the three bridesmaids. These kids soon got bored sitting at the table and were allowed to go wandering. Modern parents don't seem to have much control, or these didn't. Their offspring had the run of the place for an hour or more. They came back after Joe had made his speech and just before the bridegroom stood up to speak and they were over-excited and claimed they'd found a dead body. The mothers dismissed it and I thought much the same, but I checked the time, just in case. It was ten-twenty. With hindsight we know the kids were right and this gives us one of the parameters for the incident. Ten-fifteen is the very latest it could have happened.'

'But you were with Irving all through the evening,' Leaman said, repeating Ingeborg's point.

'I'm coming to that,' Diamond said. 'Obviously we need to establish the earliest the fatal shot was fired. The Roman Baths were open to the public all day. People are coming through all the time. There's no chance the shooting happened before closing time, which is six p.m. The reception started at seven-thirty. I was there at the start and as John just reminded us I kept tabs on Joe Irving from then until the party ended.'

'Which narrows it down to the ninety minutes between six and seven-thirty,' Ingeborg said.

'If Irving killed him,' Leaman put in, ever the sceptic on the team.

Ingeborg didn't allow him to divert her. 'There will have been people around the complex for some of that time, mainly caterers and security staff, but an area like the hypocaust is closed and gets left alone. An ideal place for the gunman to hide until the reception gets underway.'

'Does that fit your timescale?' Leaman asked – and the 'your' made clear that he wasn't yet convinced. 'When did Paul last see him?'

Paul Gilbert was shaking his head. 'The wedding was well over. That's all I can say for sure. I asked him what time it was, but he wouldn't say. I'd lost track by then.'

Diamond said, 'He must have waited for the baths to close. I reckon he went in shortly after six.'

'So, like I just said, we have a time slot,' Ingeborg said. 'Next question: where was Joe Irving? Did he arrive early? Presumably he went home after the wedding to get ready for the evening event.'

'There wasn't much getting ready,' Diamond said. 'He was wearing the same clothes he'd been dressed in at the Abbey. Some of us had taken the trouble to go home and change.'

Looks were exchanged among the team. Almost everyone had seen the suit the boss had changed into, but nobody was bold enough to comment.

'And I can tell you something else I heard from the cousins at my table. Joe wasn't at his house that afternoon. He had a caller, a woman friend apparently, and one of the cousins went to the door and told her he was out. They made a joke of it, saying he'd cleared off because his house was full of excited females.'

'I'm with him there,' Halliwell said.

'Sexist,' Ingeborg said.

'Three small girls, their mothers and the bride, all getting ready for a big night out? Give me a break.'

'The bride was back home with her new husband.'

'Okay, only five females.' Halliwell's eyes rolled at the prospect. 'I grew up with sisters. How much longer is she taking in the bathroom? What happened to all the clean towels? I just ruined my tights. My lashes won't stay on. I brought the wrong shoes. I forgot to bring my extensions.'

224

'Give it a rest, Keith,' Diamond said. 'I was telling you about Joe Irving being out all afternoon. He was free to turn up early at the Roman Baths and make his own security check. If he found the gunman and killed him, it was reasonable to expect no one would discover the body until next day.'

'Which brings us to the crunch,' Leaman said. 'How did he do it? How could anyone have done it?'

'Faking a suicide? You surprise your victim and get close enough to put your gun to his head and pull the trigger. Then you clean your prints off the grip, wrap his hand around the gun and drop it somewhere near him. Obviously, you relieve him of his own weapon before leaving the scene.'

'Not so easy as it sounds. He was a professional hitman, agreed?'

'Irving is a professional, too.'

'Yes, but is any hitman so dozy that he lets himself get ambushed like that? He's alone in the hypocaust and keyed up to kill. He's going to be hypertense.'

Diamond couldn't fault that. And Leaman hadn't finished.

'It's just about impossible to creep up on anyone in that big space with all the columns of tiles and the uneven footing. I've studied it online. It's an obstacle course. All those columns built on plinths in states of disrepair. Ridges to step over. Cavities between them. You'd have a job staying upright.'

'I know,' Diamond said. 'Some of us have been there. But it will have been in near-darkness.'

'Even more difficult to step through.'

'True.'

'And in silence? No chance.'

Leaman must have been taught by the Jesuits. He found the weak points in any theory. Typical of him to have checked the footings on his screen. He hadn't even been inside the hypocaust. Diamond had stumbled through it himself and couldn't deny that his main critic on the team was right.

'Fair enough. It must have happened another way.' How feeble was that? He knew as he said the words that he hadn't thought of another way. He'd lost the plot.

Ingeborg came to his rescue. 'John, you talked about this guy being a professional. In that case you've got to explain why a professional killer turns the gun on himself.'

'I haven't got to explain anything.'

'Someone has to if it was suicide.'

Leaman wasn't backing down. 'We'll know more about that when the tests come back. Until then it's all speculation.'

'Some of the biggest discoveries in history began with speculation,' she said. 'We ought to be asking ourselves why a hard man like this would take his own life. If we can't come up with a plausible theory, then murder has to be a serious option.'

'Try this for size, then,' Halliwell said. 'He was hired by Sid Felix to kill Irving. He'd botched the job and he knew what would happen to him.'

'A contract killer?' Ingeborg said. 'I don't buy it. He was well placed to shoot Joe at the reception. Any pro would see it through rather than give up at this stage.'

Halliwell shrugged. 'Anyone got a better theory?'

Nobody took up the challenge.

The only way to wrest back control was by ordering some action. 'Is that the verdict of you all?' Diamond demanded of them. 'He didn't top himself and he wasn't murdered?'

'Pending the results from forensics,' Leaman said.

'Fuck forensics.' As the words came out, Diamond caught a horrified look from George Brace. Easy to forget he was in the presence of the DCC. 'I only say that because I expect results from my own team. We're detectives, in case it slipped anyone's mind. We investigate. Joe Irving has questions to answer and I'll see him today. And if you're right, Keith, and the gunman was a contract killer, someone in the underworld will know.'

'A snout?'

'Right. Get your pet canaries singing. Who put a notice on Joe Irving? Who acquired an AK recently? Who is our dead gunman?'

30

If any more proof were needed that Joe had not been impoverished by his years in prison it was his Georgian house in Sion Hill Place. At a hundred and fifty metres above sea level, the highest point the eighteenth-century builders had risen to on the northern slopes, the location was the most secluded in Bath. The palace-fronted terrace of nine four-storey houses faced a lawn and long-established trees, copper beeches blending with the greener foliage. Most of the building was divided into apartments but Joe had an entire house to himself. The upper floors afforded unmatched views of his empire.

Diamond stared and despaired. The war against crime was lost if felons like Irving could live like this. He turned to Ingeborg, who was his support for the visit, and shook his head. Nothing needed to be said.

A gleaming white front door. Boxwood in a tub at either side. Respectability objectified.

Joe didn't come to the door. He appeared like the Pope at a window upstairs. But he wasn't wearing vestments. He was in boxer shorts. And he didn't say, 'Buongiorno.' He said, 'Piss off.'

Diamond cupped his hands to be heard. 'Better let us in, Joe. We have something to discuss.'

'Like what?'

'You won't want me telling the whole of Sion Hill Place.'

'I'm not bothered.'

'Are the bridesmaids and their mothers still with you?'

Joe shook his head. 'Left early.'

'Because they weren't mistaken, those little girls.'

After a moment's reflection, Joe decided he didn't wish to play this balcony scene after all. 'Hang on.'

When he opened the front door he was in a black bath-robe and flip-flops. His joyless eyes looked more alert than at any time in the past twenty-four hours. 'Are you saying there really was a stiff?'

'Can we do this inside?'

Bringing him to the door had been a small victory, Diamond told himself. The man had cultivated this persona of indifference. The immediate aim was to keep him curious.

'Gone, but not forgotten,' Diamond said when Joe let them in.

'What are you on about?'

'Your overnight guests.' The chandelier in the hall was festooned with streamers. Confetti was liberally scattered. Moving about involved crunching little items underfoot that turned out to be Love Hearts. To find a seat in the drawing room, they needed to clear the sofa of bath towels smelling of hairspray.

Oblivious to the bear garden his home had become, Joe had flopped into an armchair. The strains of the day before – or the pains of a hangover – or both – were etched in his face. 'Who is it, then?'

'Who are you talking about?'

'The stiff.'

'You disappoint me, Joe. Don't you know?'

'Why should I?'

'He was coming after you with a handgun.'

Joe propped his feet on a low table and kicked some empty beer cans off to make room. 'Why didn't he use it, then?'

'He did – on himself.'

'What a berk.'

'Fair comment, but we're checking the evidence in case someone else pulled the trigger and fitted up the scene to look like suicide.'

'One bullet?'

'Only one, yes.'

'To the head?'

Diamond nodded twice. These were reasonable assumptions by Joe, safe to confirm. Give the suspect a little information and he might volunteer the extra detail that nailed him. Or was Joe already bossing the interview, hammering home the points that made the case for suicide?

'Hard to fake,' he said.

'Just about impossible with modern forensics,' Diamond said. 'Makes our job easier.'

Joe didn't comment.

A movement at Diamond's arm startled him. Claude the kitten had jumped on to the sofa and was looking for someone to play with. Diamond remembered Joe's offer to care for Claude while the bride and groom were on their honeymoon.

With Claude licking the back of his hand, the head of CID tried to stay on message. 'But the scientists won't be hurried. In the meantime, we use up a lot of shoe leather talking to witnesses.'

'I didn't witness nothing,' Joe was quick to say.

'Okay. Did you kill him yourself?'

A twitch and a glare. The question had caught Joe off guard. 'You've got to be joking.'

The kitten had pricked its ears at Joe's reaction and dug its needle claws into Diamond's thigh. He winced and lifted it clear. 'I had to ask. I may ask again. Failing a confession, will you point us in the right direction if it turns out there was a second person involved?'

Joe yawned and tried to look nonchalant again. He wanted it known that suicide was the only possible cause of death.

'And we do need to eliminate you from our enquiries.'

'Me?' Joe said in amazement as if he really was the Pope. 'You was watching my back the whole fucking day.'

'I wish it were as easy as that,' Diamond said. 'There were three to four hours when I wasn't with you, between the end of the wedding and the start of the reception.'

'I came back here.'

'But you weren't here long.'

'Who told you that?'

'My sources.'

'Your sources,' he said with a sneer. 'My bloody nieces.'

'I shared a table with them. One of them told me you were out most of the afternoon.'

'That's family for you,' Joe said, unsurprised by the betrayal. He didn't seem troubled that he'd been caught out. Literally caught out.

'You won't mind telling us where you went?'

He sidestepped the question. 'What time is this jerk supposed to have topped himself?'

'That's just it. We don't know yet. Most probably while you were out and about.'

'Bollocks.' He stamped on the suggestion with more force than a simple denial warranted.

'Didn't you call at the Roman Baths, then?' Diamond asked. 'It was a reasonable thing for the bride's father to do, making sure the place was ready for the party.'

'I did not.'

'I know what you're about to say, Joe. The place was open to the public until six, so the hitman couldn't have been shot without someone seeing and raising the alarm. But there's still a slot we can't account for between the time the baths closed and seven-thirty, when the reception started.'

'I got there five minutes early and no more.'

'Where from? Where did you disappear to all afternoon?'

Joe looked down at his left hand and turned one of the gold rings on his fingers. 'That's private.'

'Visiting a friend?'

No answer.

'Or silencing an enemy? We're going to think the worst if you don't tell us.'

'You ever made a wedding speech?' Joe asked.

This time Diamond didn't answer and neither did Ingeborg. The question sounded like a blatant evasion.

'It ain't easy, standing up in front of eighty people,' Joe continued. 'I was out practising, trying to get laughs from the bloody trees in Henrietta Park.'

So ridiculous that it might actually be true.

Best to take it seriously and probe.

'Whatever you did, it worked,' Diamond said to butter him up. 'Yours was easily the best speech. How long were you there? Not the whole afternoon?'

'No, mate. I moved on to Victoria Park.'

'The trees there have a sharper sense of humour?'

Joe raised a warning finger. 'Watch it.'

'While you were out, did you meet anyone who can vouch for you being in the park?'

'I got no need to lie about it.'

'We need to double-check everything.'

'I been banged up for five. People round here don't know me no more.'

'Okay, let's see if you can help us identify the victim.' Diamond nodded to Ingeborg, who took a photo of the dead man from her back pocket and handed it to Joe. A fine likeness, the features unmarked by the bullet.

He gave the picture a glance, shook his head and handed it back.

Diamond expected nothing else but he said, 'I'm disappointed. There aren't that many local hitmen. I thought you knew them all.'

'You thought wrong.'

'Could he be a recent associate? Someone from Horfield nick?'

Silence.

'Or from further back? Did you do time in other prisons?'

'Why ask me when you've already looked at my bloody record?'

'Because I'd rather hear it from you.'

'I lose track.'

'Before you arrived in Horfield where were you?'

'I done the Scrubs for a month and before that I was at some hellhole in Gloucester called Bream.'

'Bream. That's a fish, isn't it?'

'It stank of fish and a whole lot more.'

Ingeborg was quick to say, 'Wasn't there a riot at Bream a few years back?'

'Nothing I would call a riot,' Joe said. 'It was all over in one day.'

Full marks to Ingeborg for making the connection. Her former career in journalism had given her a keen memory for detail. Who needed search engines when she was around?

'You were there? Is that why you were moved?' Diamond said.

'The whole of our wing got ghosted after the fire.'

'A riot and a fire?'

Joe grinned. 'A riot without a fire don't deserve to be called a riot.'

'Did you have anything to do with it?'

'Me?' Joe shrilled in denial. He'd have you believe he was no more responsible than the prison chaplain. Fortunately it didn't matter because there must have been an inquiry and they could check the report.

'Was the riot squad called in?'

'Everyone was except the Girl Guides.'

'Was anyone badly hurt? Prison officers?'

He shrugged. 'Collateral damage.'

Ingeborg was checking the internet on her phone. 'That's one way of putting it. Says here that two prison officers were beaten and taken hostage in a riot at HM Prison, Bream, Gloucestershire, in July 2015. And in a related incident, two men were killed in a car crash outside, after kidnapping the governor at home and forcing her to drive there. One died instantly and the other in hospital. The governor was driving the first of two cars at gunpoint and bravely caused the collision by braking at high speed. She was later awarded the OBE. Her own life-changing injuries forced her to retire from the prison service.'

'The worst collateral damage, as you called it, occurred outside the prison?' Diamond said to Joe.

'So I heard, yeah.'

Ingeborg scrolled her phone. 'The Ministry of Justice inquiry into the incident concluded that the kidnap was coordinated with the riot in an attempt to stage an escape by one or more of the inmates. That's all it says here.'

'And you had nothing to do with it?' Diamond said to Joe.

'You heard what she just read out,' Joe said. 'Did you hear my name?'

'That's only a summary. The fact that you were transferred to another prison begs the question.'

'Weren't you listening? We was all shipped out, the whole bang shoot.'

'How much was added to your sentence?'

'Not one day. You can bet your life they would have thrown the book at me if they could.'

234

'Who was behind the riot, then?'

'Why ask me? I was out of it.'

'I expect you were questioned later by the inquiry team.'

'They came out to Horfield and saw me and some others.'

'There must have been a suspicion that you were the man all this was arranged for – the one the rioters wanted to spring.'

'Why do you say that?'

'Now come on, Joe. Don't play the innocent. You're the main man wherever you go.'

'My bad luck, ain't it?'

He was going to go on denying any part in the incident however long they questioned him. There was no specific evidence that the Bream riot had any connection with the body in the hypocaust. Diamond returned to the line of enquiry he'd originally meant to pursue. 'I'm thinking your release from prison creates a problem for your old rival, Sid Felix.'

'Him,' Joe said with scorn.

'I don't need to tell you he took advantage while you were banged up. And now you're a threat.'

'To that toerag?' He shook his head.

'Don't underestimate him, Joe. The reality is that the pecking order has changed. He runs Bristol and most of Bath now.'

'Is that supposed to worry me?'

'Your worries don't concern us. We're interested in what's been worrying Sid Felix, and that's you, fresh out of prison. He hears about your daughter's wedding, a good chance to rub you out, and he sends a hitman.'

'You think so?'

'It's one scenario. And you know as well as I do why I was watching your back.'

Joe wasn't going to pass up this chance of sarcasm. His

mean eyes gleamed like drops of molten solder. 'And the hitman sees you and says Jesus Christ they sent Peter Diamond as a minder. I'm fucked. I'm shaking in my shoes. I'm so scared I'm going to turn the gun on myself.'

Diamond clenched his teeth. 'Let me repeat the question I asked earlier. Did you shoot the guy in the hypocaust?'

This time, Joe wasn't caught off guard. 'Pathetic. Is that the best you can do?'

'I'm not sure how you managed it, but we have ballistics experts checking that gun as we speak.'

'On a Sunday morning? Pull the other one.'

'There's an autopsy to come. There are people checking the scene for your DNA.' He moved Claude off his lap and let him take over the warm spot on the sofa. 'I'll be back with the evidence, Joe. I'm not a quitter.'

31

'W hat do you think?' Diamond asked Ingeborg as they were driving away in her small Ka. 'Is that a guilty man?'

She laughed. 'Is the sky blue?'

'Guilty of murdering the hitman?'

'That's more problematical, isn't it?'

'Why?'

'It's difficult to see how a murder was committed.'

'It's either that or suicide – and that's even more unlikely.'

There was a long pause for thought.

'But how can it be murder?' Ingeborg said eventually.

'I refuse to rule it out.'

'That's not what I asked.'

'There was a famous Victorian murder,' Diamond said. 'The beautiful widow Adelaide Bartlett was put on trial and acquitted of poisoning her late husband with liquid chloroform found in his stomach, but no traces of burning were found in his mouth or throat. An impossible crime. Afterwards a leading pathologist wrote, "Now that Mrs Bartlett has been acquitted of murder and cannot be tried again, she should tell us in the interest of science how she did it."'

'You and your famous crimes from the past.'

'I only brought it up because we have an impossible crime here and Joe Irving isn't likely to tell us how it was done in the interest of science or anything else.'

'But you told us at the meeting, guv. The killer fired at point-blank range and arranged things to look like a suicide.'

'Yes, and John Leaman pulled the rug from under my feet by pointing out that no one could have approached the victim without being noticed. You and I have both tried doing the snake-walk between the tiles and we know he's right. What did he call it? An obstacle course?'

'Let's think laterally, then,' she suggested. She had a personal mission never to allow Diamond to sink into pessimism. At his best he was amusing company, but he could be a world-class grouch. 'We need a reason why Joe Irving was able to get close enough to the gunman without being shot, right?'

'Go on.'

'Why was the gunman in the hypocaust? He wasn't expecting to shoot Joe from there.'

'He was lying up,' Diamond said. 'It was closed to visitors and a good place to hide until the wedding reception started.'

'Agreed. Here's what I think could have happened. Joe also arrived early to check round and satisfy himself that everything was safe. He came to the hypocaust and saw the gunman without the mask and recognised him.'

'That's possible. He knows most of the career criminals round here.'

'Both men were armed, but at this time neither of them drew a gun. They talked.'

'What about?'

'Joe guessed why the other guy was there. He offered to double whatever he was being paid. The hitman said he wanted to see the money. Joe said he could have it now. He was carrying several grand in cash to pay off people like the string quartet and the DJ.'

'I think I see where this is going,' Diamond said.

'That's good,' she said, 'because it's believable, isn't it? Joe climbs over the plastic wall and makes his way between the pillars to where the hitman is and instead of producing a wad of banknotes takes out the gun and holds it to his head and fires. Then he sets up the scene to look like a suicide just the way you told us. And takes away the hitman's gun.'

'Not bad,' he said.

'What's wrong with it?'

'The psychology, for one thing. I can't see any hitman falling for a trick like that. It's not impossible, I grant you, but unlikely. And Joe would be taking a huge risk as well. He's savvy enough to know he's giving the gunman the chance to shoot him first and take the money, too.'

She gave a sharp sigh. 'Put like that, it does seem far-fetched. What else is wrong with it?'

'You said the mask was off, yet the fatal shot was fired through it.'

'Shucks.'

'If there's anything in this theory, the tests should confirm it. There will be traces of Irving's DNA on the gun or the body however careful he was to fake it.'

'Can we arrest him?'

'On what we've got so far? No chance.'

'He may do a runner.'

'He's too smart for that,' he said. 'It would really give him away.'

They were heading west on the Upper Bristol Road.

'Back to base, is it?' Ingeborg asked.

'Yep. To find out what that bunch of layabouts have dug up so far – if anything.'

She didn't rise to the slur on the team. Typical Diamond bluster. She didn't need to defend her colleagues. Deep down, he respected them more than he ever admitted.

239

'Shouldn't we be making enquiries about some of the other people who were in the Roman Baths between six and seven-thirty?'

'Such as?'

'The security staff who toured the building making sure all the visitors were gone.'

'We had two armed policemen doing the rounds. George Brace made sure of that.'

'And what did they report?'

'Nothing suspicious.'

'They can't have been all that good if they didn't find the gunman.'

'That's the catch,' he said. 'People who can handle a gun aren't always blessed with brains. Who else are you talking about?'

'The caterers.'

'True. They'd need to get the room ready. Can't argue with that.'

'Quite a good number of them to look after the champagne reception and get the meal ready upstairs.'

'I suppose.'

'The florists, to decorate the room.'

'All right.'

'The string quartet will have wanted to get there early to be playing as people arrived.'

'I'd forgotten them, I admit.'

'Not that you'd expect classical musicians to be murderers.'

He smiled at a memory. 'It's not unknown.'

'The DJ will have needed to get his equipment in before it started.'

'You're making this sound like the rush hour.'

'And the photographer and his assistant would be setting up.'

'I met them. Former crime scene photographer by the

name of Maurice Ableman. The assistant was a pushy young lady called Dixie who really had me under the cosh.'

'I can't believe that.'

'You should have been there. I'm glad you weren't. You're right, Inge. We should be treating these people as potential witnesses at the very least.'

'Suspects, possibly?'

'I wouldn't go that far. The clever money is on Joe.'

She drove in silence for a while before asking, 'That Victorian woman you spoke about, with the chloroform. Did she ever confess?'

'Did she hell. After the trial, she vanished.'

Ingeborg's smartphone buzzed. 'Would you mind?' she asked. 'It could be important.'

He unclipped the phone from the dashboard. He still treated mobile phones as suspicious objects but he'd mastered the basics. 'You've got a new text. Shall I open it?'

'Go ahead.'

'It's from Georgina. "Kindly ask DS Diamond to call me directly." What's she doing at work on a Sunday? She should be at church.'

'Why didn't she call your number?' Ingeborg asked.

'Mine is switched off.' A trick he'd learnt to protect his privacy.

'Why?'

'I told you. It's the weekend. What does she want, do you think?'

'Better ask her, hadn't you, guv?'

'When I'm ready. We'll be there in twenty minutes.'

Joe Irving took a slow shower after the police had left. If he'd had the energy he'd have cleaned the house as well. Uniformed or in plain clothes, the police were the filth as far as he was concerned.

He was towelling himself when the doorbell rang again. Bloody cheek. They'd go on bugging him until they got a result.

He would ignore it.

In the full-length mirror in the en suite shower room, he studied his physique. The remnant of a six-pack was still apparent when he flexed. Not bad, considering. He sprayed himself liberally with Beckham Homme, a luxury it hadn't been wise to enjoy in jail, and stepped into his boxers just as the bell disturbed his peace for the third time that morning.

Persecution, that was what this was.

When the ringing began once more, a doubt crept into his head. Could the caller be someone else, some person he actually wanted to see? Offhand, he couldn't think of anyone on this earth.

They weren't giving up.

Should have fitted CCTV to get a look at whoever it was. Now that he was likely to be living here some time he'd get around to it. Meanwhile he had his own non-electronic security system: the view from the balcony.

He went out and looked over.

A woman, alone.

Not the blonde female cop.

This one was in a suit and with a shoulder bag. Difficult to tell her age from this angle. She hadn't seen him yet and he was hoping she'd go away. He guessed she was some sort of do-gooder wanting his money. The only charity he supported was the prisoner's aid society and the only prisoner it aided was himself.

The woman stepped back from the door and moved along to the next house. Good riddance, lady.

He went inside to look for a clean shirt. Now that he was out of jail, he put on a fresh one each day and felt better for it. There was a heap of used shirts and underpants in the bedroom waiting to be washed. Freedom came at a cost.

Would you believe it? He was on his way downstairs when the fucking doorbell went for the umpteenth time. The reason she'd called at the neighbours' must have been to confirm that he was at home.

The way to deal with someone like this was to get in their face and tell them to piss off.

He marched through his confetti-strewn hall and flung open the door.

And Claude the kitten came from behind him and dashed out, trailing a pink streamer caught in its leg.

'Fucking hell, that's my daughter's kitten.'

The woman in front of him turned to look as Claude streaked across the road and under a car that was fortunately not moving.

'That's your bloody fault,' Joe shouted as he pushed past and went in pursuit. 'Claude, come here. Heel.'

Kittens don't behave like dogs.

Joe clapped his hand to his head. 'Caroline will kill me.'

The woman had remained where she was, plainly annoyed at being blamed for the escape.

Joe crossed the road and knelt to look under the car. He wouldn't have wanted any of his underworld contacts looking on as he put on a silly squeaky voice and called, 'Pussy, pussy, come to Uncle Joe.' Turning to the woman, he growled, 'Come and help me catch him. That's the least you can bloody do.'

She didn't move a muscle, except to say, 'You'll panic him, doing that. He'll run for the trees and then you're really in trouble.' She seemed to know what she was talking about.

'What am I going to do, then?'

'Who's Caroline?'

'My daughter.'

'And she's the owner, right?'

'She's on her honeymoon. She left him here for me to look after. He's not used to me yet.'

'Tempt him back. Have you fed him yet?'

'I only just got up.'

'Back away from the car slowly. Fetch his feeding bowl and some moist food.'

The prospect of losing Claude had robbed Joe of his dignity and banished every other thought from his head. He stood upright. Moving as silently and smoothly as the moon, he did as the woman had suggested, glided past his visitor and into the house, pausing only to murmur out of the side of his mouth, 'For Christ's sake keep your eye on him.'

When he emerged with a bowl of freshly opened minced chicken in gravy he could see the kitten still under the car and now resting on its haunches. Probably it felt safe there.

'Slowly now,' the woman said. 'Place the bowl just this side of the car where you can pick him up. Give him a few seconds to start on the food and then grasp him round the middle with both hands and draw him up to your chest. He'll wriggle, so get a firm grip, but don't squash him.'

The advice was good. Claude watched Joe's approach and didn't run away. When the food was within sniffing distance he ventured out, took a few licks and was snatched. Joe carried his captive triumphantly into the house, through to the kitchen and closed the door.

The woman had picked up the bowl and followed him into the hall. 'We'd better give him the food now, poor mite. He can't escape. I closed the front door.'

Joe couldn't escape either. Obediently he carried the bowl into the kitchen and set it down for Claude. Then he emerged and said, 'What do you want from me – a donation?'

244

'Don't insult me,' she said. 'I want the truth out of you, Joe Irving.'

Hearing his name spoken like that was a shock. Now that their eyes met, her tone of voice reminded him who she was.

Georgina was waiting in Diamond's chair, drumming her fingertips on the only space she could find on his cluttered desk. 'You could have called me.'

'We were on the road, ma'am,' he said, standing in front of the desk like the schoolkid told to report to the headmistress. And like the cocky schoolkid he had once been, he said, 'I'm a careful driver, as you know.' Which was entirely true. She wasn't to know Ingeborg had been at the wheel.

'You could have pulled over.'

'Not on the M4.'

'You didn't come by the motorway. We tracked Ingeborg's phone. You were on the A4.'

Harder to wriggle out of that. 'Slip of the tongue.' He moved on fast as if he'd just gone past an amber light. 'Anyhow, I'm here the quickest I could have been. What did you want me for, ma'am?'

'I would have thought it obvious. The suicide last night.'

'That's why I'm on duty,' he said, noting her use of the word suicide. 'I was visiting Joe Irving.'

'I know. I heard that much from your team. Did he have anything germane to say?'

Germane. What a headmistressy word, 'Not really. He doesn't know the dead man, or so he says. He gave an account of his movements yesterday afternoon.'

'An alibi?'

'I wouldn't call it that.'

'I was told by DI Leaman that you're toying with the notion that the man was murdered.'

'"Toying" is about right,' he said, planning to have words later with John Leaman. 'I wouldn't put it any stronger.'

'I'm glad to hear it. Anyone who has ever seen that place with all the tiles will know there's no possibility that it was anything else but suicide. My information is that the muzzle of the gun was held to his head.'

'That's right.'

'No one else could have pulled the trigger for the simple reason that he would have seen them coming.'

'Could have been taking a nap.'

'On a mission to kill? Are you serious?'

'He won't have had much sleep.'

'When you get a bee in your bonnet you won't give up, will you?'

'Not until the bee has buzzed off.'

'Face up to it, Peter. This one doesn't exist. It's in your imagination. I can't stop you from thinking about it, but keep your thoughts to yourself. We don't want this sensationalised by the media. They're already asking questions.'

'Who are?'

'The local press. The *Chronicle*. A suicide in the Roman Baths is a strong story for them, regardless of what we know. We must manage it with extreme care, for obvious reasons.'

So that was what was behind this summons. 'Covering for George and his family?'

'I wish you wouldn't call him that.'

'He started it.'

'Yes, and I'm sure he'd rather we returned to normality now that the wedding is over. To get back to the point, I believe we should we put out a short press release confirming that a man was found dead in the hypocaust early this morning with the gun beside him, without, of course, linking it in any way to the wedding.'

'Will you be doing that?' he asked.

'Good Lord, no. That's your job.'

'Because I'd like to issue the photo of the victim at the same time and make an appeal for help in identifying him.'

She consented to that. 'We can't do otherwise.'

'Has the Chronic put anything online about the wedding itself?'

'Mercifully only a short piece. The rain came to our rescue there. If they got a picture, it wasn't good enough to publish. A few lines of text are easy to miss without a photo to go with them. We can be grateful for that.'

'And nobody from the media has picked up on what happened to DC Gilbert?'

Suddenly her small brown eyes turned into avocado stones. 'Peter, that must not get out. I shudder to think what the press would say about us. Your CID people are the only ones in the know. They had better not leak anything of this.'

Diamond saw red, shocked by such distrust. 'My CID people – as you call them – are *our* CID people, and they aren't blabbers, ma'am.'

'Perhaps I should have expressed myself another way,' Georgina said. 'We're all a little frayed at the edges today.'

And you weren't on duty all day yesterday and up half the night, he thought, but stopped himself from saying so.

Georgina seemed to sense that her moment had passed. Headmistresses don't apologise. She got up and left, muttering something about phone calls to make.

After drafting a press statement as innocuous as a baby's smile, Diamond, too, moved out of his office, interested to discover if any of the team had yet dug up any useful intelligence on the gunman. They all had their contacts and most of the contacting was being done over a beer. Sunday lunchtimes saw a lot of business done in the local pubs.

Several were still out. Expenses would take a hit today.

Keith Halliwell was looking pleased with himself, so Diamond went over. 'What have you learned, then?'

'May be nothing,' Keith said in a tone suggesting the opposite. 'How did you get on, guv?'

'As I expected. Irving playing the innocent. At the critical time between six and seven-thirty, he was in the park talking to trees, rehearsing his father-of-the-bride speech.'

'Couldn't he come up with anything better than that?'

'It's so off the wall it might be true. He hasn't got much imagination. And I've just had my ear bent by Georgina. She wants to hush everything up. Come on, what's your news?'

An artful gleam came into Halliwell's eye. 'What's it worth?'

'A kick where it hurts most if you don't cough up.'

'Well, the word on the street is that a shipment of military weapons was smuggled into the country four weeks ago from Hungary and delivered to an arms dealer in Swindon. They included several cases of ex-army AK-63 assault rifles.'

Diamond whistled in appreciation. 'What's his name?'

A shrug. 'You know how it is working with snouts. Everything is guarded with a triple lock. I offered some extra and this Swindon guy is being tapped for more information.'

'As we speak?'

'I made it very clear how urgent this is.'

'It's likely you've found the supplier. These weapons aren't much used.'

'I'll give you a shout as soon as.'

This wasn't the full breakthrough, but it was promising.

'One more thing,' Diamond said. 'Where's Paul Gilbert?'

'I sent him home. He looked knackered.'

'I'll give him a call. I forgot to ask something.'

He returned to his office and called Paul's number and got a female voice. The young officer lived with his parents. In the economy of modern Britain he'd be drawing his pension when he finally got his own pad.

'Paul is asleep,' Mrs Gilbert said. 'He was on duty all day yesterday in that dreadful rain and I'm wondering if he caught a cold.'

He caught worse than that, Diamond thought, but the lad can't have mentioned it to his mother. 'Feeling below par, is he?'

'He was a bit out of sorts when he got in last night, insisting on wearing his baseball cap in the house, which he's never done before. His clothes were wet through and he went to bed almost at once saying he had a headache. I gave him two Ibuprofen tablets but he was up at seven this morning, still in the baseball cap, insisting he would be needed at work. You'd like to speak to him, I'm sure.'

'That's all right, Mrs Gilbert. Don't disturb him now. Ask him to give me a bell when he surfaces.'

'He wouldn't like that. If you're calling him here it must be important. He admires you enormously, Mr Diamond. He'd hate to keep you waiting. Hang on and I'll get him.'

Very little time passed before the young constable's voice came through. 'Something wrong, guv?'

'Not at all. Relax. It could have waited, but your mum insisted on waking you. There was something I meant to ask you and didn't. My fault entirely. But first, what is it with the baseball cap?'

'That? It's to hide the stitches on my head. If my parents saw them, they'd be sure to ask questions. I tried brushing my hair over the patch the nurse shaved, but it still shows.'

'They don't know what happened?'

'It's my work, isn't it?'

Diamond wished Georgina had been on the line to hear that.

'Good man. Now, this may be difficult for you, but I'd like you to cast your mind back to when you were on the roof

249

with the gunman. Try and picture him handing you the water to drink. Was the bottle in his right hand or his left?'

Paul took a few seconds to answer. 'His right, guv. He was right-handed, if that's what you're asking.'

'You're certain?'

'Positive. I can't tell you much else about him, but I know that much. I was with him for more than ten hours, on and off.'

Diamond's grin was wider than the Royal Crescent. He thanked Paul and put down the phone.

All doubt was removed from his mind. This was murder. A right-handed man doesn't shoot himself in the left temple. Call it an impossible crime as many times as you want. You'd be wrong. There had to be a way the hitman had been shot at point-blank range.

The only conceivable explanation so far had been Ingeborg's: a cat and mouse set-up in which the cat didn't realise he was in fact the mouse until too late. He'd allowed his killer to get near under the pretext of a large wad of money changing hands. A bribe to buy him off. A fatal mistake.

The theory hadn't washed with Diamond when he'd first heard it and still didn't. A hitman doesn't fall for a trick like that. He was a well-armed professional who had made an elaborate plan to kill. Through no fault of his own, the shooting from the rooftop hadn't been possible and he'd been forced to improvise. Down in the hypocaust he was still committed, still armed and still primed for his opportunity.

Okay, he should have fired first. Why didn't he?

Could it be the Joe Irving factor? Diamond had seen enough of the gang leader to know he was as cunning as any villain he'd encountered, like a large lizard sunning itself, poised to strike while giving the impression it didn't much care. He'd insisted on this wedding despite the danger of putting himself in the public eye and at risk of being killed by a contract killer hired by a rival. Instead of surrounding himself with bodyguards, he'd allowed George Brace to manage the security. He'd conducted himself throughout with confidence, as if he was in control and not the police.

At the end of the day, Irving had survived and the gunman was dead. How on earth had he engineered that? Could he cynically have used his own daughter's wedding as a trap?

Presumably, he'd been given a tip-off by someone in the criminal world that a hitman was definitely gunning for him. Yet in the evening he'd behaved with the supreme confidence of a man who knew any danger had been dealt with. He'd lined up boldly at the edge of the Great Bath for the photos and he'd stood for his speech and taken his time making it. It all suggested he knew his would-be killer was already dead.

So going by Irving's behaviour, the killing had been done in the time slot after the wedding and before the reception. And his alibi for the afternoon was flakier than the confetti that littered his house.

Diamond lingered in the office another hour and a half in the hope of more information coming in from the team's boozy lunch dates with the CID's top grasses, but there was little of help. No one in Bristol seemed to have heard anything about Sid Felix for several weeks. He'd done a disappearing act. There was no word about anyone issuing a contract.

He shut up shop for the day.

32

P atience had never been a virtue of Diamond's. As soon as he got in on Monday he phoned the firm who had carried out the crime scene inspection.

'It's far too soon,' the pitiless voice on the end of the line said. 'You have no idea how long our procedures take.'

'Oh, but I do,' Diamond said. 'I know from bitter experience and that's why I'm asking.'

'You can ask as much as you like, but—'

'You and I are batting for the same team, you know.' He was second to none at winkling out information.

The voice underwent a subtle change, from implacable to faintly regretful. 'We can't under any circumstances reveal our findings until they're validated.'

'My friend, I wouldn't dream of asking for unvalidated findings. A hint of progress would be good. Have you actually made a start?'

Unwise to ask. There was petulance in the answer. 'People like you don't seem to realise calls like this are counter-productive. Of course we've started.'

'And one of the first things you do is examine the firearms for prints and DNA, because they need to be handed on to ballistics for test firing, right?'

'Yes, but—'

'Excellent. And are there signs someone made an attempt to wipe the handgun?'

Shock, horror. 'I can't possibly tell you that. I'll be in trouble with my supervisor.'

'He will never know.'

'She – and she sacked the last guy who messed up.'

'You're not the sort to mess up. I can tell from your voice you're encouraged by what's been found so far.' A little applesauce never went unappreciated.

'You could be right about that.'

'About you?'

'About what you said.'

Diamond waited for more. He knew the pressure a pause can bring.

'About the gun.'

'Well, that's a relief.' He waited again.

The urge to share good news is a basic human trait.

'You aren't mistaken about the gun. There was a clear set of prints, too clear, in fact.'

'Really? It was wiped? After the shot was fired?'

'That's impossible to tell. The victim's prints were present, as you'd expect . . .'

'And?'

'Very little else.'

'But something else?'

'We also found a trace of a second person's DNA.'

'Nice work.' He pressed the phone harder to his ear. 'Well done.'

'What I just told you is off the record.'

'As far as I'm concerned, we never had this conversation. I haven't even asked your name, have I?'

'We won't know whose DNA it is until the samples have been checked at the profiling lab against the national database, and of course there's no guarantee either sample will match anything.'

'You'll have to be content to sit back and wait – like me,' Diamond said. 'The story of my life.'

Whilst sitting back and waiting, he used the back of a Home Office circular about rises in crime and falling detection rates to summarise the case for murder.

Joe's unlikely alibi.
Victim was right-handed. Entrance wound left.
Gun had been wiped.
Trace of different DNA.
Victim was a hitman. Kill or be killed.
Joe's confident demeanour after the killing.

Then his phone buzzed. He was expecting a call from Halliwell to report on the autopsy but this was the office downstairs. Someone in Bath had asked to speak to the officer in charge of the suicide investigation.

At first he was thrown. He'd forgotten that the rest of the world wasn't thinking of the death as murder. He was streets ahead.

'Put them on, then.'

'She isn't there any more.'

'Where exactly is "there"?'

'The One Stop Shop.'

The police's only public presence in the city ever since dear old Manvers Street police station had been sold off. Diamond's blood pressure rose whenever the One Stop was mentioned.

'You took her contact details, I hope?'

'I didn't speak to her. I'm just passing on the message. Apparently, she wouldn't give her name, sir. She said she had some shopping to do and she'd return at noon and she expected to find you there.'

'At the One Stop?'

'Yes.'

'Who does she think she is – the Chief Constable?'

'I got the impression she was someone rather important.'

'And did you also get the impression she was playing games, wanting to see a senior policeman jump to her command?'

'I don't know about that, sir.'

'Did she say why she wanted to meet me personally?'

'I didn't speak to her myself. I believe she'd been online and seen your press release and the photo.'

'Had she recognised the dead man?'

'I don't know.'

'Has anyone else got in touch yet?'

'Not that I've heard.'

He looked at his watch. 'I'd better see this Lady Bracknell. Okay, I'm sorry I lost my rag. My fault entirely. Pass on this message, would you? If I'm late, I'll be on my way.'

Going out, he met Keith Halliwell, fresh from the autopsy.

'That was quick.'

'One of the quickest I've attended, guv. I've had haircuts that lasted longer.'

'What did Dr Sealy have to say?'

'The bullet in the head did the job, as if we didn't know. The skin around the wound was burned from contact with the gun. He was a fit man in his forties, reasonably well nourished.'

'No other injuries?'

'Abrasions to his arm, elbow and hip, consistent with falling on the uneven surface where he was found. Superficial skin damage to his palms and fingers.'

'From climbing over that wall, we think. Did Sealy come up with anything suspicious about the shooting?'

'You mean evidence of someone else being involved? Sorry, but no.'

'Good thing we've got some pointers of our own. I'm heading out to the One Stop Shop to meet a woman who may know who the victim is. That's my hope. She could be an attention-seeker.'

'Good luck with that,' Halliwell said.

Every trawl for information brings in a high percentage of dross, most of it from responsible, well-meaning citizens who are genuinely confused. Bath, being the genteel place it is, has more than its share of them. And then there are the time-wasters who want to be part of the action. You have to cultivate the patience that Diamond found so elusive. He didn't have high hopes that this imperious lady would have personal knowledge of a professional hitman.

He parked outside the railway station and marched the few yards up Manvers Street to where Bath and North East Somerset had concentrated its council services and where the police had been allocated a space that to his jaundiced eye was a hole in the wall.

Two officers were visible behind the counter. There wasn't room for more. One was sharp enough to recognise him.

'Thanks for coming over, sir. The lady is in the meeting area with the small white dog.'

'There's a dog as well?'

She was at one of the round tables staring at her phone, most likely checking how late he was. Dark-haired, maybe forty (as he got older he found it more difficult to tell younger people's ages), no make-up he could detect, black top with a glittery motif and white jeans.

The dog was a West Highland terrier.

He went over. 'I believe you asked to see me. I'm Peter Diamond, Bath Police.'

256

'Magda Lyle,' she said. 'Ex-governor of Bream Prison.' She handed him a business card that said as much.

His brain played rapid catch-up. Ingeborg had been on about a riot at Bream a few years ago when Joe Irving was detained there. This was more promising than he'd dared to hope.

He offered coffee. 'Don't know if it's any good here. I'm based at an outpost up near the motorway.'

'Lucky you. I won't, thanks, but Blanche would appreciate a bowl of water.'

Fetch for the dog? he thought briefly and irritably. I'm not one of your inmates, madam. Then he looked down and happened to notice the woman's foot and shin and the solid surface of a prosthetic leg.

He fetched the dog's water.

He had remembered with a stab of self-reproach what he'd heard about the riot – the prison governor crashing her car deliberately to thwart her kidnappers. This woman wasn't a freeloader. She was a hero.

Humbled, he sat opposite her.

'Your dead man,' she said. 'I know who he is. He was in Bream when I was one of the governors there. I saw the photo you issued and I'm certain I'm right. His name is Jack Peace. He was serving five years for grievous bodily harm. His DNA will be on record. You can check it.'

This was a breakthrough. He wanted to jump on the table and shout, 'Yes!' Instead of which, he controlled himself and said with the calm of a Buddhist monk, 'Do you remember him personally?'

'Quite well. Not so well as some of the others who were sent to me regularly because of behavioural problems. Peace was no trouble at all. That was my judgement, for what it's worth.' She paused and looked away, as if deciding how much she would tell. Clearly there was more to her story than this. 'There was a serious riot in 2015 that brought my career to a sudden end. I should have been on duty, but I was prevented from going there. I saw none of it. I was involved indirectly, but outside the prison walls, so I'm unable to comment on any of his actions on the day.'

Diamond was careful not to lead her. If he'd realised she was going to be a key witness he'd have asked for a formal statement and made sure one of his team was present. Now she'd started, he'd hear her out and arrange the formalities later.

'You'll need to read the report,' she said. 'It wasn't a spontaneous incident. There was planning and communication with the criminal community outside. Let's not pretend our prisons are secure. As everyone knows, offenders and their contacts smuggle in drugs and they improvise weapons if they can't smuggle them in as well. Our staffers do their best, but it's out of control in all the prisons I've known. We have poorly trained officers trying to deal with sophisticated technology. Phones get smaller and easier to bring in. Drones are used increasingly. I can't tell you how the riot was plotted and the report doesn't have much to say about it either. We take it as a given that prisoners are in touch with the underworld. I don't need to tell you this.' She stiffened in her chair. 'Blanche!'

The small white dog had drunk its fill and was showing its gratitude by resting its front paws on Diamond's thigh and licking the back of his hand with a bright pink tongue cool from the water.

'She's no bother,' he said.

'Have you got one of your own?'

'No, but animals seem to like the taste of me.'

'They know more than we give them credit for,' she said. 'I wouldn't be without her. On that morning three years ago, I was fearful that they'd shoot her. I shake when I think of it, even now. They tied her in a sack and left her in my garden shed. One of them was slightly more civilised than the other. He exercised restraint.'

'It looks as if Blanche came off better than you did in the end.'

'My own fault. I was kidnapped in my own garden and forced at gunpoint to drive to the prison. When we got there, one of the wings was on fire and there were men on the roof. The man beside me told me to drive into the prison after the gates opened to let the fire engine in. They were using their phones and it was clear to me that the riot had been staged to allow an escape.'

'You crashed your car.'

'Correction. I braked my car and the crook behind crashed into me, but I won't quibble over who was responsible. Everything that happened after is the direct result of my own actions. I woke from a coma more than a week later and was told both my legs needed to be amputated.'

'Both? That's awful.' Whatever you say about an event like that will sound crass.

She shrugged. She must have experienced every show of sympathy before. 'But here I am, alive, unlike my passenger and the man in the car behind. Fortunately, my stumps are strong and I owe my recovery so far to the medical professionals who got me upright and walking again.' She'd spoken without self-pity. 'I can move on now, literally. I drive a specially adapted car.'

Diamond had been scrupulous in letting her tell the story as she wished. It seemed to have come to an end. 'Do you live here?'

'No. I'm staying at the Abbey Hotel, one of the few dog-friendly places. I have a nice ground-floor flat in Gloucester.'

'You're here for a reason. A connection with the riot?'

'Indirectly.' She seemed reluctant to expand on this.

259

'With Jack Peace?'

She shook her head. 'I didn't know he was here until I saw your appeal for information.'

A promising avenue closed.

There was more to come, he was confident. She was waiting for him to contribute. He dredged deep in his brain and remembered something the cousins had told him. 'Did you by any chance visit a house in Sion Hill Place on Saturday afternoon?'

She looked startled. 'Who told you that?'

'It's true, then?'

'Unfinished business. I said something about moving on, but I can't until this is settled. I came here to track down someone I knew from my time at Bream.'

'Joe Irving?'

'You know him?' Her tone became more relaxed, as if she'd needed some assurance that this was going to be productive. 'I discovered on the internet that his daughter was getting married here. You must understand that for a long time after the riot I was bed-bound, too much of a basket case to think of anything except my own troubles. Only when I was learning to walk again did I start to wonder what happened inside the prison that day. I read the official report of the inquiry and it didn't tell me what I wanted to know. Have you seen it?'

'No.'

'Understandably it's more about underlying causes and recommendations than personalities. Gloucestershire police interviewed everyone, including me in my hospital bed, but I couldn't tell them much. I'm one of four governors who shared responsibility for the prison and I was supposed to be on duty that morning, but I never got there, as you know. I had my suspicion who the ringleaders were and I didn't hold back when I was asked, but it was only my opinion. They were never charged.'

'Joe Irving and his friends?'

'You get no prize for working that out, I'm afraid, except a copy of the official report, if you want it.' She reached for her bag.

'Do you have one with you? It would save me some time.'

She handed across a thick Ministry of Justice tome of the sort that would normally have been chucked straight into his waste bin. 'Every word of every witness statement is in there. You don't have to wade through it all. There's a summary of the findings.'

'And they failed to see that Joe was implicated?'

'His witness statement reads like Snow White's CV. He gets one short paragraph in the possible causes bit. Every prison wing has its hierarchy and Joe bossed C Wing, no question. They worked that out and decided blaming him was the easy solution, too obvious. They needed to delve deeper. Have you met big Joe?'

'Several times.'

'He's a much-feared gangland chief outside prison, isn't he? All my experience of him is inside. The entire community went in fear of him, including some of my staff. Yet he's a complex personality, extremely well-defended, able to project himself as the soul of innocence to anyone in authority. Clearly it works in the courts, because he wriggles out of the high-tariff offences by admitting to relatively minor crimes.'

'He can afford the best lawyers,' Diamond said.

'That I can believe. My personal belief is that he orchestrated the riot as a distraction. In the ensuing chaos he and perhaps some others were to escape. The two thugs who kidnapped me were going in to spring him. I know from what was said to me that their mission was to get someone out and Joe would surely have been first in the queue. Unhappily I can't prove a thing.'

261

'He must have come under strong suspicion.'

'But the evidence wasn't there. The wing was a no-go area for hours. The only witnesses were inmates who still go in fear of him.'

'Weren't some prison officers held hostage?'

'Yes, and locked inside a cell. That was the start of it. They seem to have been ambushed without even knowing who attacked them. It wouldn't have been Joe Irving dirtying his hands, I guarantee. When the only people who know the truth are offenders, you're up against lies and distortions. Frightened men will say anything for fear of reprisals. When the evidence was taken, one name came up – from as many as four sources.'

'Jack Peace?'

'You know?'

'I could see where this was going. You think he was set up?'

'I'm convinced of it,' Magda Lyle said. 'He was no angel. He had a history of violence and serious crime but from my perspective he was a model prisoner. He was coming to the end of quite a long term and he had high hopes of early release. His probation officer and I were actively planning his resettlement. Why would he have put that at risk by becoming involved in a riot? He was charged with prison mutiny and causing damage. He was cleared of the mutiny, but given three more years for the damage. I felt so strongly about this injustice that I decided to try and trace Joe Irving and find out the truth.'

'Big risk.'

She smiled. 'I don't have much more to lose. I knew he had been released and was probably back in Bath or Bristol, but I didn't have an address. I suppose I could have contacted the probation service but I wanted to deal with this in my own way.'

She must have seen a look of misgiving flit across Diamond's features. 'I'm a peaceful woman, Mr Diamond.'

'Peaceful,' he said, 'and brave. Not a safe combination.'

'The safe option isn't always the right one. And then an online newspaper had a short piece about the forthcoming wedding at Bath Abbey. I packed a bag and came here to try and find out more. Irving was paying for the wedding and it was sure to be lavish, so I got his address from the main florists in town.'

'And went to the house?'

'On Saturday afternoon. I thought I could count on him being there, getting ready for the reception, but he wasn't. Some woman came to the door in a dressing gown and was unfriendly, to say the least, as if I was the floozy, not her. He hasn't long been out of prison. I can't believe he's in a relationship already.'

'She was a cousin of the bride, staying overnight for the wedding.'

'Ah. You know more about it than I do.'

'Some of it.'

'I've spoken to him,' she said.

'When?'

'Yesterday afternoon. I want to his house a second time and managed to get inside. I won't bore you with how it happened. I tried everything I know to get a confession but I was wasting my time. He could stonewall for England.'

He was shaken. 'You shouldn't have gone there. He's dangerous.'

She was unimpressed. She stared at him for a moment in silence. 'Do you know where I think he was when I first called there and spoke to the woman?'

'Tell me.'

'The Roman Baths. I reckon he knew by then that Jack

Peace was planning something. He found him there and shot him. I believe the suicide was faked.'

'I'm not sure if he knew Peace was gunning for him,' Diamond said, 'but he knew he was putting his head above the parapet. Major criminals don't usually break cover. They have too many enemies.'

'This was exceptional. The biggest occasion in his daughter's life.'

'Exactly. But he wasn't unprepared for an attack. I spoke to him myself after the service and without quite admitting he was armed, he confirmed as much in coded language.' The 'coded language' Joe had used was 'Does a bear shit in the woods?' Magda Lyle must have heard worse than that, but Diamond had an old-fashioned care for language in female company.

She rolled her eyes. 'Armed – at his daughter's wedding?'

'We're thinking along the same lines as you, but there's a difficulty. It's almost impossible to fake a suicide like this.'

'Can't you trace his DNA?'

'We're looking at that. The gun had been wiped.'

'Even more suspicious.'

'But there's a problem. Peace's body was found in a place where you couldn't creep up on him without giving yourself away.'

'Could Joe have immobilised him first?'

'How?'

'With a taser.'

None of the team had thought of that. Crooks, just like the police, used tasers. Anyone could buy them on the dark web. For a short interval, Diamond gave it serious consideration before realising the catch.

'The effects of a taser last about five seconds, no more. The person tasered feels intense pain and often falls down, but the recovery is quick. His attacker might just get to him in the time to kill him, but the taser gun fires these little barbed electrodes that lodge in the clothes or the skin and deliver the volts. He was wearing a T-shirt and they'd have ripped straight through and left tell-tale marks that would show up at the autopsy.'

'Not a taser, then?'

'Nice try, though.'

'How else could it be done? Hypnosis?'

He smiled. 'That's another one I hadn't considered. Isn't that a slow process, putting someone into a trance?'

She smiled back. 'Can't win, can I? But I agree really. Joe Irving is scary, but he's no Svengali. What's your best theory?'

'We think Joe conned him in some way, maybe with the offer of cash. When he got close, instead of handing over money, he drew the gun, pressed it to the side of Jack Peace's head and fired. There are obvious flaws in this.'

'Jack was no mug,' she said.

He couldn't argue with that. She'd known the man.

She added, 'When I saw his picture online, I called the present governor to make quite sure he'd been released, and he had, only a short time ago. I also spoke to his probation officer. They didn't know what he was planning, but both confirmed how bitter he was when he came out. Three extra years in prison, three long, festering years to brood over the injustice and plan his revenge. I'm as sure as anything he blamed Irving and planned to kill him, but I can't believe he'd be taken in by the trick you just outlined.'

'I have to agree,' Diamond said. 'I said there were flaws. You asked for our best theory and that was it, unconvincing. Would you do something for me?'

'What's that?'

'Visit the hospital mortuary and identify the body.'

'Willingly.'

He told her she was right to identify Jack Peace as the

gunman planning revenge, and about the trouble he must have been to, taking delivery of the assault rifle and picking the ideal vantage point for the killing. 'If it weren't for the monsoon weather, Irving would be dead meat by now.'

'Instead of which he walks free, leaving an unexplained death and you with a case you can't solve.'

33

'Peter, have you eaten?' George Brace asked Diamond when he returned to Concorde House. For the second time in recent weeks they'd met in the staff car park. Diamond was beginning to wonder if the DCC lurked there because he was uncomfortable inside the building. There wasn't much sympathy among the staff for his new family situation.

'Been quite busy.'

'The Folly does excellent lunches, I'm told. You must let me treat you. The least I can do after all your efforts.'

'I've got a murder case now, George.'

'No promises, but I may be able to help with that.'

'Really?'

'A quiet chat away from the coalface. Two heads better than one. What do you say?'

They did the short drive in George's Volvo, ordered their food and took their drinks to a table outside. After going through his pipe-lighting ritual, George said, 'Down to business. I know you're keen to get back and hear the latest from your team. What's your thinking on Joe Irving? Did he shoot his stalker?'

'That's our belief,' Diamond said. 'In the last hour we've identified the victim as Jack Peace, an ex-convict who served time with Irving in the same prison, same wing.' He reported on his meeting with Magda Lyle. 'So we have a motive for the gunman, a long-standing grudge, and more importantly we have an even stronger motive for Irving.'

'Needing to stop this fellow who was sure to stalk him until he made the kill?'

'Right. If it wasn't achieved at the wedding, Peace was never going to give up.'

'Joe shot him and faked the suicide?'

Diamond swayed to his left to avoid a gust of pipe smoke. 'The thousand-dollar question is how he managed it.'

'Thousand-dollar question or three-pipe problem?' George said with a smile, tapping the stem of his briar. 'Let me see if I can assist. What are your best guesses so far?'

Diamond didn't care for that word 'guesses'. First, he listed the yardsticks: the location, the timing and the need for the killer to get close enough to fake a suicide. Then he went through the various theories, starting with the con trick with the payment and ending with the taser, and explained the difficulty with each. He omitted Magda Lyle's suggestion of hypnosis as too far-fetched.

What time did you say the fatal shot was fired?'

'We don't know for sure, except it was before ten-twenty. The best estimate is between six and seven-thirty, after the baths closed and before the reception.'

'Didn't anyone hear the gun go off?'

'Apparently not. Most people were some distance away. The hypocaust is more than six metres below ground level. The closest to it were the photographer and his assistant beside the Great Bath, but they were separated by several solid stone walls.'

'Could the shooting have happened after seven-thirty, when the party was in full swing?'

'In theory, yes, but I personally watched Joe all evening.'

'Have you considered whether he had an accomplice?'

'Somebody else who fired the shot?'

George nodded. 'Joe doesn't put himself in danger much, from all I've heard. He's more of a delegator.'

Good one, George. It was a fresh angle, and a persuasive one that fitted most of the facts. No question Irving had the clout to call on some assistance. He could have sat through the long hours at the reception knowing someone else was doing his dirty work. 'He'd have needed to issue the order at short notice.'

'Unless he always had his own back-up waiting in the wings,' George said. 'I remember you half expected it. You couldn't understand him relying on you alone.'

'Couldn't understand him relying on me at all if I'm honest,' Diamond said. 'He was always more likely to trust one of his own. I was there to make sure the wedding went off peacefully, not to kill his enemy.'

'Does the proxy killer answer your problem, Peter?'

'It might well – if there was any evidence of this extra gunman – a sighting, or some traces.'

'Forensics may help there.'

'We can hope so. And we still haven't explained how it was done.'

'The shot through the head at close quarters? Let me think about that.'

Their rib-eye steaks and chips arrived and were consumed before George Brace had anything useful to add. Then he said, 'Perhaps we should be thinking outside the box.'

'How exactly?'

'Well . . .' George had lit up again. He exhaled a plume of smoke that made sure the thinking outside the box wasn't blue-sky thinking. 'Let's go back to the one thing we've been avoiding: the possibility that Jack Peace really did kill himself.'

'We haven't avoided it. We have a duty to examine the alternative,' Diamond said.

'And quite rightly,' George said, picking up on the note of irritation. 'But we ought to apply the same rigorous standards to the chance of it being suicide, don't you think?'

Diamond wanted to yell in the DCC's face that suicide was out of the question because the dead man had been right-handed, but he restrained himself and said a tame, 'All right.'

'The method, means and opportunity are obvious. The timing fits the same parameters, between six and ten-twenty p.m.'

'Agreed.'

'The hard part is the motive. Why would he have shot himself when he was there to shoot Joe?'

'Because he knew he'd failed,' Diamond said. 'That's the only explanation I can think of.'

'Come now, Peter.'

'If you can suggest something else . . .'

'Try this for size,' George said as archly as if he was about to reveal that there is life on Mars. 'He'd always intended to shoot himself after taking out Joe. That's not so far-fetched. A good proportion of people who murder others by shooting will turn the gun on themselves. Am I right?'

Diamond nodded. 'But he *hadn't* taken out Joe.'

'He changed his mind. The bottled-up anger dissipated when he saw the wedding going on, the joy of the bride and groom on their special day.'

'You're saying he had a road to Damascus moment?'

'You've got it. He saw how destructive killing Joe would be to everyone concerned and it made him look into his own embittered heart. In self-disgust, he put the gun to his own head.'

Diamond was thinking you wouldn't put this into a 1950s B movie, but he had enough tact to say, 'Thanks, George. I'm keeping all options open in the expectation that forensics will report back soon.'

'Very wise. We need more evidence. In the end, it may be the coroner who settles the matter.'

Back in the CID office, Halliwell said, 'Have you been hiding, guv? We were expecting you two hours ago.'

'I was waylaid by the DCC.'

'Anything we should know about?'

'Relax, our jobs are safe for this week, anyway. Why did you need me? Something in from forensics?'

'Still waiting.'

'Idle bastards.'

'But there is something. I don't know if it will amuse you. It made me smile. I got it from Bristol CID. You know Sid Felix hasn't been seen for a while? Well, his mob have been keeping this under wraps. Felix has been suffering from stress.'

'Sid Felix? Stress?'

'Early in August, he went into a retreat somewhere in Dorset and he's been there ever since trying to get his mojo back.'

'Since before Irving was released?'

'Right. He's not in contact with any of his gang. He can't have ordered anyone to kill Joe Irving.'

'And we've been in a mucksweat about him for nothing. Felix is out of the equation. I bet bloody Irving knew about this. His jungle telegraph is better than ours. It explains a lot. Do I want to laugh or jump off a bridge? I wish to God we'd known from the beginning.'

But at least it clarified his thinking.

He told Halliwell about his meeting with Magda Lyle, the governor. 'I'm in no doubt now that this all goes back to the riot at Bream and Peace being named as the ringleader. He served three more years as a result.'

'Stitched up?'

'Well and truly. Apparently four of the inmates named him. The governor was still in hospital when the investigation took place and didn't know he was being held responsible until after the report was published. She would have spoken up for him. She's convinced Joe Irving was behind the whole thing. He ruled the wing and was expecting to be sprung by his friends, but it went wrong. When the investigation followed, Joe and his cronies made Jack the scapegoat.'

'No wonder he was bitter, poor sod.'

'When I visited Irving yesterday, I showed him the picture of Peace and he denied even knowing the guy. He's lying, Keith. They were on the same wing. I want him nicked and brought in for questioning. A dawn raid.'

'Tomorrow? Why not right away?'

'Do you want another long night on duty?'

Halliwell grinned. 'Not really.'

'So we start the fun and games with the six o'clock knock. Tonight I must do my homework.'

34

Statement from Prisoner A, taken at HMP Chelmsford, 8 December 2015:

'I was in C Wing at Bream when the riot happened. Conditions was bad there. We was banged up for hours and the food was crap and most of them was doing drugs, but I been in worse. The first I heard of what was going to happen was someone (I forget who) telling me Warren on the middle landing wanted to see me. Warren is a silent guy with mean eyes you don't want to upset. His cellmate was massive, a lifer known as Muscles, who was supposed to have nicked a Spiderman toy from some supermarket and karate-chopped a security guard who stopped him at the exit. He snapped the bloke's neck with one blow and got sent down for life. With Muscles as his heavy, Warren got what he wanted in Bream. He was definitely running the show that morning, giving orders to everyone. He told me to go up on the roof, so I did. I didn't do no damage. The hole was already made when I climbed up. I stayed up there a few hours, until it was all over. I didn't lay hands on no one, cons or screws.'

Statement from Prisoner B, taken at HMP Wormwood Scrubs, 9 December 2015:

'I had no reason to play any part in what happened at Bream. I'm on my second year of five and looking for parole as soon as I can get it. The centre of activity was the end cell on the middle landing of C Wing, occupied by a surly prisoner called Warren. We all had nicknames, so that may not have been his real identity. He had a henchman known as Muscles, for obvious reasons, who was much feared. There is no doubt that these two were the ringleaders, although I doubt whether Muscles was involved in the planning. I stayed clear of trouble until the smoke from the fire in the association area downstairs was getting on my lungs and then I moved to the top landing and waited there until order was restored.'

Statement from Prisoner C, taken at HMP Wormwood Scrubs, 15 December 2015:

'The action started on the middle landing after unlock. I heard a load of shouting and someone told me two of the screws had been attacked and tied up in the last cell but one. Their belts with all their gear was taken and a prisoner called Warren was using the keys to open up the kitchen and the gym and the other places that was trashed. He was the ringleader. I was on the top landing trying to mind my own business, but the fumes got too much in the end and I had to leave the cell and run for it.'

Statement from Prisoner D, taken at HMP Cardiff, 16 December 2015:

'My cell was on the middle landing where the trouble started and I heard something was being planned. I was surprised. It's the quiet ones you have to watch. I can't think what got into Warren, thinking he could mastermind an escape. He let a few of us know he had friends outside and none of us believed him, but in the end he was proved right about that, even if these mates of his cocked up. I mean, the riot went to plan. He knew there were plenty of idiots happy to join in smashing up furniture and lighting fires. Personally, I stayed out of it. I may have done a bit of shouting to show solidarity, if you know what I mean, but I didn't throw nothing or start a fire and I wasn't on the roof.'

Such innocence. Diamond read the statements a third time. They had more vitality than the dull prose making up the rest of the report. If Magda could be believed, they were mostly fiction, but they conveyed something of the chaos inside the prison that morning three years ago. He was fairly sure Prisoner C – interviewed at the Scrubs – was Joe Irving. The hard man of C Wing had certainly been transferred there in the mass relocation after the riot.

The surprise was that someone called Warren was apparently the prime mover in all this. Diamond had expected Jack Peace to be named, or else why had Magda insisted he studied the report?

He found her business card and called her mobile number.

'Miss Lyle?'

'Magda, for pity's sake. Is this DS Diamond?'

'It is. Sorry to disturb your evening but I've started reading the report of the riot.'

'Best of British with that.'

'One thing puzzles me.'

'Only one?'

'These statements that were taken later all mention a prisoner called Warren.'

'Yes.'

'Who was he?'

She laughed. 'Haven't you worked that out? It's Jack Peace. Everyone inside is given a nickname. His was Warren, get it?'

'Oh.' Said flatly in a tone showing he didn't get it.

'Warren Peace.'

'War and Peace.' He winced at the pun and then rather enjoyed it. 'I was way behind you there.'

'What did you make of those statements?' she asked. 'Was that collusion, or what?'

'Could well be.'

'To me, they shouted stitch-up.'

Diamond was trying to keep emotion out of it, but he could understand Magda's heartfelt need to prove her case. 'To be fair, they were taken months after the event. The prisoners had been dispersed to other prisons. And the wording isn't similar.'

'That would be too obvious,' she said. 'You've got to understand how Irving's influence extends outside the walls of any one prison. People go in fear of him wherever they end up. They'll do as he orders. No one would dare name him as the organiser.'

'Did the investigation team speak to this man Muscles?'

'They wouldn't have got anything out of him. Believe me, Muscles doesn't have the IQ of a jellyfish.'

'Was his sentence increased?'

'He's a lifer already. I think he lost some privileges. I don't suppose he noticed.'

'Were others punished besides Jack Peace?'

'A few got their terms increased by short amounts. Nothing compared to what he was given.'

'Presumably he was interviewed and given a chance to defend himself?'

'I'm sure he must have been, but I wasn't there. I was getting over a double amputation.'

He paused. In his eagerness, he was overlooking the suffering she'd endured and would for the rest of her life. 'I know, and I'm sorry to be pestering you. You were interviewed by the inquiry team, you said.'

'Some jerk with a tape recorder who asked me about my

kidnapping and damn all else. He didn't want my take on the inmates and he wasn't there to tell me about the riot. I'm not sure I wanted to know at the time. I had my own troubles.'

'But you became interested since.'

'Because they got it wrong and an innocent man took the rap for that ogre Irving. And I don't mind admitting there's a personal edge to this. I'm angry about losing my legs. You'll be thinking the car crash was down to me and you're right, but I'm not happy that Irving walks free. Can't you arrest him now?'

'It's coming soon. Very soon.'

'Still looking for the smoking gun?'

'We found that. We're waiting for forensics to tell us who fired the bloody thing.'

He went back to reading the report. Every anodyne word from the terms of reference to the summary of conclusions. Most of it was about as interesting as a mug of cold tea. Then he looked for anything he might have missed. Two hours later, he knew for certain who had fired that gun. Without any help from forensics.

In the morning, he was at his buoyant best, ready to wrap this up. Georgina stood in his way before he even got to the CID room. 'Peter, the key results are in from forensics and ballistics.'

'My favourite double act. Forensics and ballistics. Shame you can only ever catch them on the late, late show.'

She frowned. 'Are you complaining? It's only three days since the body was found. They have to be thorough.'

'What do they say?'

'We have a DNA result for the victim.'

'Jack Peace?'

She blinked. 'You know his name already?'

'Information received, ma'am. I take no credit. And did they identify the other scrap of DNA found on the gun?'

'I'm sorry to disappoint you, but no. Not known on the national database.'

'Anything else at the scene apart from the mask and the handgun?'

'Plenty of unrelated scraps of rubbish. After all, hundreds of visitors pass through there every day. The only things I noticed that may be relevant are several scraps of confetti.'

'Most likely from the bridesmaids. Can't get excited about that.'

'You'll be able to read the findings for yourself, emailed to us both at my request.'

'No traces on the victim's clothes?'

'Evidently not. The one small oddity is that the bullet-holes in the mask didn't quite match the positions on the head. They weren't just above the level of the eye-holes, as you'd expect. They were higher up. I'm thinking he may have pulled the mask down over his eyes before firing the gun.'

'Why would he have done that?'

'The stress of the moment. I don't think it's significant. On balance, we have a case of suicide here.'

The blood pressure soared. 'What sort of balance is that, ma'am? For a start, the entry wound suggested he was left-handed and he wasn't.'

Georgina nodded. 'I heard this was troubling you and I spoke to the pathologist.'

'Sealy?' He uttered the name as if it had been scraped off the road.

'He said it's not by any means unknown for a right-handed person to use the left hand to shoot himself. In fact, he told me it was quite possible Peace had damaged a tendon in his right hand when climbing the wall.'

Diamond didn't dignify that hypothesis with a comment. He vibrated his lips in disgust. 'Did he also have a theory as to why a hardened criminal on a murder mission changes his mind and ends his own life?'

'There's no need for sarcasm, Peter.'

'Excuse me, ma'am, but there's every need for suspicion about what happened. Did forensics confirm that the gun had been wiped before the prints were made?'

'They don't appear to regard it as significant. You may have to accept, Peter, that you're reading too much into the circumstances.' She drew a sharp breath in the way she had of delivering the knockout. 'I've had the coroner on the phone about setting a date for an inquest. He's far too discreet to give an opinion, but he must have read the papers and he remarked that we've had quite a spate of suicides this summer.'

Even the bloody coroner was putting on the squeeze.

Shaking his head, he walked away from Georgina. Nothing he'd heard had changed his mind.

Inside the CID room, he put all that behind him, rubbed his hands and pumped himself up for the face-to-face with Irving. 'Did you pick him up? Where are we holding him?'

Keith Halliwell looked up. 'Bit of a setback there, guv. We had to force an entry into Sion Hill Place. He's done a runner.'

35

An all-units call was put out for the arrest of Joe Irving. Most units wouldn't need the description and mugshot. The Baron of Bath was well enough known already.

'He couldn't have learned about the dawn raid,' Diamond said. 'We only made the decision last night.'

'I expect he knew the net was closing in,' Halliwell said.

'How? He put on a good front when I saw him. This is out of character.' He trusted his team. It was unlikely any of them had leaked the news. 'Could he simply have spent the night at a friend's house?'

'He shouldn't, under his probation order.'

'Since when did that dickhead pay any attention to the law?'

Ingeborg, across the room, said, 'Is the kitten gone?'

Halliwell said, 'Are you talking about Irving?'

'Oh, come on. Kitten, as in cat. Black and white, only a few weeks old. Big Joe is supposed to be taking care of it while his daughter is on her honeymoon.'

'I didn't see one.'

'Did you look round? It's a large house.'

'We were looking for a bloody great gangster, not a kitten.'

'If little Claude is there, Joe will be back. He wouldn't dare lose it. His daughter Caroline is the only person in the world he's scared of.'

'Cats are curious,' Diamond said. 'It would have made itself known.'

'If the kitten isn't there, Joe really is on the run.'

'You broke down the door, right? Maybe it made a bolt for freedom, too.'

'Now you've got me really worried,' Ingeborg said.

'I can't get worked up about a kitten,' Halliwell said. 'We boarded the place up before we left.'

'That's so cruel,' Ingeborg said in a rare outburst. 'If he's in there, he'll starve. If he's out, he'll be killed by a fox.'

Diamond wasn't thinking about Claude's survival. He was still trying to work out how Irving had got wind of their plan. The arrest team would have been briefed ahead of time and they'd include some uniformed men, but they'd understand the importance of security. Who else could have known apart from the dependable Halliwell?

With a stab of guilt, he recalled last evening's phone conversation with Magda Lyle. He'd told her the arrest was coming soon. The leak – if it was such – had come from him.

Without a word to anyone, he went into his own office and phoned her.

'After we spoke, did you have another go at Joe?'

'I phoned him, yes. I'm not in Bath to enjoy the sights, you know. I came here to get the truth out of that serpent. I wanted it when I came and now I know he murdered Jack Peace I want it even more.'

He was trying to contain his fury, as much with himself as Magda. 'I wish you'd left him to us.'

'Why? What's happened?'

'He's gone missing.'

She was silent for a few seconds. Then the defiant note changed to self-reproach. 'My big mouth.'

'Did he admit anything?'

'No.'

'But you warned him he would be arrested?'

'He was so damned pleased with himself, positively

gloating, telling me I have no power over him any more. I wanted to strike back at him. I'm sorry. That was unprofessional. I'm too closely involved to take a measured stance as you do. I won't interfere again.'

'We'll find him,' he said. 'I doubt if he's really on the run. It would dent his hard-man reputation. My reading of this is that it amused him to think of an early-morning police raid that came to nothing.'

He hadn't needed to soften the blow, but he empathised with Magda. His own career had been peppered with impetuous outbursts. She remained a brave woman he respected. He thanked her for being so frank and ended the call.

He genuinely believed what he'd told her. Joe was playing games.

The plan of action now forming in his own brain was not a game.

He opened those emails from forensics Georgina had taken such comfort from. His boss would always give her backing to whatever caused the least upheaval. Nothing short of an earthquake would shake her conviction that Jack Peace had taken his own life.

Dr Sealy and the coroner appeared to be of the same mind.

Was this one of those days when everything went belly up?

Point by point, he studied the findings from the lab. The scientists weren't under any obligation to prove Jack had put a gun to his head. They presented the facts they found and left it to CID to interpret them.

All the pressure was on him to explain how those same facts pointed to homicide. His trump card until a few minutes ago had been the unlikely event of a right-handed man shooting himself in the left temple. Now Sealy, an expert, had said such a thing was possible.

A second opinion would help.

Somewhere he had a phone number for Jim Middleton, forensic pathologist now retired. Middleton had attended several of the homicides Diamond had investigated in his earlier years in Bath. In CID he was known as Motormouth, but his knowledge was unquestioned.

He found the number in a dog-eared address book in the bottom drawer of his desk. Good thing he threw nothing away except official bumf.

'Peter, how are you?' Jim's familiar voice said and started a monologue of reminiscence it was impossible to stop for some minutes.

At length, Diamond staunched the flow with his query.

Middleton actually paused to think. 'The site of election was the left temple, was it? Certainly that suggests a left-handed man, but it's not an absolute rule, old friend. I came across three or four exceptions in my years in the job. Don't ask me why it happens.' Without pause for breath he supplied a theory. 'None of us can get into the thoughts of a man who shoots himself, thank God. Could be nervousness pulling the trigger. He can't will himself to do it straight off, so he changes over and tries with the less dominant hand. Does that make sense?'

'Thanks, Jim,' Diamond said, anything but thankful, and ended the call as soon as he could.

His trump card was unplayable.

36

If Diamond was right, and Joe Irving hadn't panicked and disappeared over the horizon, he would still be in Bath and it wouldn't take much detective work to track the creep down. Go alone and unarmed, he had decided. The dawn raid had been a mistake.

He was confident where he would find him. He had driven out to Camden Crescent, where Caroline and Ben lived. Currently, of course, the newlyweds were honeymooning in the Bahamas, funded by Irving.

After one glance at the house, Diamond phoned the CID room and told Halliwell to call off the hunt. He'd spotted Claude the kitten sunning himself at a ground-floor window.

Fortune favours those who use their judgement.

'Are you alone, guv?' Halliwell asked. 'Do you want back-up?'

'No thanks. I can handle Claude.'

'It's not Claude I'm thinking of.'

'Trust me, Keith. I know what I'm doing.'

He left the phone in the car, marched up to the door, pressed the bell and heard chimes and the tread of a large man.

'Found you.'

Irving raised an eyebrow.

'A condition of your release is that you reside permanently at the address you supplied. That isn't here.'

No answer.

'Are we going to speak inside?'

A shrug and he was admitted to the gracious sitting room he'd last entered the day he'd walked up the hill with George Brace.

Claude jumped off the sill and scampered over.

A sitting room it was, well furnished with chairs, but the two remained standing, facing each other like gunfighters.

'You lied to me about not knowing Jack Peace. You were on the same wing in Bream Prison for – how long? Six months? A year?'

'Who the fuck are you talking about?'

'The man found dead in the Roman Baths. I showed you his picture and you made out you'd never seen him before. Jack Peace got shafted for masterminding the riot in 2015.'

'That was Warren.'

'One and the same. Warren was his nickname.'

'You're confusing me,' Irving said.

'Don't try that. You made a statement to the inquiry naming him. I've read the report. You said Warren was the ringleader and you were on the top landing minding your own business. Familiar?'

'I forget.'

'Warren, as you call him, had his sentence increased by three years on the perjured evidence of you and a few others. No wonder he was bitter. The poor sucker was stitched up.'

'You been listening to that governor bitch,' Irving said, spurred finally to say more than the minimum. 'She don't know nothing. She weren't even there that morning.'

'Two prison officers were. You and your mob attacked them and banged them up in a cell.'

'With bags over their heads.' Slyly he added, 'I was told.'

'You were told,' Diamond said in a tone that exposed the claim for the lie it was.

'They saw shit all.'

'They're willing to testify that you ran C Wing.' Diamond waded chest-deep into fantasy. The men had testified no such thing to the inquiry and he hadn't sought them out. 'And so are plenty of others who were serving at Bream.'

'Too late now, ain't it?' Irving said, still unfazed.

'The riot was all your doing, to set up your escape.'

'Careful what you say, copper.'

'I'm being careful,' Diamond said. 'I'm doing you the favour of saying it to you in private. I'm not wired up, in case you were wondering, and my phone is in the car outside.' He opened his jacket wide. 'You planned the whole thing with your friends outside. They kidnapped Miss Lyle and drove her to the prison and then it all backfired because she was brave enough to cause the crash.'

'All done?' Irving bent down and scooped up the kitten with one huge hand. 'Are you going to leave me in peace now?'

'I've barely started,' Diamond said. 'There's the killing of Jack Peace.'

Keith Halliwell checked the time again. More than an hour had passed since that phone call from the boss. He was worried. He understood the reason Diamond had chosen to go unaccompanied to interview Irving. The two men were poles apart in the eyes of the law, but some sort of rapport had been forged between them during the weekend. Irving was more likely to open up without a third person being present. However, the CID protocol of only ever visiting suspects in pairs was founded on good sense. Aside from safety in numbers, the officer in support was a witness to everything that was said.

Why wasn't Diamond answering his phone? He ought to be out of Camden Crescent by now. An hour for an interview was excessive. He always came quickly to the point.

'Maybe he's gone for a drink,' Ingeborg said. 'He's had a pig of a morning.'

'He doesn't drink alone.'

'A late breakfast, then. Comfort eating. He knows the best places in town for a fry-up.'

'I don't know how you can be so flip. Joe Irving is evil and dangerous.'

'He's no fool. He's got more sense than to injure a cop.'

'We can't even tell for certain if Irving was inside. He could have left the kitten there with someone else in charge. His henchmen wouldn't think twice about putting in the boot.'

'In his daughter's house? I can't see it.'

Halliwell was still uneasy, chewing obsessively on his thumbnail.

'If you're so concerned,' Ingeborg said, 'you could check whether his car is still outside the house.'

'Good thinking.' Halliwell was on his feet, car key in hand, in need of immediate action.

'And if it's gone,' Ingeborg called out to him before the door swung shut, 'my theory of the late breakfast comes into play.' She found Halliwell's concern for the boss endearing and also amusing. Some men of that generation were like old hens over each other's safety.

Not long after Halliwell had left, John Leaman came in looking as if Miss World had asked him for a date. 'Where's the guv'nor?'

'Camden Crescent when we last heard from him.'

'And Keith?'

'Gone looking for him.'

'I need to speak to one of them. I've been talking to my snout, the guy with tabs on the Swindon arms smuggler.'

'Something new came up?'

'The boss will like this. Jack Peace was supplied with two weapons, the AK-63 and the Glock 17.'

'John, he knows this already,' Ingeborg said. 'We recovered both of them.'

'No, we didn't,' Halliwell said. 'The Glock found in the hypocaust was generation five, the latest model, remember? The guy in Swindon swears that the handgun he supplied to Peace was gen three, first issued in 1998.'

She thought about that for a couple of seconds. 'Is he reliable?'

'My snout? Sure.'

'The Swindon guy.'

'Absolutely. You see what it means?' Leaman said, more animated than she'd ever seen him. 'The gun found beside the body wasn't the one he was carrying. It was brought in by his killer. He can't have committed suicide. There's no argument any more. It was murder.'

'Smart work.'

'Can we call him?'

She shook her head. 'We've been trying. He's on voicemail.'

'Who's he with?'

She told him and he said, 'Bloody hell.'

Diamond's car was still parked in front of Camden Crescent, a full hour and a half since he'd gone in.

Halliwell was more troubled than ever, faced with a real dilemma. Knock on the door and interrupt a crucial interrogation and get the full force of Diamond's fury. Do nothing and miss a chance to save the boss's life – if it wasn't already too late.

He wasn't armed. Another option was to ask for armed assistance and storm the place – with the same risk of fouling up a delicate operation.

Undecided, he got out of the car and walked slowly towards the house and past it.

Not a movement was visible through the casement windows of the front room.

He took a few more tormented steps, turned and tried for a second look, hoping to God that this time it would be different and he'd see a sign of life as he walked past.

And God delivered.

Just when Halliwell drew level with the house, the front door opened and Joe Irving emerged, hands behind his back. Then – praise the Lord – Diamond stepped out as well. He was carrying what appeared to be a box-shaped canvas bag. He closed the door behind him, turned and noticed Halliwell rooted to the spot a few yards from him.

'Ah, Keith,' Diamond said as if he'd been expecting nothing less than one of his team to be waiting outside the door. 'You can carry this.'

He handed over the bag, now revealed as a pet carrier. Through the mesh window, Claude the kitten was visible, sitting serenely.

And it was now apparent that Joe Irving was handcuffed.

37

Advance news had reached Concorde House that Diamond was bringing in the crime baron, so there were interested faces at the plate-glass windows of the CID room when the car came up the drive. It was unusual for any prisoner to be brought here. They were supposed to be taken to the custody suite at Keynsham. But as John Leaman remarked to Ingeborg Smith with a shake of the head, if there was a rule the guv'nor hadn't broken in his time, he'd like to know what it was.

Diamond was out first and opened the car door for his prisoner, who had the look of a defeated man, head bowed and wrists cuffed. Diamond took a grip on Irving's arm and steered him towards the main entrance. From the back of the car, a sheepish Keith Halliwell emerged with the pet carrier.

'Yay,' Ingeborg said. 'They arrested the kitten as well.'

'I'm going down to meet them,' Leaman said, eager to share his sensational new information about the existence of a second handgun.

'I wouldn't,' Ingeborg said.

'Why not?'

'See the look on his face?'

'You've got good eyesight if you can tell from here.'

'I'd call it his take-no-prisoners look, except he's actually taken a prisoner.'

Leaman took her advice. She was the best in the team at judging Diamond's moods.

Not a word was spoken when the boss and his sullen captive entered the CID room. They crossed to Diamond's own office and the door slammed behind them – a sure sign that interruptions wouldn't be welcomed.

When Halliwell walked in a few seconds later, he placed the pet carrier on Ingeborg's desk. 'Do you mind?'

She unzipped the sidepiece and lifted Claude out. 'Poor little scrap – he's terrified.'

She was a better judge of people than cats. Claude was in no mood to be comforted. He squirmed free and strutted across her desk to investigate the box of tissues she kept beside her computer screen.

'Is it house-trained?' Leaman asked.

'Must be,' Ingeborg said.

'I don't want it on my desk.'

'I don't suppose he's interested in your desk unless he wants to leave his calling card.'

Unamused, Leaman turned to Halliwell. 'Has Irving confessed yet?'

'I'm not sure. Not much was said in the car. I didn't dare ask. I could feel the electricity between them.'

'Why has he brought him here?'

'More questions, I guess.'

'Why not at Keynsham?'

'His decision.'

'It ought to be done properly and on tape. The CPS won't be happy with this.'

'I'm sure he knows what he's doing. This may be a way of buying more time. We can hold the bastard for breaking his probation order and hit him with the murder charge when we're ready.'

Leaman didn't look impressed. He went back to his desk.

291

Halliwell left the room to see if he could get a lift back to Bath to collect his own car, still parked at Camden Crescent.

'Looks as if I'm left to take care of Claude,' Ingeborg said with a sigh.

'That'll be no hardship,' Leaman said from across the room.

The kitten was still on Ingeborg's desk, nudging her computer mouse across the shiny surface, when the Assistant Chief Constable, Georgina, made an unexpected entrance.

'What's that animal doing here?'

'I'm keeping an eye on it, ma'am, while DS Diamond is in conference with Mr Irving.'

'In *conference?*'

'Questioning him, we believe. He brought him here in handcuffs.'

'Under arrest? Why wasn't I informed?'

Tricky.

Ingeborg said. 'They only came in a short while ago.'

'If there were plans to bring in a major criminal like him, I should have been consulted first and so should head-quarters.' She started towards Diamond's door, thought better of it, and said, 'He's put me in an impossible position. I don't want to question his authority in Irving's presence. It would undermine us all.'

'Yes, ma'am.'

'Ask him to report to me as a matter of urgency as soon as you see him alone.'

'I will, ma'am.'

'And put the kitten back in its box, or whatever it arrived in.'

She strode out, powered by her own invective.

Leaman looked over his screen. 'Rather you than me, asking him to report to her.'

'What's going on in there?' Ingeborg asked.

Leaman's desk was against the wall of Diamond's office and occasionally he heard things. He pressed his ear to the plasterboard.

'He's making phone calls. They've stopped talking and he's been on and off the phone. I can't hear what he's saying, but he's saying it to a lot of people.'

'Maybe he'll phone Georgina and save me the job of telling him to report to her.'

'You can hope.'

Diamond did eventually emerge, only to put his face around the door and say to Ingeborg, 'Be an angel and nip out for two packs of sandwiches. I can't leave him alone. A BLT and an egg mayo preferably. Some crisps and a six-pack of lager. Do you have money?'

She nodded. Normally anyone of any rank asking her to run an errand like that would get an earful from Ingeborg, but she sensed that this was an exceptional request. 'Guv, the ACC looked in.'

'I know,' he said. 'I've calmed her down on the phone. Thanks.' He closed the door again.

'Doughnuts for me,' Leaman said as she was reaching for her bag.

'Piss off.'

When she returned and tapped on the boss's door, he shouted for her to come in.

Joe Irving was slumped in the armchair in the corner, apparently no happier than when he'd arrived, but he wasn't wearing the handcuffs. Diamond was seated behind his own desk.

She handed across the bag.

'Who's outside?' he asked.

'John and me. And Claude.'

'Keith?'

'He went to fetch his car. And Paul's still getting over the attack. Guv, John would like a word. He has some more news from his snout and he thinks it will help.'

'Send him in.'

'With present company in the room?'

'You heard what I said.' There was a real sense of urgency about him. 'And rally the troops. I'll brief them individually. I'm going to need everyone I can get tonight. I've arranged to do a reconstruction in the hypocaust at six-thirty. All interested parties are being invited and Mr Irving here will be cooperating.'

You could have shelved the Encyclopædia Britannica on the jut of Mr Irving's lower lip. If that look promised cooperation, she could only hope Diamond would be bringing a cattle prod to the reconstruction.

38

'What sort of stunt is this?' Leaman complained. 'In all the years I've endured in CID I can't remember him doing such a thing. It's like the last chapter of an old-fashioned detective story.'

'Detective stories are the new cool,' Ingeborg said. 'I'm sure he knows what he's doing. I've been given my instructions and I expect you've got yours.'

They were in the palatial entrance hall of the Roman Baths, where the wedding guests had been received on Saturday evening. The gathering wasn't as big as before. Diamond hadn't brought in the string quartet, or the champagne and canapés, but there was likely to be a speech. All of CID had turned up, even Paul Gilbert, no longer sporting a surgical dressing but with three stitches visible in his head wound. Georgina, frowning a lot and clearly of the same mind as Leaman about this jamboree, was watching from the side with George Brace, who appeared more forgiving and willing to see what emerged. Both were still in uniform. The two armed policemen who had patrolled the building before the reception were present with their Heckler and Koch assault rifles across their chests, trigger fingers poised, no doubt conscious that they were under the scrutiny of the top brass and trying hard to appear reassuring rather than threatening. They still got some uneasy looks.

Maurice the photographer and Dixie, his fixer, were

looking lost without a camera and groups to organise. Diamond had asked them to attend in case this re-enactment triggered a helpful memory. They had been closer than anyone to the scene of the killing at the time it was supposed to have happened.

George's wife, Leticia, was the only other one of the principal guests able (and more than willing) to attend. Her outfit in shocking pink was as dressy as the one she'd worn for the wedding, even running to another spectacular hat. She was treating the occasion as if she attended crime reconstructions every week, mingling and chatting animatedly to everyone.

'Where's your sexy superintendent?' she asked Ingeborg, who couldn't at first think who was meant. 'Peter Diamond, my dear.'

'Oh.' Lost for words, Ingeborg could only assume Leticia was using irony.

'You're lucky enough to be on his team, aren't you?'

'I'm sure he'll be here presently with Mr Irving.'

'Joe, you mean, the father of the bride? A dark horse, that one. Surprised us all.'

'How was that?'

'His speech. Perfect for the occasion. Witty and wise and so sincere. He had us eating out of his hand.'

Difficult to picture, but Ingeborg knew what was meant. She'd heard about Irving's speech from Diamond, her sexy boss. Sexy? She couldn't wait to share that titbit with the rest of CID.

'I thought Joe Irving was a man of few words.'

'So did we all until he opened his mouth.' Leticia's grasshopper mind hopped to another subject. 'And are you the young lady looking after the kitten?'

'For the time being.' Ingeborg switched her own thought to the furry visitor currently installed at home in her bedroom with a good supply of kitten food, a catnip toy and a litter tray. He ought to be all right for an hour or so.

'From all I hear, you could be its permanent owner soon.'

'I don't think so. Claude belongs to Caroline. She'll get him back after the honeymoon.'

Leticia's attention had moved on again. 'Who's the woman with artificial legs who just came in?'

'Miss Lyle. She was governor of the prison where Joe Irving and Jack Peace did time together.'

'Thought so. My husband told me about her. Got the OBE, and deserved it. Strictly between ourselves, there are some sour grapes. George would dearly love to get an honour himself. It's not for want of trying. I must meet her.' To Leticia this was a networking exercise no different from a cocktail party. She moved off in Magda's direction.

Finally Diamond arrived with Joe Irving. Big Joe wasn't in handcuffs any longer. His body language – head bowed and shoulders sagging as if he was trying not to stand out as the tallest man in the room – suggested he was unlikely to make a dash for freedom. The spirit that had fuelled the best speech at the wedding had drained from him.

Diamond did the right thing and spoke briefly to George and Georgina before calling everyone to order by rapping the black case he had brought in with him. It was about the size of a large book and the thermo-moulded plastic made an arresting sound.

'Thank you, good people,' he said. 'I'm Peter Diamond, head of Bath CID, and I've just been asked to make clear that this get-together is entirely unofficial. Avon and Somerset Police are not responsible for anything that happens. Guns are present, as you may have noticed. We're in the business of law and order. But you are free to leave at any time unless you work for me or commit a crime in the next ten minutes.'

Some nervous laughter greeted this.

'Some of you – not all – were present in this building on Saturday night when a fatality occurred downstairs in a part of the baths called the hypocaust. Not everyone knew at the time that a man's body was discovered late in the evening. He'd died from a head wound inflicted with a handgun at point-blank range. There was some question whether he committed suicide or was murdered. Suicide was hard to explain in the circumstances, but then so was murder. Presently we'll all go down to the hypocaust and I'll point out the difficulty we have.

'I want to tell you about this unfortunate man. I say "unfortunate" and you're probably thinking anyone who ends up dead is unfortunate. Actually, Jack Peace was also a villain, an armed gunman intent on committing murder at an event that should be entirely joyful. He'd recently been released from prison and he had a massive grudge. Three years had been added to his sentence for organising a prison riot in 2015 that resulted in serious damage and minor injuries to prison officers. Two people also died outside the prison gates, but Peace couldn't be held responsible for their deaths, or he would have faced a charge of manslaughter at the least. The inquiry into the incident took evidence from several of the prison inmates and they named Jack Peace as the main man. I can tell you tonight that those convicts lied to the inquiry. There was a conspiracy to get Peace blamed. I have it on the best possible evidence.' He turned towards Joe Irving. 'Shall I tell them or will you?'

Joe shook his head slowly, eyes as animated as crushed beetles.

'In fact,' Diamond resumed, 'Jack Peace played no part at all in the violence at the prison. He was coming to the end of his term and was due to be released. The others were so angry when he refused to join in that they left him and

298

another man locked in a cell throughout the riot. Peace had good reason to be bitter.'

Diamond paused and looked around the room, assessing the response. 'You're wondering who was really behind the riot and I can tell you now. He's standing here beside me and his name is Joe Irving. He was the father of the bride and he's well known to us in Bath Police. Whether inside jail or out, he runs various rackets in the city. He's a crook, powerful and dangerous.'

Joe's bowed head showed no reaction. He must have been warned what to expect.

'I can tell you he was the organiser because he confessed to me under questioning this afternoon. The whole point of the disturbance at the prison was to create a diversion so that his lordship Joe Irving could make an escape bid. There's never any shortage of prisoners willing to join in a riot and he ruled the wing with a group of thugs who made sure his orders were carried out. Anyone brave enough or reckless enough to refuse could expect trouble – and that's what happened to the unfortunate Jack Peace and his cellmate, a mentally challenged man known as Muscles. They were left in their cell and they could have died there if the flames had really taken hold on the middle landing.'

Someone called out, 'Shame!'

Diamond said, 'Am I telling it right, Joe?'

Irving was a spent force, like some captive chief being paraded and goaded in the Colosseum.

Leaman said in a muttered aside to Ingeborg, 'What's got into the boss? Why is he doing this?'

'There's got to be a good reason,' she said, but her loyalty was under strain. She didn't like the way this seemed to be heading. Playing on people's emotions wasn't Diamond's style.

'No wonder Peace was an angry man,' Diamond went on. 'No one can justify what he did next, but I can understand why he did it, and perhaps you can as well. Not long after he was released, he heard about the forthcoming wedding here in Bath of Joe Irving's daughter, Caroline, to Ben Brace, the son of the Deputy Chief Constable, and he saw it as the perfect opportunity to right the injustice he'd suffered. Two charming and innocent young people prepared for their big day with no inkling of what was being planned. Peace went to someone who traded in illegal weapons and armed himself with an assault rifle and a handgun. He scouted the Abbey and its surroundings for a place to use as a sniper's vantage point and chose one on the roof of this building, just above where I'm standing. It overlooked the Abbey front, where the wedding guests would arrive and emerge and pose for photographs. He climbed the side of the building after dark the night before and set up the gun.'

His audience would know that Jack Peace's plan hadn't succeeded, but they hadn't been aware until now how close it came to success, and the thought of what might have happened was obvious in their faces.

'You'd expect some level of security at a wedding involving the families of a senior police officer and a gang leader and that's how I came to be involved. I was asked to be present as a precaution. Of course, we had no inkling at that stage of what Jack Peace was planning, but we had to be ready in case some rival crime baron decided to make an attack. On the day, a number of officers in uniform and plain clothes were posted at key points near the Abbey. I myself attended the wedding and the reception. Unknown to any of us, the young officer posted on the Roman Baths roof was attacked by Peace, beaten with the butt of the rifle and knocked unconscious. He was tied up and gagged and he's lucky to have escaped with his life. He almost drowned at one stage, lying in a gutter.'

Keith Halliwell nudged Paul Gilbert and said, 'Take a bow.'

Gilbert reddened and did a fair imitation of a tortoise retreating under its shell.

Diamond had moved on. 'Well, anyone who was at the wedding will know it was held in a rainstorm, a right cloudburst, in fact. Your typical British summer afternoon. Umbrellas were out and nobody lingered outside the West Door – which was fortunate, because the would-be killer couldn't get an accurate shot in, before or after the service. The photography was postponed, but we make the best of a weather crisis, don't we, and it was decided to have a photo session instead at the evening reception here at the baths.

'What does Jack Peace do about that? He isn't going to be beaten by the weather. After all the trouble he's gone to, he won't give up now. The blood lust hasn't gone away. He knows there is sure to be another opportunity if he can find a way inside this building and he has a few hours to plan his next move. There's a ten-foot wall that separates the roof above us from the Great Bath. If he can climb that, he'll be inside the baths and have the run of the place. He leaves the assault rifle and most of his equipment behind. A single handgun will do the job. He waits for the baths to close, when not many people are about, and climbs over.'

Diamond paused. He'd picked this moment to leave them in suspense. 'And now I'd like to show you where he got in. The best view is from the side of the Great Bath. Follow me down there, but please go carefully on the stairs – especially you guys with your fingers on the triggers.'

The joke fell flat, judged by the response. There was some hesitation before anyone moved, but once a few had gone, the others followed.

The giant manta that was Leticia's latest hat flapped into Ingeborg's field of vision. 'Isn't he a star?' the smitten lady said, still bedazzled. 'He makes it all so real. I was at the

301

wedding and I hadn't the foggiest a gunman was stalking us and we were in danger of our lives. None of us would have guessed. And to think we worried about nothing more than getting a few spots of rain on our clothes.'

'Puts it in perspective,' Ingeborg said, consumed with her own concerns about the wisdom of what Diamond was doing.

Keith Halliwell passed them on the stairs at a speed of knots. He was under instructions to move ahead and take up a position in the hypocaust.

Beside the Great Bath, the gas flares had been turned on and were mirrored in the water. Here at the Roman level it required no imagination to travel two thousand years into the past. The attendees clustered around three sides of the end where Diamond positioned himself.

'This was where everyone assembled for the delayed photo session,' he resumed, resolved to keep the minds of his audience on the recent past. 'The obligatory picture of all the guests first, followed by family groups and finally the bride and groom themselves. You will understand how anxious I was feeling in my role as security adviser. The armed police had made their check of the building and left. We didn't want them standing around all evening frightening everyone. But take a glance behind you and you'll see any number of shadowy places where some evil-minded person could be hiding. Where are our photographers, Maurice and Dixie?'

Two hands went up on the left side.

'You may remember trying to bring me into line for the group picture, calling my name through the loud-hailer when I was skulking in the background. Now you know why I was camera-shy. You never did get me in the photo. Mr Irving here came to my rescue and announced in colourful terms that I was indisposed, isn't that so, Joe?'

Irving, still at his side, managed a nod, no more at ease

302

than he had been at the beginning. Diamond was keeping him in the spotlight at every opportunity.

'I had the same misgivings through the wedding breakfast and the disco. Little did I realise that the emergency was over and the only person who presented any danger was already dead. As I told you upstairs, he climbed over the wall from outside. If you look above the arched windows where I'm pointing you can see the slope of a tiled roof. That's where Jack Peace got in. He will have climbed down the drainpipe at the far end and then used the stairs. This happened shortly after six when the last of the afternoon visitors had left. At this stage he was looking for a place to lie up and wait. He may have thought about hiding here, behind the masonry at the back, but he will have changed his mind when he saw our friends Maurice and Dixie setting up their tripod for the photos. Did you happen to notice anyone lurking in the shadows, Dixie?'

'Only you, Peter,' Dixie called across the water and got a laugh. In case he took it badly, she added, 'Sorry, but we had our minds on the job.'

'You don't have to be sorry. Our gunman was a pro as well, used to staying out of view. Best to find a place well away from you two, he thought, so he went through the open doorway at the end to explore the west baths, by now deserted and in darkness. He'd wait there until all the guests were in and settled, either for the photographs or the meal. Then he'd sneak in and get close and fire the fatal shot. In the confusion he'd have a good chance of escaping. Let's move on to the hypocaust and see what really happened.'

Ingeborg stood back with Paul, letting the others file through.

Leticia said, 'Aren't you coming in for the final bit?'

'We have to make sure no one trips over,' Ingeborg improvised. In truth they were acting as sheepdogs.

303

'Is it really dark in there? Where's my better half? I'm getting nervous.'

George Brace heard, left Georgina's side, and came over.

'Take my arm, dear,' he told her. 'I'm sure there's some form of lighting.'

'If anyone jumps out from behind a pillar I'll scream.'

The last of the party took the paved way through the next room and past the thirty-foot-wide circular bath where the Romans once cooled off after a dip in the thermal water.

John Leaman was acting as marshal in the viewing area that overlooked the hypocaust, urging the early arrivals to move along and make room for the rest. Once in, they were distributed comfortably along the Plexiglass barrier. Just as George had promised his wife, there was subdued lighting, yet the stacks of terracotta tiles in the large space below still cast shadows that made it an eerie place to be after the violent death a few days before.

Diamond stood among his listeners with the sombre Joe Irving still so close that they might have been handcuffed together, his height a help to anyone wanting to know where Diamond was standing.

'Everyone in? Welcome to the tepidarium, to use its proper name, a little chilly this evening, but warm when the Romans were here because of the underfloor heating. You modern visitors will have to rely on the hot air I'm giving out.'

Another joke bombed.

'It must be the way I tell them. Joe made a better fist of it at the wedding. His speech had them rolling in the aisles, didn't it, my friend?'

The curl of Irving's lip wasn't the response of a friend.

Diamond motored on. 'So this was the place Jack Peace chose to hide in. It was supposed to be off-limits after six p.m., and it would have been deserted and in semi-darkness when he found it. He hunkered down in one of the rows between the stacks.' He took a torch from his pocket. 'I'll show you exactly where.'

Some shocked cries were heard when the beam picked out a crouching human form three-quarters of the way back.

'No cause for alarm. That's one of my team, DCI Halliwell. For this demonstration he's standing in for Mr Peace, who can't be with us. Show us you're alive, Keith.'

Halliwell's hand appeared above the stacks and waved.

'The question we had to ask ourselves was this: did Peace commit suicide or was he murdered? We can discount an accident. People don't hold a gun to their heads and pull the trigger by mistake. If he shot himself, why, for heaven's sake? He was on a mission and he'd found a good hiding place. He'd had some setbacks, but he was still well placed to get revenge for those lost years in prison.

'No, it was murder. Jack Peace had to be stopped. He was bent on committing murder himself, creating mayhem at the wedding. He couldn't be allowed to do it. This was clear to me from early on. What I couldn't understand was how it was done.'

Diamond swung the torch beam slowly across the hypocaust revealing the narrow spaces where the heated air had circulated. The stacks of square tiles, ten or twelve high, some cracked and broken, some clearly rebuilt from the debris found in the excavation, were about as sturdy as towers of playing cards. Too slender to provide cover, they were too close to move through with any confidence. 'Peace was well defended here. He had sightlines all around him, the full 360 degrees. Getting close to him without making a sound and giving yourself away, knocking down a tile, crunching on stone, tripping on the uneven floor, was impossible. I've tried crossing that floor and, believe me, you can't do it unseen and unheard. I couldn't do it. A man Joe's size certainly couldn't. I doubt if a cat could.

'So how did it happen? I'll demonstrate. The killer enters just as we did a moment ago, except he creeps in unnoticed. That's possible in the viewing gallery here. Not down among the tiles. He's on the lookout for a gunman, so he's ultra-careful. He senses this is a likely hiding-place and he catches sight of Peace's dark form skulking among the stacks. He's come prepared.'

With the flourish of a magician performing his best trick, Diamond raised his arm and held high the black plastic case he'd been carrying from the beginning, turning each way so that everyone had a sight of it. 'Any guesses?'

'A gun,' someone said.

'Correct.' He lowered the case and placed it in the hands of the main suspect, the man who'd been shadowing him throughout, Joe Irving.

There were gasps.

'Open it, please.'

Joe unfastened the double-throw latch and raised the lid. Diamond reached in and took out a black pistol. 'A Glock 17, the weapon of choice for law enforcement around the world, including our own police authority. And, regrettably, the criminal world. Peace's handgun was also a Glock 17. But this little beauty in my hand has an extra attachment I learned to use recently on the firearms course, a laser sight. It projects a laser beam that shows on the target as a red or green spot. With a laser, even a cack-handed shooter like me can't miss.'

He aimed the gun into the hypocaust and instantly a red spot found Halliwell and glowed on his shirt.

'Relax, everybody. This isn't loaded, but if it was, I'd know I could hit Keith from here. And he'd know, too. If he looked down and saw the red spot on his shirt, he'd better do as I say, or else.

'And that, ladies and gents, solves the first mystery of what happened here on Saturday night. Jack Peace sees the laser spot on his body and knows it will be curtains if he even thinks about reaching for his own gun. Simple as that. He may even have the Glock in his hand, but it's too late to aim and fire. He's told to drop the gun and stand up straight with his hands held high. He obeys. That's your cue, Keith.'

The sound of a gun clattering on the floor was audible in the viewing area. Halliwell surfaced with hands up. He was wearing a black balaclava.

'But you're thinking Peace was shot at close range, and you're right. Still pointing the laser, the killer mounts the barrier and lets himself down into the hypocaust. That isn't easy one-handed for a man of my girth. I'll try and show you how it was done.'

He gripped the top of the Plexiglass barrier, hauled himself up and swung his left leg over, then his right. It wasn't a pretty sight, but he managed, still in control of the gun. From a sitting position he was able to lower himself to the top bricks of the original Roman wall and step down the damaged part to floor level.

The bright red spot had remained on Halliwell's shirt front throughout.

'Can you still hear me?' The sound quality of Diamond's voice had changed, but it carried easily to his rapt audience. 'You may be wondering why he doesn't shoot Peace from here when the aim is so accurate. He's already decided to stage a suicide and he needs to hold the gun to his victim's head. So he threads his way like this.'

Moving at a steady rate that enabled him to keep the laser spot on Halliwell's chest, he crossed the floor and closed in.

Standing beside Halliwell, he said, 'I can't tell you what was said. Very little, I suspect. Poor Jack Peace was expecting to be taken prisoner. Instead, his balaclava was tugged down, unsighting him. He felt the gun jammed to the side of his head, like so . . .'

Leticia said, 'Oh my God,' and covered her eyes.

The gun clicked.

'. . . and that was all he knew of it.'

Halliwell was no actor, but sudden deaths in shootouts are familiar to us all from gangster films and westerns. He played the scene with gusto, yelled in pain, dived to his right, twitched and lay still.

Diamond allowed that part of the reconstruction to speak for itself. 'This is when the crime scene needs fixing to confuse the forensic scientists. The killer unclips the laser sight from his gun and pockets it.' He wasn't slick at separating the two, but he managed it. 'He wipes his weapon clean –' he produced a cloth and performed the action – 'and then presses it into the dead man's hand with the fingers turned around the grip and trigger before letting it rest on the ground nearby.' He stooped beside Halliwell's fine imitation of a corpse, but he knew he couldn't be seen, so he used the moment to feel inside his own jacket for another item he'd brought with him, a taser. When he stood up again, he kept his grip on this unseen weapon, looking rather like Napoleon. And his commentary continued smoothly. 'He remembers to pick up the victim's own gun and hide it in his pocket. He's cool. Got to be.

'But three things are wrong. First, he's shot Peace in the left temple and made him left-handed. Mistake. He was right-handed. Okay, I've been told right-handers have been known to shoot themselves with their left, but that's unusual, an indication, if not proof.

'Second, we traced the supplier of Jack Peace's handgun. He told us the weapon Peace was carrying was a Glock 17, the same as he was shot with, but it wasn't the latest model, like the one found by his body. It was generation three, a type used in the late 1990s. Still popular, still lethal, but different in several details from the gen five found at the scene.

'The gun I brought here today is a gen five, a police-issue weapon on loan from the firearms training unit at Black Rock. We use the latest models. The guns in circulation among criminals like Peace tend to be older. I have to tell you that the murder weapon was a police-issue gun held and fired by' – a pause – 'one of our own.'

Watching his audience keenly, he took a couple of steps towards them.

'When I said Jack Peace expected to be taken prisoner it was because his pursuer was a police officer in uniform. And now—'

A voice from the viewing gallery yelled, 'No you don't.'

George Brace had produced a gun.

But in the same split-second, Diamond whipped out the taser and fired it. Like the handgun he'd demonstrated, the electroshock weapon had a laser sight. The barbed electrodes on conductive wires hit Brace in the chest and delivered fifty thousand volts.

He screamed and keeled over.

He wasn't the only one who screamed.

In the ensuing panic, Georgina's voice was clearest. 'Oh my sainted aunt! What's he done now? He's tasered the Deputy Chief Constable.'

A taser incapacitates the person targeted for about five seconds. In that time, Ingeborg and John Leaman knelt on George Brace and disarmed him. Others reverted to type. Leticia hyperventilated. Joe looked faintly bored. Georgina vowed to murder Peter Diamond. Maurice took out his smartphone and photographed the scene. Dixie attempted to salvage some order from the chaos.

Explanations would have to wait.

39

Magda Lyle and Georgina joined Diamond in his office next morning. Magda had brought her West Highland terrier, Blanche, who settled by her feet and went to sleep.

Diamond didn't mind defending his handling of the case. He'd need to be convincing in his report to the Crown Prosecution Service.

'I know the tasering and the arrest came as a shock to you, ma'am, and I'm sorry for the chaos at the end. The reconstruction was a poppy show, but something dramatic had to happen to force the issue. I had a marathon session yesterday afternoon with Joe Irving. Eventually I wore him down and he agreed to cooperate.' He grinned, remembering. 'He didn't have much choice when I told him the charges we could bring for the false statements he made to the inquiry into the prison riot. The whole point of the reconstruction was to give the impression Irving had already admitted to murdering the gunman. George Brace could relax, believing he was in the clear – so the shock of being named at the end would be all the greater. When he reacted like the guilty man he was, we'd have him.'

'And you did, spectacularly,' Magda said.

'I would never have agreed to such a trick,' Georgina said. 'A senior officer tasered like a common criminal . . .'

'He might be uncommon, but he's a criminal, ma'am.'

'I can't understand what drove him to this.'

310

'Early on, when I was getting to know George Brace, he sat in the same chair you're in now and told me how he rose through the ranks from when he first joined the police as a graduate. Ambition runs through his veins. Towering ambition. It's his fix and it governs everything he does.' He turned to Magda. 'His wife, Leticia, told me he was jealous of your OBE.'

Magda shook her head. 'That? I'd rather have my legs back.'

'I can understand, but Brace wouldn't. His reputation came before everything. So the prospect of his son marrying the daughter of a career criminal was a massive blow. You saw that, ma'am,' he told Georgina.

'Indeed. I sympathised.'

'So did I at the beginning. There was no way he could come out of it without his status being damaged beyond repair. What neither of us realised at the time was that there was history with Joe Irving.'

'Oh? In what way?'

'I'll come to that. Brace told me himself he got a name at headquarters for volunteering to serve on key committees.'

'Nothing wrong with that,' Georgina said.

Diamond opened a desk drawer and took out the report of the inquiry into the prison riot. 'Miss Lyle kindly loaned me this and I read it more than once before I thought to look at the names of the people on the investigation team.' He opened the page and handed it across.

Georgina studied it. 'Well I never. "*The inquiry was conducted by the Gloucestershire Police and the chairman was Chief Superintendent G. Brace.*"'

Magda said, 'I didn't know that.'

'You were in hospital when the evidence was taken.'

'Someone came to see me, but it wasn't him.'

'George Brace was in charge and wrote the thing.'

'He wasn't much good, then. It stinks.'

'Yes, it was done in double-quick time and came to an entirely wrong conclusion, blaming an innocent man for masterminding the riot. Jack Peace was stitched up by Joe Irving and his henchmen on C Wing.'

'Why? What was the point?'

'For Irving, the point was that he didn't get blamed and have his sentence increased. For Brace, the findings marked up another triumph in his stellar career, a clear result, a named culprit and witnesses to back it. Just what everyone wants from an official enquiry but hardly ever gets. His reputation for efficiency soared and he landed the DCC job here. He admitted freely to me before I knew he was involved at Bream that he pushed the boundaries and took short cuts. I remember his words: "You should be more like that, Peter, ambitious."'

'That's appalling. Are you sure?'

'I'm sure and, more importantly, Joe Irving is sure and admitted it to me. Brace knew at the time of the inquiry that false evidence was being presented about the riot and chose not to question it. He was looking for a tidy result and Irving and his cohorts were happy to manufacture one. But their collusion had an unintended consequence. The main victim of all this, Jack Peace, came out of prison fixated on taking revenge on the corrupt police officer he blamed for his three extra years inside.'

'He wasn't out to kill Irving?'

'Joe acted according to type. Brace was the shocker, the main architect of the injustice, and Peace believed he could shoot him and get away with it. The wedding presented an ideal opportunity. If the rainstorm hadn't come when it did, he would have succeeded.'

'Do you think the DCC knew he was under threat?'

'Not at the start. I'm sure he'd dismissed Jack Peace from

312

his thoughts after the report was written. But the wedding was a huge problem for a man who had risen to such a high position without a stain on his character.'

'He made that very clear to us.'

'What he didn't make clear was that he and Joe Irving had met in prison when he was conducting the inquiry. Because of the collusion, they both had something on each other, but Brace faced far worse: the prospect of his meteoric career being shattered. Dismissal and shame if someone pulled the plug. And neither of them knew what Peace was planning. The first inkling of that came in the interval between the wedding and the reception when we found my officer Paul Gilbert tied up and attacked by a masked gunman armed with an assault rifle. Naturally I informed George. He was shaken to the core. The wedding service had passed without a hitch and now this. He kept saying, "Oh my God."'

'He guessed it was Peace?'

'He did then. If the truth about the rigged inquiry came out, he'd be sunk for sure. He decided to act first. He was good with a gun. Told me himself he'd trained regularly at Black Rock.'

'I remember.'

'He had a weapon in case of trouble, a new Glock 17 from Black Rock with the laser sight that gives such an advantage. As someone involved in the wedding, he had no difficulty getting into the baths. He hunted the gunman down and put the spot on him. Jack Peace saw who it was and knew it was game over. But he didn't know how desperate Brace was. He didn't expect a uniformed officer to shoot him through the head. That's why he made the mistake of allowing Brace to get close up. And it played out as you saw.'

Gentle snores from Blanche were the only sound in the room for several seconds.

Magda sighed and said, 'I suppose bloody Irving will walk away without any further action being taken. The Ministry of Justice, bless their little cotton socks, will decide any new enquiry into the riot isn't worth pursuing now Peace is dead.'

'I'm not going to say you took the words out of my mouth,' Diamond said. 'My lips are sealed, aren't they?'

'What will happen to George Brace?' Georgina asked.

'That's up to the Crown Prosecution Service. Don't get up your hopes. Nobody was present in the hypocaust except those two. A clever defence lawyer has heaps to work with.' Diamond took a deep, world-weary breath and sat back in his chair. 'The one thing it's safe to say is we'll be needing a new Deputy Chief Constable.'

A lightbulb came on in Georgina's head.

'Oh!' she said so loudly that the little dog woke up and barked.